Planned by Zhuang Zhixiang Edited by Pan Wenguo

READINGS OF CHINESE CULTURE SERIES

ACADEMICS Ⅳ

Choice Blossoms of Literature and the Trends of Premodern Poetry and Prose

Translated by Zhang Deshao & Huang Pengnian

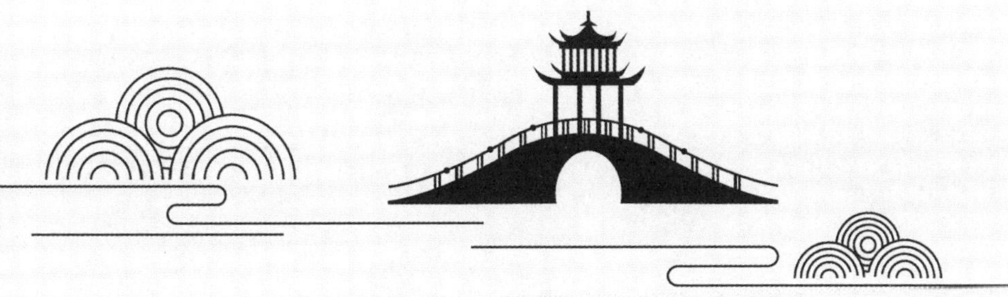

中国经典文化走向世界丛书

学术卷 四

庄智象◎总策划 潘文国◎总主编

张德劭 黄彭年◎译

图书在版编目(CIP)数据

中国经典文化走向世界丛书. 学术卷. 四/张德劭，黄彭年译.
—上海：上海外语教育出版社，2018
ISBN 978-7-5446-5513-2

I. ①中… II. ①张… ②黄… III. ①中国文学—综合作品集—英文
IV. ①I211

中国版本图书馆CIP数据核字(2018)第162836号

出版发行：上海外语教育出版社
（上海外国语大学内） 邮编：200083
电　　话：021-65425300（总机）
电子邮箱：bookinfo@sflep.com.cn
网　　址：http://www.sflep.com
责任编辑：李振荣

印　　刷：上海盛通时代印刷有限公司
开　　本：635×965 1/16 印张 11.5 字数 184千字
版　　次：2018 年 11月第 1版 2018 年 11月第 1次印刷
印　　数：1 100 册

书　　号：ISBN 978-7-5446-5513-2 / B
定　　价：36.00 元
本版图书如有印装质量问题，可向本社调换
质量服务热线：4008-213-263 电子邮箱：editorial@sflep.com

PREFACE

"Cherish one's own beauty, respect other's beauty, and when both beauties are respected and cherished, the world will become one", said Fei Xiaotong, a famous Chinese sociologist at a celebration party in honor of his eightieth birthday about thirty years ago. In a time of growing interest in intercultural communication today, these words sound especially wise and far-sighted. Translation, as one of the most important means for cultural communication, is usually done into one's mother tongue from other languages by native translators. This largely guarantees the quality of translated text, so far as the linguistic readability is concerned. However, this method implies a one-sidedness in correspondence, as only the translator's "respect for other's beauty" is concerned, regardless, though not completely, of how the local people look upon and cherish their own beauty. It should be compensated by translations on the other way, that is, works selected, interpreted, and translated by the local people themselves into languages other than their own. This approach may go directly against the prevalent views in modern translation theories but, in my opinion, is worthy of practicing. It is perhaps an even more effective way to bring about successful communication in cultures, and the beauties of the world can really be shared by the world's people. It is with such understanding that the Shanghai Foreign Languages Education Press is organizing a new series of books, entitled *Readings of Chinese Culture*, to introduce Chinese culture, past and present, to the world, with works selected and translated by the Chinese scholars and translators.

The series will cover a wide range of writings including but not restricted to works of different literary genres. For the first batch, we are glad to provide three books of essays and one book of short stories, all written by authors of the 20th century. They will be continued by a batch of serious academic writings on premodern Chinese classics in philosophy, literature, and historiography, written by influential scholars of our time.

Later, we will offer more books on classical Chinese drama, classical Chinese poetry, etc.

Some of the books in the series have been published before, but they have been revised and rearranged for the new purpose to meet the current needs of broader readers. We are looking forward to hearing comments and suggestions on the series for future improvement.

Pan Wenguo

CONTENTS

INTRODUCTION

Through years of efforts of the authors and translators, the Chinese-English Series of Premodern Chinese Classics and Traditional Culture has finally come under publication. The word *premodern* here refers to a specific period in Chinese history between *ancient* and *modern*, starting, as I propose, from the Song Dynasty.

The Song Dynasty is a very important period in China which, in a sense, marks the end of the classical China and the beginning of the premodern China. Before the Song Dynasty, China had always been a society of aristocrats when all important persons known to us, even the humblest ones like Tao Yuanming or Du Fu, had an aristocratic or noble background, whereas from the Song Dynasty on, common people from grassroots might have a chance to enter the elitist gentry; in fact, certain people from poor families had even become prime ministers or esteemed scholars in the Song Dynasty. The reason is that the imperial examination system which was founded in the Sui and Tang Dynasties was brought into full play in the Song Dynasty and yielded its best effect. "A muddy-footed farmer in the morning, an official in the emperor's court in the evening" became a realizable dream and the social strata became a convective and lively one. At the same time, thanks to the imperial policy which lay more emphasis on culture than on army, education and cultural undertakings were highly encouraged, which made the Song Dynasty the most wealthy and prosperous period in the history of China or even the world. What was described in the famous genre painting of *A Clear Bright Day on the River* by Zhang Zeduan and the famous tune-poem *Watching the Sea Tide* by Liu Yong, or recorded in the memoirs of *The Prosperous Days in Kaifeng* by Meng Yuanlao and *The Past Memories of Hangzhou* by Zhou Mi reflected the thriving and vigorous civil life never found in earlier dynasties, and gave us a direct impression that the Song and the Tang belong to two different epochs with the Song much closer to us. The much talked-about "four great inventions of China", with the exception of *paper*, were achieved in the Song Dynasty and introduced to the West, leading to the great Renaissance in Europe.

Culturally speaking, the Song Dynasty is an epoch of historic importance which creates the future by inheriting the past. This is a time when all the past cultural achievements were inherited and summarized; it is also a time when people made cultural achievements to influence the coming times till today in China as well as in East Asia. It might not be everybody's knowledge that the "traditional China" or "Chinese tradition" we talk about proudly today was not that of the Han, Tang or pre-Qin as we imagine or believe, but was actually created from the Song Dynasty, or reshaped by the Song people in the name of earlier periods. For instance, in the May Fourth Movement in 1919, people raised the banner of "Down with the Kong stash (Confucian doctrines)", but their criticism should actually be targeted at the "Zhu stash", as what they repudiated was not the doctrines of Kong Zi or Meng Zi, but the doctrine of Cheng Yi and Zhu Xi, only disguised as the former. And the Confucianism or neo-Confucianism many people have been advocating since the 1930s till today is actually a resurgence of the Song-Ming Principlism. Using the method of "elaboration instead of creation", Zhu Xi successfully transformed Kong ideology into Zhu ideology, which later became the dominant ideology especially since the Ming dynasty as it was adopted as the only authorized standard for imperial examinations. The methodology of Zhu Xi is a typical example of Song scholars, which was adopted by other people in other fields as well. Everyone is familiar with the stories of "two Sima's". The former refers to Sima Qian of the Han Dynasty who created the chronological-biographical style in writing history, thus laying the foundation of the 25 orthodox histories in China, whereas the latter refers to Sima Guang of the Song Dynasty who, by continuing the tradition of *Spring-Autumn Annals* of the ancient time, revived the annalistic style in history writing, thus not only successfully inheriting the achievement of the past 17 *Histories*, but also opening a broader way for later history writing such as the event-focused style and the outline-focused style. Zheng Qiao of the Southern Song Dynasty found another new path by emphasizing the memorandum part of *Historical Records* and *History of the Han Dynasty* and spent his whole life finishing the book *Comprehensive Study of Memorandums,* a vital complement to Sima Guang's book which merely reorganized the biography part of *Histories.* The two books formed another tradition in historical studies, working side by side with the orthodox 25 *Histories* and impacting the historical study till today.

From the above examples we conclude that one cannot really understand China and Chinese tradition without studying the Song Dynasty and its cultural contribution. However, for a very long time in our translation and introduction of Chinese culture to the world, we lay too much emphasis on the pre-Qin part and neglect the Song Dynasty. The pre-Qin classics and philosophical works have had more than scores of translations while important books since the Song Dynasty, save poetry, plays and novels, have drawn little attention and translation. We translated *Confucian Analects* and *Mencius*, but did not know that the "feudal ideology" which had restrained the Chinese nation for centuries did not come directly from them but from the Song-Ming Principlism; we translated *Laozi* and *Zhuangzi* but did not know that what influenced the thoughts of intellectuals after the Song Dynasty was already an amalgam that merged Daoism, Confucianism and Buddhism, with the Chan Buddhism playing a very important role. Realizing this, we planned to do something to fill in the blank so as to draw attention from home and abroad to the introduction of the *premodern* cultural literature, of which the present series is the initial step.

The role of the Song Dynasty as a linkage between the ancient and the modern can be seen principally in the several "great" books or anthologies. In the early Northern Song period there already appeared the "four great works" of *Taiping Imperial Encyclopedia, Referential Records from Imperial Archives*, *Taiping Miscellany* and *Choice Blossoms of Literature*, three out of the four containing 1,000 volumes. These were doubtlessly the representative establishments of the Song culture. The *Kaibao Tripitaka* laid the foundation for the Buddhist pitaka compilation. The *Enlarged Rhyming Dictionary,* the

Collected Rhyming Dictionary, the *Enlarged Sinographic Dictionary* and the *Classified Sinographic Dictionary* marked new achievements in dictionary compilation. The *History as a Mirror for Governance* opened up a new path for historiography. The *Comprehensive Study of Memorandums* served as an important continuation in the formation of the ten *Comprehensives*. Hong Mai's *Miscellaneous Notes from the Tolerance Study,* Shen Kuo's *Pen Talk in the Dreamed Creek Garden* and Wang Yinglin's *Record of Observances from Arduous Studies* marked the beginning of premodern academic research. Although the *Complete Works of Zhu Xi* was compiled just recently, most of the works contained therein were already popular in the late Song Dynasty. Among them, the *Collected Annotations to the Four Books,* the *Close Reflections,* and the *Classified Analects of Zhu Xi* even became the most important textbooks of Principlism during the 700 years from the late Song Dynasty to the beginning of the 20th century. And from Zhu Xi one would naturally relate to Wang Yangming whose Mindology had played no less important role since the mid-Ming Dynasty. Thus we decided to introduce the premodern classics and their influence to Chinese culture by way of introducing some "great books" and their developments. In the present series we have chosen six books. They are respectively, the *Complete Works of Zhu Xi*, the *Records of Instructions and Reviews*, the *History as a Mirror for Governance*, the *Choice Blossoms of Literature*, the *Taiping Miscellany*, and the *Buddhist Tripitaka.* And we invited established experts in relevant areas to write concise, introductory books in the manner of "big heads preparing small pamphlets", before asking English experts with Chinese study background to translate them into English. Specifically, the authors and translators of the six books are:

Complete Works of Zhu Xi and Its Inheritance, written by Fu Huisheng, annotated & translated by Pan Wenguo

To Attain Innate Knowledge — Records of the Instructions and Reviews and Yangming's Mindology, written by Yang Guorong, translated by Gong Haiyan

History as a Mirror for Governance and Chinese Historiography, written by Zhuang Huiming, translated by Zhang Chunbai

Choice Blossoms of Literature and the Trends of Premodern Poetry and Prose, written by Chen Yinchi, translated by Zhang Deshao and Huang Pengnian

The Buddhist Tripitaka in Chinese and Its Cultural Concern, written by Li Xiangping, translated by Fu Huisheng

You may find in the list not a few names very familiar to the academic circles. For example, Professor Yang Guorong is the Changjiang Scholar of the State Ministry of Education and dean of the School of Humanities and Social Sciences of East China Normal University (ECNU), Professor Zhuang Huiming is the ex-vice-president of ECNU and dean of Meng Xiancheng Academy, Professor Chen Yinchi is head of the Department of Chinese Language and Literature of Fudan University and "Talent of the New Century" assigned by the State Ministry of Education, Professor Chen Dakang is the former head of the Department of Chinese Language and Literature, former head of the ECNU Library as well as member of the Discipline Appraisal Group of the Degree Committee of the State Council, Professor Li Xiangping is head of the Department of Sociology of ECNU and vice-chairman of Shanghai Society for Religious Studies, Professor Zhang Chunbai is the former dean of the School of Foreign Languages of ECNU and member of the Guidance Committee for Teaching Foreign Languages of the State Ministry of Education, as well as the vice chairman of the Shanghai Society of Foreign Languages, Professor Fu Huisheng is head of the Department of International Chinese Studies of ECNU and standing council member of China Association for Comparative Studies between English and Chinese, so on and so forth. Their participation is an important guarantee of the success of the present series. Here I would like to express my personal gratitude to these eminent scholars!

The plan for this series actually started a dozen of years ago and many authors handed their manuscripts rather early. It's mainly my delay and the difficulty in translation that had kept the process so long. Now, with the efforts of all the authors and translators, this series is finally under publication. Special thanks must go to Professor Fu Huisheng who personally took up the writing of one book and the translation of another two books. Besides, he has helped me to read over most of the manuscripts of translations. Without his persistence the series would not be successful.

Finally I would like to extend my thanks to Shanghai Foreign Language Education Press and its president and editor-in-chief, Professor Zhuang Zhixiang, who has been unswervingly in support of the country's foreign languages teaching cause, and who, in recent years, has shown special concern for promoting the traditional Chinese culture to the world. Without their support, this seemingly unpopular title would not have an opportunity to go to the public.

Pan Wenguo
Shanghai
June 28, 2016

Chapter One

Choice Blossoms of Literature and Anthologies of Ancient Poetry and Prose

*Choice Blossoms of Literature*① (*wen yuan ying hua* in Pinyin), a big anthology of 1,000 volumes, is of great importance and value in the history of the Chinese documentary study.

It is no easy work to edit such a voluminous book, which was a product of the imperial cultural policy in the early period of the Northern Song Dynasty. Throughout the Chinese history, it was a convention for the new emperors to engage themselves in cultural construction right after their enthronement as a part of their agenda to attain both cultural prosperity and military supremacy. On top of it, the compilation of comprehensive anthologies of classics in a new dynasty served another purpose, that is, to rope in intellectuals and scholar-officials. To take *Choice Blossoms of Literature* as an example, Liu Xun of the Yuan Dynasty once expressed his disapproval by quoting someone's saying that its compilation was none other than a scheme of the conqueror to entrap the surrendered officials of the newly-conquered dynasties. At that time, there were many surrendered scholar-officials in the court, and they usually kept missing their old times. The ruler of the Song Dynasty was afraid that

① *Choice Blossoms of Literature* is an anthology of poetry and prose from the Liang Dynasty to the Five Dynasties (the 6th century to the 10th century). Compiled by a team of officials headed by Li Fang (926 – 996) under an imperial order from 982 to 986, the book contains nearly 20,000 pieces of works by 2,200 authors.

they might have rebellious thoughts in such a state for long, so they were assigned to work in the imperial institutes and libraries to edit different huge books, and bestowed with substantial emoluments; hopefully all their aspirations and energies would be spent on the piles of old books. That is all. (*Generalities in Reclusion*) Such spiritual imprisonment was not originated in the Song Dynasty. According to Zhang Duanyi of the Song Dynasty who had a crystal clear analysis of the underlying motive, Emperor Taizong of the Tang Dynasty had set up an institute of literature of this nature to accommodate the former officers of the preceding Chen and Sui Dynasties. (*The Collection of Gui'er*, vol.2) Another well-known example is the compilation of *The Complete Library in Four Treasuries* in the Qing Dynasty. Lu Xun denounced this kind of cultural construction as "ideological control" deeply embedded in political intentions. (*Note on Buying the Complete Collection of Philological Studies* and *Some More Notes of the Miscellaneous Talks after Discovery from Disease*)

Apart from the political background, the relatively stable social environment created the situation for accumulation of classics, which also provided the conditions for the great compilation programs in the early Song Dynasty. Otherwise, where could sufficient materials be made available for the compilation of the big, 1,000-volume books such as *The Taiping Miscellany*[①], *The Taiping Imperial Encyclopedia*[②], *Choice Blossoms of Literature* and *Important Events Archived in the Imperial Library*[③]? The ancient classics underwent a history of being scattered and recollected repeatedly. They totaled up to about 80,000 volumes in the Kaiyuan Period of the Tang Dynasty and were subject to holistic destruction during the turmoil

① *The Taiping Miscellany* is a 500-volume collection of stories compiled in the early Song Dynasty under imperial direction by Li Fang. The work was completed in 978 but wasn't published until much later in the Ming Dynasty. It helps to preserve a lot of lost stories before the Tang Dynasty.

② *The Taiping Imperial Encyclopedia* is a massive encyclopedia compiled by a number of officials under Li Fang from 977 to 983. It consists of 4.7 million Chinese characters in 1,000 volumes and includes citations from over 2,000 different kinds of documents ranging from books, poems, odes, proverbs, steles to miscellaneous works.

③ *Important Events Archived in the Imperial Library* is the largest encyclopedia compiled during the Song Dynasty. The work was started in 1005 and finished in 1013 by Wang Qinruo (962 – 1025) and numerous other scholars. It consists of 9.4 million Chinese characters in 1,000 volumes and includes political essays, biographies of rulers and subjects, memorials, and decrees.

and wars of the late Tang and Five Dynasties. In the early Song Dynasty, the classical collections of the Southern Tang Dynasty and the Western Shu Dynasty were gathered after the conquest of the States. When *The Chongwen General Catalogue* was composed in the reign of Emperor Renzong of the Song Dynasty, there were already more than 36,000 volumes in store, which laid the foundation for the successful compilation under the title of the "Four Big Books" of the Song Dynasty.

Among the "Four Big Books", *The Taiping Miscellany*, *The Taipin Imperial Encyclopaedia* and *Important Events Archived in the Imperial Library* were classified in the ancient bibliography as "category books", a class of works that combines the characteristics of encyclopaedias and concordances, but *Choice Blossoms of Literature* was regarded as the general collection of literature. Its compilation followed directly *Anthology of Poetry and Prose*[①], including the works from the end of the Liang Dynasty to the late Tang and Five Dynasties. Even the title of the book could have been inspired by Prince Zhaoming (Xiao Tong[②]), the chief editor of *Anthology of Poetry and Prose*. The evidence came from *The Catalogue of Classics and Books* in the *History of the Sui Dynasty* which recorded two books edited by Xiao Tong and lost today: *Choice Blossoms of Prose* in 30 volumes and *Choice Blossoms of Ancient and Modern Poems* in 19 volumes. Even their names are so similar! In order to have a thorough understanding of the quality, characteristics and status of *Choice Blossoms of Literature*, we should review the history of its anthological compilation.

1. The Origins and Illustrations of Ancient Anthologies of Literature

Articles were composed one by one of individual words and

① *Anthology of Poetry and Prose*, or *Wen Xuan*, is one of the earliest and most important anthologies of Chinese literature. It collects poetry and prose from the late Warring States Period (circa 300 BC) to the early Liang Dynasty (circa 500). The work was compiled in 520 – 530 by Xiao Tong and a group of scholars he had assembled.

② Xiao Tong (501 – 531), or Prince Zhaoming, is the Crown Prince of the Liang Dynasty in the Southern and Northern Dynasties. He is well-known for his legacy, the literary compendium *Anthology of Poetry and Prose*.

sentences, and went into circulation in single copies at the early times. Han Fei① of the pre-Qin times, for instance, had many proposals to cope with the turmoils in the late Warring States Period. In contrast to Meng Zi who was an eloquent orator and could persuade the kings with his oral skills, Han Fei had a stammer and was clumsy in expression. Consequently, he had to resort to writing. When King Zheng of the State of Qin, i.e. later the Emperor Shihuangdi of the Qin Dynasty, read his "Solitary Resentment" and "Five Moths", he exclaimed, "I would die with no regret if I had the chance to meet this man and be his friend." To this end, he dispatched troops to take over the State of Han and seized Han Fei. (*Biographies of Lao Zi, Zhuang Zi, Lord Chunshen and Han Feizi* in *Records of the Historian*) This incident suggests that the articles of Han Fei, Meng Zi, and many others were not edited into any form of anthology in the pre-Qin times. As a further proof, Sima Qian② listed separately the articles by Zhuang Zi③ — "The Fisherman", "Zhi the Robber", "Pry Open a Suitcase" — in his *Records of the Historian*. A legitimate hypothesis would be that there were no books consisting of all the articles of Zhuang Zi or Han Feizi at that time. In other words, the articles were compiled at a later time into the well-known books we are now familiar with. Then, what is the case with the literary works? In *Records of the Historian*, Qu Yuan④ was credited as the author of "Departure of Sorrow", "Inquiring Heaven", "Spirit Calling", "Plaint for Ying", "Thinking of Sha", etc., and there was no mention of an anthology. In the case of Sima Xiangru⑤, the greatest rhapsodist of the Han

---

① Han Fei (circa 280 – 233 BC), or Han Fei Zi, a philosopher of the Legalist School in the Warring States Period. He was a nobleman of the State of Han and his works were very influential on the First Emperor of the Qin Dynasty, or Qin Shi Huang.

② Sima Qian (circa 145 BC – circa 86 BC), a historian of the early Han Dynasty. He is the author of the influential history work *Records of the Grand Historian*, or *Shiji*, which covers more than 2,000 years from the legendary Yellow Emperor to his time, during the reign of Emperor Wu of the Han Dynasty.

③ Zhuang Zi (active in the 4th century BC), or Zhuang Zhou, a philosopher in the Warring States Period. His eponymous work *Zhuang Zi* is one of the foundational texts of Taoism.

④ Qu Yuan (circa 340 – 278 BC), a prominent poet in the Warring States Period. He is known for his patriotism and contributions to classical poetry and verses, especially through the poems of *Chu Ci* (*Songs of the South*). His works include *Li Sao* (*Encountering Sorrow* or *Suffering Throes*) and *Nine Songs*. The Dragon Boat Festival is dedicated to his memory.

⑤ Sima Xiangru (circa 179 – 117 BC), a poet and musician of the Western Han Dynasty. He was a great composer of *fu* (part prose and part poetry, a dominant literary form of the time) and was versatile enough to write in the *Chu Ci* style.

Dynasty, his works were unnoticed by Emperor Wu of the Han Dynasty before his hometown fellow, Yang Deyi, made the introduction. It was via Yang, who took care of the dogs in the royal family at that time, that Sima's talent as shown in his "Rhapsody of Nowhere" captured the attention of the emperor (Biography of Sima Xiangru, *Records of the Historian*). It may be quite safe to conclude that the anthologies of the Han Dynasty were not compiled contemporarily. Liu Shipei, a distinguished scholar of the early modern times, put it this way, "The works of men of letters, up to the Eastern Han Dynasty, were treated in terms of articles, not of anthologies." (*Miscellaneous Notes on Poetry and Prose*) *The Book of the Later Han Dynasty*, written by Fan Ye of the Southern Dynasty, is the first official history book to embody the biographies of literary men, probably under the influence of *The Biographies of Men of Letters* by Zhang Zhi of the Western Jin Dynasty (Yao Zhenzong: *Textual Research on Book of the Sui Dynasty*: *Bibliography of Classics and Books*). But the individual literary works were still treated as poems and rhapsodies separately. It can be said that only after the Six Dynasties did the anthologies gain popularity. *The Book of the Sui Dynasty*: *Bibliography of Classics and Books* said: "After the Jian'an Period, rhapsodies and poems multiplied constantly and the anthologies increased day by day." This is in conformity with the fact.

The general anthologies came into being right because the collections of individual writers were increasing rapidly.

It is worthwhile to make the distinction between the general anthology titled as such by the later bibliographers and the personal anthology. Any collections representing more than two writers' works could have been labeled as general anthology. Now we may regard *Book of Poetry* as the first general anthology of Chinese poetry. Due credit can be given to this argument. However, the compilation of *Book of Poetry* was completed before Kong Zi, and it had established itself as one of the Confucian classics in the Western Han Dynasty. Though there might have been little variance in terms of compiling methodology in the later ages, *Book of Poetry* was not taken as an anthology by the ancient scholars and consequently had negligible influence upon the practice of anthology compilation. In fact, there was hardly any prevailing norm of what an anthology should be like in the Han Dynasty. To think of it, the people in the Han Dynasty did not have any consciousness about anthologies yet.

Then what about the *Songs of the South*? The synopsis of *The Philological Study on The Songs of the South*①, which was included in the collection part of *The Synopses of the General Catalogue for the Complete Library in Four Treasuries*② (hereafter referred as *The Synopses*), recorded that Liu Xiang collected the works of Qu Yuan, Song Yu, Jing Chai, Jia Yi, Huainan Xiaoshan, Dongfang Shuo, Yan Ji, Wang Bao and his own, "as the first general anthology". This statement certainly has some truth in it. Liu Xiang was indeed a conscious documentalist to collect all the previous works. But *The Song of the South* was never formally credited as a general anthology in ancient times. In *The Book of the Sui Dynasty: Catalogue of Classics and Books*, for instance, there were three subdivisions in the category of anthology: "The Songs of the South", individual anthologies and general anthologies. Note that *The Songs of the South* received its own classification in parallel with the other two types. According to the *Catalogue of Classics and Books*, the general anthologies were represented by *The Collection of Literary Writings in Genres*③ attributed to Zhi Yu④ of the Western Jin Dynasty. As increasing amount of proliferation in poetry and prose surged after Jing'an Period, "Zhi Yu of the Jin Dynasty considered it an arduous work for readers to extract the essentials from such a large mass, so he picked out the highlights by clearing undesirables and arranged the selected poems and rhapsodies in an orderly fashion to compile *The Collection of Literary Writings in Genres*. Later collections of poetry and prose began to follow its example and the men of letters learned from it as a treasure trove of poems."

---

① *The Philological Study on The Songs of the South* is first complete annotated version of *The Songs of the South*. Wang Yi (active in the 2nd century) of the Eastern Han Dynasty made the annotations on the basis of previous collections.

② *The Synopses of The General Catalogue for the Complete Library in Four Treasuries* is a 200-volume general catalogue of *The General Catalogue for the Complete Library in Four Treasuries*. It was compiled by Aixinjueluo Yongrong (1743 – 1790) and Ji Yun (1724 – 1805) and first published in 1789.

③ *The Collection of Literary Writings in Genres* is an anthology of ancient writings divided by their genres. The original texts are lost now.

④ Zhi Yu (250 – 300), courtesy name Zhongqia, a literary cataloguist of the Western Jin Dynasty.

Besides *The Collection of Literary Writings in Genres*, there is another book by Zhi Yu recorded in *The Book of the Sui Dynasty: Catalogue of Classics and Books*. Its title is *On the Collection of Literary Writings in Genres* (in 2 volumes), which has unfortunately been long lost. The only remaining pieces (up to a dozen) can be found in *The Collection of Beitang*①, *Classified Collection of Poetry and Prose*②, *Records of First Learning*③ and *The Taiping Imperial Encyclopedia*, which included discussions on the different genres of poetry, hymn, rhapsody, epigraph, dirge, ode in sevens, question-answer, tablet inscription, etc. *The Collection of Literary Writings in Genres* (together with *On the Collection of Literary Writings in Genres*), by inference, must have been a sizable collection (in either 40 or 60 volumes), representing different literary genres with critiques and comments attached. It was really a great advancement. Nonetheless, Zhi Yu is not the first one to make a collection of one literary genre. *The Song of the South*, for example, appeared much earlier than his book. Other examples can be found in *The Book of the Sui Dynasty: Catalogue of Classics and Books*: *Collection of Essays* by Ying Qu; *Collection of Sevens* by Fu Xuan, *The Songs and Poems of the Jin Dynasty* and *The Lyrics of Yan in the Jin Dynasty* by Xun Xu; *The Memorials of the Famous Officials in the Han Dynasty* and *The Memorials of the Famous Officials of the Wei Dynasty* by Chen Shou; *The Ancient and Modern Five-Syllable Poems and Excellent Essays* by Xun Chuo, and *Miscellaneous Inscriptions* and *Tablet Inscriptions* by Chen Xie, etc. In regard to the origin of the compilation of collections in genres, Zhang Taiyan held that it should be traced back to Du Yu's 50-volume *Good Essays* as it was listed in the *Catalogue of Classics and Books* in *The Book of the Sui Dynasty*. (*Random Comments on Genres in Collected Writings from Taiyan*, vol.1) But we have very little knowledge about this book. Only some citations about it in "The Letter to Zhang Han" by a hermit at the end of the Qin Dynasty were available from *The Collected Explanations of the Records of the Historian* (in *The Biography of Li Si*)

① *The Collection of Beitang* is an encyclopedia compiled by Yu Shinan (558 – 638).

② *Classified Collection of Poetry and Prose* is the first officially made encyclopedia extant in China. The lead compiler is the famous calligrapher Ouyang Xun (557 – 641).

③ *Records of First Learning* is an encyclopedia compiled by Xu Jian (660 – 729).

and *Indexes to the Records of the Historian* (in *The Chronicle of Grand Ancestor of the Han Dynasty*). It might not be a collection with emphasis on literary achievements. There is still another book edited by Hua Yi, which has the same title as Du Yu's. *The Book of the Jin Dynasty* explicitly stated that it "collected the essentials of Confucian classics" and therefore was not considered to be an anthology of literature.

Another noteworthy anthology prior to Zhi Yu's book was the one edited by Cao Pi①, Emperor Wendi of the Wei Empire for "Pleiade of Jian'an". In the twenty-second year (217) of the Jian'an Period, a plague struck the land, and Xu Gan, Chen Lin, Ying Yang, Liu Zhen, et. al. "all died at that time". Cao Pi was very much distressed and "compiled their works into a posthumous anthology" (*A Letter to Wu Zhi*). It has not been preserved to now. He might have put together their poems, essays and rhapsodies, etc. into one book, possibly without critical selection.

In conclusion, there were quite a few anthologies in only one genre after the appearance of *The Songs of the South*. The anthologies with several individual collections were initiated by Cao Pi, while the first anthology extant of different genres and multiple writers was *The Collection of Literary Writings in Genres*. It is the latter that connects with the *Anthology of Poetry and Prose*. When he edited the *Classified Collection of Poetry and Prose* in the early Tang Dynasty, Ouyang Xun② said, "I choose only from *The Collection of Literary Writings in Genres* and *Anthology of Poetry and Prose*." He was very insightful to draw a parallel between the two books.

2. From *General Anthology of Poetry and Prose* to *Collection of Essays and Poems*

After the Wei and Jin Dynasties, literary consciousness grew increasingly and its development greatly accelerated. This led to the increasing growth of individual collections and the compilation of anthologies as well. In

① Cao Pi (circa 187 – 226), courtesy name Zihuan, second son of the warlord Cao Cao and later made King of Wei in the Three Kingdoms Period. He was also an accomplished poet.

② Ouyang Xun (557 – 641), courtesy name Xinben, a Confucian scholar and calligrapher of the early Tang Dynasty.

the above examples, we have listed some titles of anthologies in single genres in the Wei and Jin Dynasties, which could still be seen in the Southern Dynasty, for example, *The Collection of Rhapsodies*, and *Collected Poems* composed by Xie Lingyun. Before compiling *The Anthology of Poetry and Prose*, Xiao Tong, Crown Prince Zhaoming of the Liang Dynasty and supervisor of *The Anthology of Poetry and Prose*, had compiled *Choice Blossoms of Ancient and Modern Poems* specifically in five-syllable poems, but he was not satisfied with it. In a letter to his younger brother, he said: "In the past leisure time, I searched and collected materials to compile *Choice Blossoms* for several decades long. Although I have yet to get familiar with the subject and still have some regrets for the book, the book has already been in circulation." (*In Reply to Prince Xiangdong's Request for the Collection of Essays and the Anthology of Choice Blossoms of Poetry*) Based on the practice of the previous compilers and his own personal experiences, Xiao Tong carefully designed the guide, established the criteria and accomplished the compilation of *The Anthology of Poetry and Prose*.

The Anthology of Poetry and Prose is a milestone in the history of anthological compilation. It is not only because it is the earliest extant anthology but also because it was compiled under a definite literary principle which is evidenced by a mere glance at the title. Wang Shihan of the Qing Dynasty said in the "Preface to *The Basic Principle of the Anthology of Poetry and Prose*" that "General anthologies emerged in the Jin Dynasty, but none of them had 'selection/anthology' in the title." Indeed, the books listed in *The Book of the Sui Dynasty: Bibliography of Classics and Books* were all "collections" — *Collection Garden*, *Collection Forest* and *A Copy of Collection Forest* by Liu Yiqing, *A Copy of Collection* by Shen Yue and *A Copy of Collections*, *Concise Collection* by Qiu Chi. The title of *The Anthology of Poetry and Prose*, compared with them, was obviously new. Afterwards the books named "selection/anthology" were countless.

The Anthology of Poetry and Prose was attributed to Xiao Tong of the Liang Dynasty, who was posthumously known as Prince Zhaoming. In the historical literature, Xiao was an honest and kind-hearted nobleman and had a keen interest in arts and literature. He liked to make friends with the men of letters and discussed literature with them, among whom up to over thirty were well-known writers. There was a collection of 30,000 books in the prince's palace, and Xiao, sitting in the piles of books, "often read and wrote and contemplated upon them as a routine." Besides the books he compiled, Xiao composed a 20-volume anthology, of which few are available now. Under his leadership, "the literature was in an unprecedented prosperity since the Jin and Song Dynasties." (Biography of Xiao Tong in *The Book of the Liang Dynasty*).

Some scholars believed that when ancient demoted high officials or noblemen wanted to compile a book, they mainly depended on the scholars in their patronage; similarly when Xiao Tong compiled *The Anthology of Poetry and Prose*, it was mainly accomplished by the famous literary men in his patronage, particularly Liu Xiaochuo. Kukai[①], a Japanese monk, wrote a well-known book on Chinese literature, *The Secret Repository as a Mirror of Literature*[②] after his visit to China in the Tang Dynasty. In the book there was a quotation from Yuan Jing of the early Tang Dynasty: "Crown Prince Zhaoming of the Liang Dynasty, Xiao Tong, led Liu Xiaochuo, et.al. to compile *The Anthology of Poetry and Prose*." This story may not be totally a hearsay. We can learn, however, from Xiao Tong's keen interest in literature and, more importantly, the extant Preface to *The Anthology of Poetry and Prose* by him that *The Anthology of Poetry and Prose* was completed under his auspices and to his literary taste. The preface stated explicitly why the Confucian classics, philosophical and historical works were excluded: the Confucian classics were too lofty in position to be split into articles, the philosophical works "concentrated on thoughts and not on literary grace", and the historical books were not identifiable with the single articles. What *The Anthology of Poetry and Prose* opted for were individual poems, rhapsodies and articles, well constructed and polished, and rich in style. The preference revealed the literary ideals of that time.

---

① Kukai (774 – 835), also known posthumously as Kōbō-Daishi, a Japanese Buddhist monk, civil servant, scholar, poet, and artist who founded the Shingon or "True Word" school of Buddhism. He was also a great calligrapher and engineer. In 804 – 806, he studied Buddhist sutras in China.

② *The Secret Repository as a Mirror of Literature* is a collection of poetics and literary criticisms from the Southern and Northern Dynasties to the middle Tang Dynasty.

The writers whose works had more entries in *The Anthology of Poetry and Prose*, for example, Cao Zhi, Lu Ji①, Xie Lingyun, Yan Yanzhi, Xie Tiao, Jiang Yan, Shen Yue, et.al., were indeed the distinguished men of letters in the evolution of the scholarly literature since the Wei, Jin, and Southern Dynasties. *The Anthology of Poetry and Prose* may be taken as the culmination of the tradition of scholarly literature of the medieval times.

The genre classification of *The Anthology of Poetry and Prose* exerted great influence upon the subsequent compilation of general anthologies, and its role in linking the past and the future cannot be trivialized. The evolution in genre classification is indicative of the progress of the ancient literary concepts. The articles were divided into four categories in Cao Pi's *On Scholars* in *On Classical Writings*② as memorial, commentary, inscription and elegy, and poetry and rhapsody, and their stylistic characteristics were discussed respectively. Lu Ji's *Rhapsody on Literature*③ divided literary writings further into ten categories. For instance, Cao Pi claimed "poems and rhapsodies should be beautiful", while Lu Ji declared more exquisitely, "Poems tend to be ornamental in expression of emotions, and rhapsodies tend to be lucid and bright in portraying things." Zhi Yu's *The Collection of Literary Writings in Genres* has been scattered and lost. But from the remaining fragments we know that there were at least such classes as hymn, rhapsody, poem, ode in sevens, exhortation, epigraph, elegy, memorial speech, memorial discourse, tablet inscription, augury, etc. Liu Xie gave even more detailed classification in his *Literary Mind and Carving the Dragon* and labeled 33 categories. And there are 38 categories in *The Anthology of Poetry and Prose*: rhapsody, poetry, *sao* (poems by Qu Yuan), ode in sevens, edict, conference of posthumous title, order, admonishment, discourse, memorial, memorial to the throne (emperor), report, impeachment, letter to a noble, written report, letter, written summons

① Lu Ji (261 – 303), courtesy name Shiheng, a writer and literary critic who lived during the late Three Kingdoms Period and the Jin Dynasty.

② *On Classical Writings* is the earliest anthology of literary criticisms. Written in the 3rd century, it is incomplete today.

③ *Rhapsody on Literature*, or *Wen Fu*, is an anthology of literary criticisms written in the *fu* form, in which the author expounds the philosophical basis of poetry and its rhetorical forms.

to arms or written denunciation, question and answer, supposed question and argument, criticism, lyrical rhapsody, preface, hymn, eulogy, military tally, historical commentary, historical evaluation, review, stringed pearls, exhortation, epitaph, elegy, mourning speech, tablet inscriptions, in-tomb inscriptions, brief biography of a deceased person, essay in memory of a dead person, and funeral oration. If a genre consists of many volumes, then they can be subcategorized with regard to different things. For example, poetry was subdivided into 23 classes: supplement, narration of virtue, exhortation and persuasion, dedication of poems, public banquet, farewell dinner on the roadside, songs of history, one-hundred-one poem, visiting immortals, summons for reclusion, anti-summons for reclusion, sightseeing, aspiration or sentiment expression, grief, reply, journey, military life, sacrifice to heaven and ancestors, music bureau, elegy, assorted songs, assorted poems, and assorted imitations, while rhapsody in 15 classes: capital, suburban sacrifice, imperial ploughing, hunting, travel notes, sightseeing, palace, river and sea, scene, birds and animals, records, sorrow, on composition, music, and emotions. Naturally it forms a unique pattern, but there are obvious disadvantages. Fragmentation occurs when some eminent writers have more than two poems and essays selected, which are scattered in the different classes. Take Pan Yue's rhapsodies as an example. "Rhapsody on Imperial Ploughing" was listed into the class of imperial ploughing, "Rhapsody on Hunting for Pheasant" into the class of hunting, "Rhapsody on Westward Expedition" into the class of travel note, "Rhapsody on Rise of Autumn" into the class of scene, "Rhapsody on Reed Pipe Instrument" into the class of music, and "Rhapsody on Memory of Virtues" and "Rhapsody on Widows" into the class of sorrow. Such malpractice was even more conspicuous in later division of categories in anthologies, for example, in *Choice Blossoms of Literature*.

The Anthology of Poetry and Prose selected over 700 pieces from more than 130 writers in 800 years from the pre-Qin times to the Liang Dynasty of the Southern Dynasties, and quite a number of poems and essays are still known to us only because *The Anthology of Poetry and Prose* preserved them, which testifies its significance as a milestone document. It also provides the proper book for the study of literature and its recognition has never failed. Lu Xun considered it one of the most influential anthologies ("On Selected Works"). As early as in the Tang Dynasty an annotated version of the book by Li Shan① was completed, and became one of the most famous annotated books of China. The men of letters were so familiar with it that some citations could pass their lips easily. There was an interesting story about it. A man named Xiao Zhizhong frequently came out and went into the mansion of Princess Taiping, and this offended Song Jing. Song rebuked Xiao satirically by citing a sentence from Pan Yue's "Rhapsody on Westward Campaign": "This is not what Master Xiao is expected to do." ("Xiao" stands for Xiao Wangzhi.) Xiao Zhizhong accepted the criticism and made a reply also by citing a sentence from Pan Yue's "Rhapsody on Autumn": "What Mr. Song said is right." ("Song" originally stands for Song Yu.) It is believed that both Li Bai and Du Fu, the great poets of Tang, had studied *The Anthology of Poetry and Prose* thoroughly. It was said that Li Bai had imitated *The Anthology of Poetry and Prose* three times (*Youyang Miscellany*), and Du Fu asked his son to study thoroughly the principle of *The Anthology of Poetry and Prose* ("On the Birthday of Zongwu"). The scholar-officials of the Tang Dynasty were chosen through examinations on poems and rhapsodies. This tradition continued until the times of Wang Anshi in the Song Dynasty. *The Anthology of Poetry and Prose*, consequently, became the desk reference book for all candidates. In the *Transformation Texts of Qiu Hu* discovered in Dunhuang, we find that besides the Confucian classics, *The Anthology of Poetry and Prose* was among the books Qiu Hu carried with him. Lu You of the Song Dynasty recorded the fashion in the early Song Dynasty:

> In the early period of this Song Dynasty, the men of letters were particularly fond of this book. Therefore, following the expression in *The Anthology of Poetry and Prose*, the grass is surely addressed as

① Li Shan (630 – 689), a scholar-official in the Tang Dynasty, best known for his work in annotating *The Anthology of Poetry and Prose*.

"wangsun" (literally noble offspring), plum as "yishi" (literally courier), the moon as "wangshu" (literally moon's driver), and the mountains and waters as "qinghui" (literally clear sunshine). After the Qingli Period, people became sick of the stale phrases and began to avoid using them. When *The Anthology of Poetry and Prose* was in fashion, the scholars even claimed that "A command of the *Anthology*, half a scholar's knowledge." (*Notes from Old Learning House*)

This refers to the excessive use of allusions in imitation of *The Anthology of Poetry and Prose*. After the middle Northern Song Dynasty, *The Anthology of Poetry and Prose* still had a strong influence, though weaker than before. Up to the early modern times, the study of *The Anthology of Poetry and Prose* was still very popular. When the May Fourth New Culture Movement was launched in 1920's, the rivals of those devotees to vernacular Chinese were branded "Tongcheng bastards" and "Anthological demons". The former refers to the ancient prose of the Tongcheng School which was very popular in the Qing Dynasty, and the latter the literary trend after *The Anthology of Poetry and Prose*. At Peking University, the best school of China at that time, several masters of the classical prose of the Tongcheng School, Wu Rulun, Ma Qichang, Yao Yongpu, et. al. dominated teaching and administration. In 1920's some distinguished scholars with revolutionary experience entered Peking University. The literary courses they offered covered the periods of the Han, Wei and Six Dynasties, which were just the epochs *The Anthology of Poetry and Prose* covered. Huang Kan hosted the lectures on "History of Chinese Literature" and "*The Literary Mind and Carving the Dragon*"; Liu Shipei, on "Mid-Ancient Literature" and "Study on the Prose of the Han, Wei and Six Dynasties". Both the former's *Notes on The Literary Mind and Carving the Dragon* and the latter's *Lectures on History of Medieval Literature* are classics in the study of literature. These two literary traditions were the opponents of vernacular literature, and naturally became its target.

There was a voluminous general anthology in the Tang Dynasty called *Collection of Essays and Poems*[①] edited by Xu Jingzong (*Bibliography of Classics and Books* of the *Old History of the Tang Dynasty* and *Bibliography of Books and Literature* of the *New History of the Tang Dynasty* both listed it in "the category of general anthology of the collection part"). It has as many as 1,000 volumes, but unfortunately it soon got scattered. In the course of compiling *Choice Blossoms of Literature* in the early Song Dynasty, *Collection of Essays and Poems* was then unavailable. There was only a record of the *Collection's* poems in one volume in *The Bibliography of Books and Literature* in the *History of the Song Dynasty*. It was not until the mid-19th century that its remaining fragments were collected and published. It totaled only 21 volumes, including a dozen volumes found in Japan. That is really a drop in the ocean in comparison with its original size.

We can learn roughly the structure of this anthology from what is extant. It was divided, like *The Anthology of Poetry and Prose*, by genres, and the genres were subdivided into classes. The genres in this book, as far as we can infer from the fragments and the list of contents, are nine categories — poem, hymn, tablet inscription, imperial edict, decree, order, prince proclamation, imperial credential, and impeachment. Most of them can find their counterparts in *The Anthology of Poetry and Prose*. There are more complex subclasses based on events in each genre. The genre of "order", for example, has eleven subclasses in the extant Volume 695; "prince proclamation" has seven in Volume 699. We have mentioned before that in *The Anthology of Poetry and Prose* only the genres covering multiple volumes are subdivided, while in *Collection of Essays and Poems*, each genre has its subclasses. This is because *The Anthology of Poetry and Prose* contains only 30 volumes, while *Collection of Essays and Poems* 1,000 volumes. It is unnecessary for the former to make a finer distinction as it may include several genres in one volume. On the contrary, one genre in the latter often takes up several volumes and therefore must be made with further distinction. The extant Volume 459 is labeled as "Tablet Inscription

① *Collection of Essays and Poems* is an anthology of essays and poems completed in 658 under an imperial order. Some of its fragments have been found in Japan and Korea.

39" and Volume 670 as "Imperial Edict 40", which indicate that there are at least 39 and 40 volumes of the genres of "tablet inscription" and "imperial edict" respectively, let alone the genres of poetry and rhapsody. As for "Tablet Inscription", it has its own sub-branches, such as "Officials", and "Officials" is further subdivided into "General" (Volumes 452, 453), "General Commander" (Volumes 457, 459) and so on. Thus it has three levels of classification, one level more than that of *The Anthology of Poetry and Prose*.

Collection of Essays and Poems has such a large size and fine classification that it must have accumulated extremely abundant materials of literature. Many pieces found in the remaining volumes are absent in the comprehensive anthologies, such as *Records of Ancient Poetry* and *Complete Collection of Prose of the Remote Ancient Times, Three Dynasties, Qin, Han, Three Empires and Six Dynasties* that were accomplished before their reappearance in the 19th century. It is a real pity that most of the volumes of *Collection of Essays and Poems* were lost, since the majority of its collection is the works of the Han, Wei and Six Dynasties. To this period of literature, the loss can no longer be compensated for. In contrast, it is fortunate that *Choice Blossoms of Literature* which preserved mainly the poetry and prose of the Tang Dynasty has survived till today.

3. *Choice Blossoms of Literature* and *The Quintessence of the Tang Poetry and Prose*

Of the Four Big Books of the early Song Dynasty, *The Taiping Miscellany*, *The Taiping Imperial Encyclopedia* and *Choice Blossoms of Literature* were all completed during the Taiping Xingguo Period. *The Taiping Miscellany* was the first one, whose compilation started under the supervision of Li Fang at the imperial edict in the third lunar month of the second year (977) in the Taiping Xingguo Period, and finished with block-print in the first lunar month of the sixth year (981). *The Taiping Imperial Encyclopedia* was also edited at the imperial edict in the second year of the Taiping Xinguo Period under the same leadership, and was completed in the eighth year (983). In the ninth lunar month of the seventh year (982) of Taiping Xingguo

Period, Emperor Taizong of the Song Dynasty ordered Li Fang, Hu Meng, Xu Xuan, Song Bai, Jia Huangzhong, Lü Mengzheng, Li Zhi, Li Mu, Yang Huizhi, Li Fan, Yang Li, Wu Shu, Lü Wenzhong, Hu Ting, Zhan Yiqing, Du Gao, Shu Ya, and others "to go over and extract the 'qintessence' of the previous anthologies and arrange them by category to make *Choice Blossoms of Literature*" (*Annotations on Bibliographies of Literature and Books in the Three Reigns of Our Dynastic History* and *Institutions and Regulations of Our Dynasty*). The editorial staff of this book, except Xu Xuan, Song Bai, Jia Huangzhong and Yang Huizhi, had other assignments and left the board in succession. Su Yijian, Wang You, Fan Gao, Song Shi, et al. were transferred in as coordinators of the project. The whole book was finished in the twelfth lunar month of the third year (Jan. 987) of the Yongxi Period (*Institutions and Regulations of Our Dynasty*, and *Sequel to the Draft of History as a Mirror for Governance*).

Choice Blossoms of Literature picked up what *The Anthology of Poetry and Prose* left off — the Liang Dynasty of the Southern Dynasties — and continued into the Five Dynasties. The voluminous book selected nearly 20,000 poems and pieces of prose by 2,200 writers, nine-tenth of which are the works of the Tang Dynasty. At the beginning of the Song Dynasty, this big book was taken roughly as the complete collection of the Tang Dynasty literature. However, such a compilation project, as complex and large-scaled as it was, didn't take a lot of time to accomplish, and the editorial staff in frequent flux included some talented writers, such as Song Bai, Hu Meng, Lü Mengzheng, Yang Li, Su Yijian, et. al. rather than erudite scholars with editorial experience. For this reason, the book as a whole fell short of high quality. Supposedly, its print would go hand in hand with *The Anthology of Poetry and Prose* in the same year, but too many mistakes and problems were found and its publication had to be postponed. In the fourth year (1007) of the Jingde Period in the reign of Emperor Zhenzong of the Song Dynasty, and the second year (1009) in the Dazhong Xiangfu Period, the book was twice ordered to be supplemented and re-proofread. However, mistakes were like fallen leaves and difficult to be swept away. After the imperial court of the Song Dynasty moved south, in the eighth year (1181) of the Chunxi Period in the reign of Emperor Xiaozong of the Song Dynasty, Zhou Bida proofread the book once. At the beginning of the Jiatai Period in the reign of Emperor Ningzong of the Song Dynasty, the book was proofread again and sent to print. Zhou Bida pointed out, "The compilation of *Choice Blossoms of Literature* at the beginning took quite a number of years to complete. Since it was not edited by one hand, there were many repetitions and discrepancies. One poem might have been split into two, or three poems combined into one, while mistakes of identification and misplacements are unaccountable." (*The Cause for Compilation of Choice Blossoms of Literature*) Peng Shuxia, co-proofreader with Zhou Bida, wrote specially a ten-volume *Collation and Correction of Choice Blossoms of Literature*, which became a classic of collative study. With Zhou Bida and Peng Shuxia's endeavors, *Choice Blossoms of Literature* became a reliable big book.

The Synoptic Catalogue of the Complete Library of the Four Treasuries pointed out clearly: *Choice Blossoms of Literature* carried on the tradition of *The Anthology of Poetry and Prose* "with basically similar editing guides of classification". That is to say, *Choice Blossom of Literature* is also a general anthology classified by genres, and altogether there are 38 genres: rhapsody, poetry, story-song, essay, imperial edict written by the Secretariat, imperial edict written by the State Academy, imperial examination with written questions, imperial credential, judgment, memorial, letter to a noble, report, war proclamation, unsealed document, impeachment, negotiation document, recommendation, letter, suggestion to the emperor, preface, thesis, comment, stringed pearls, exposition, hymn, evaluation, epigraph, admonishment, biography, narration, conference of posthumous title, suggestion for a posthumous title, elegy, tablet inscription, tomb-tablet record, tablet eulogy, in-tomb tablet of brief biography, and funeral oration. Like *The Anthology of Poetry and Prose*, the majority are poems and rhapsodies in 180 and 150 volumes respectively. Earlier we mentioned that *Collection of Essays and Poems* had a finer classification than *The Anthology of Poetry and Prose*, and such a system is also represented in *Choice Blossoms of Literature*. In *The Anthology of Poetry and Prose*, only two genres have subdivisions:

poetry and rhapsody; even the number of subcategories of rhapsody and poetry is much greater that in *The Anthology of Poetry and Prose*. For instance, in *The Anthology of Poetry and Prose*, rhapsodies are divided into 15 subcategories, while in *Choice Blossoms of Literature*, rhapsodies are subdivided into 41 subcategories: celestial phenomena, year and seasons, terrestrial phenomena, water, imperial virtue, capital, city and residence, palaces, parks, spring gathering, sacrifice, imperial travel, allegory, Confucianism, military life, state governance, imperial ploughing, music, bells and drums, acrobatics, drink and food, auspice, human affairs, will, shooting and game, handicraft, implements and apparatuses, graded official uniforms, paintings, precious objects, silk, vessels and vehicles, wood and fire, hunting, Daoism and Buddhism, travel notes, sighting, sorrow, birds and animals, insects and fish, grass and trees. The above is a good index to demonstrate the heavy and complicated classification.

As for the reason why "there is such a finer classification of the contents" of *Choice Blossoms of Literature*, *The Synoptic Catalogue of the Complete Library of the Four Treasuries* believed: "More genres emerged increasingly and the old terms were insufficient to cover them." This explanation seems inappropriate. There are 38 genres both in *The Anthology of Poetry and Prose* and in *Choice Blossoms of Literature*. Apart from their substance, the fact is that there are nearly 20 genres with similar titles, such as rhapsody, poetry, memorial, letter to a noble, war summons, negotiation document, letter, suggestion to the emperor, preface, thesis, stringed pearls, hymn, comment, epigraph, exhortation, elegy, tablet, brief biography of a deceased person, and funeral address, and no new genre is added in *Choice Blossoms of Literature*; therefore, it is not convincing to say "More genres emerged increasingly". The true reason in our analysis was the same as given in our discussion of *Collection of Essays and Poems*. That is, there was a need for subdivisions of a genre only because the excessive increase of the quantity of poetry and prose. The same conclusion follows if we compare the classification of rhapsodies in *The Anthology of Poetry and Prose* to that in *Choice Blossoms of Literature*. The 41 subclasses in *Choice Blossoms of Literature* incorporated the 15 in *The Anthology of Poetry and Prose* and added many new ones.

As the preface to the category of general anthology in the collection part of *The Synoptic Catalogue of The Complete Library of the Four Treasuries* said,

> Literary works increased fast and were scattered without collection, so general anthologies came into existence. On the one hand, they collected the works, separate poems and prose pieces together; on the other hand, they eliminated all unqualified works, and exhibited all quintessential ones.

The two different functions of general anthology mentioned above are just the two different emphases reflected in *The Anthology of Poetry and Prose* and *Choice Blossoms of Literature* respectively. *The Anthology of Poetry and Prose* was selected out of the ancient and contemporary works by Xiao Tong in his own literary taste. According to Zhu Yizun of the Qing Dynasty, the original size of *The Anthology of Poetry and Prose* had been 1,000 volumes, and was reduced later to 30 volumes (Postscript to *New Songs of Yutai*). If this is true, inference can be drawn about the stringency of the selection criteria at that time. For example, there are only eight poems by Tao Yuanming in *The Anthology of Poetry and Prose*; however, Xiao Tong liked Tao Yuanming's poems so much that he collected, revised and compiled all Tao's poems available by genres, which became the source of many anthologies of Tao Yuanming thereafter. In this sense, *The Anthology of Poetry and Prose* is indeed a general anthology of the choice, and endeavored to "eliminate the unqualified works so as to exhibit the quintessential ones". Under the same rubric of "collecting the quintessence", the compilers of *Choice Blossoms of Literature*, as Zhou Bida put it, "took in the complete works of Liu Zongyuan[①], Bai Juyi, Quan Deyu, Li Shangyin[②],

① Liu Zongyuan (773 – 819), courtesy name Zihou, a prominent writer, poet, and government official of the Tang Dynasty. Along with Han Yu, he led the Classical Prose Movement. His prose is characterized by sagacity and poignancy.

② Li Shangyin (813 – 858), an important poet of the late Tang Dynasty. He is particularly famous for his cryptic "no title" poems. The numerous allusions in his poems make translation extremely difficult.

Gu Yun, Luo Yin, etc." (*Notes on the Beginning of Compiling Choice Blossoms of Literature*), and in a sense it "collected thoroughly all the works" as historical documents. In comparison, the guides of *The Anthology of Poetry and Prose* and *Choice Blossoms of Literature* are in direct continuation, but they focused on different aspects; therefore, their qualities and values are different.

Because *Choice Blossoms of Literature* is "too voluminous for a reader to command" (Zhou Bida's words), few men would take a full-range browse, let alone keeping it as a desktop reference like *The Anthology of Poetry and Prose*, which later became a subject of "anthological study". To improve the accessibility of the best works in *Choice Blossoms of Literature*, Gao Sisun of the Song Dynasty reduced the book to 84-volume *The Essence of Choice Blossoms of Literature*; Chen Renxi of the Ming Dynasty to 26-volume *Enlarged Choice Blossoms of Literature*; and Gong Mengren of the Qing Dynasty to 60-volume *Selections of Choice Blossoms of Literature*. Despite these reductions and supplements, *Choice Blossoms of Literature* did not enjoy as much popularity as *The Anthology of Poetry and Prose* throughout the history.

Choice Blossoms of Literature was not so popular mainly for two reasons: one is its voluminous size, and the other is that soon after its completion, another anthology *The Quintessence of the Tang Prose and Poetry* was published, which reflected similar literary concepts to *The Anthology of Poetry and Prose*, and did not aim at the extensive collection of documents. Zhou Bida believed that it was "concise, therefore quintessential, and consequently widely accepted." (*Notes on the Beginning of Compiling Choice Blossoms of Literature*)

The Quintessence of the Tang Prose and Poetry[①] was compiled at the beginning of the Song Dynasty by Yao Xuan[②], who became an official candidate after his success in the imperial examinations in 983. Following *The Anthology of Poetry and Prose*'s methodology, he spent 10 years in compiling *The Quintessence of the Prose and Poetry* (the word "Tang" was added

① *The Quintessence of Tang Prose and Poetry* is a 100-volume collection of the prose and poetry of the Tang Dynasty. It prefers the classical forms of the Tang literature.

② Yao Xuan (968 – 1020), a book-collector and literary critic of the early Song Dynasty.

to the block-edition in the Southern Song Dynasty), and his hard work did pay off. The book was completed in the fourth year (1011) in the Dazhong Xiangfu Period in the reign of Emperor Zhenzong. When he passed away in the fourth year (1020) of the Tianxi Period, his son Yao Sifu presented the book to the emperor, and it was immediately decreed to be preserved in the imperial library. According to the postscript to *The Quintessence of the Tang Prose and Poetry* by Shi Changyan in the second year (1039) of the Baoyuan Period in the reign of Emperor Renzong of the Song Dynasty, Meng Qi, a native of Lin'an and an official candidate, once proofread and block-printed the book. This suggests that *The Quintessence of the Tang Prose and Poetry* went into circulation about twenty years after its completion.

The Quintessence of the Tang Prose and Poetry is an anthology of the prose and poetry of the Tang Dynasty. Yao Xuan explained clearly in the preface: "What is *The Quintessence of Prose and Poetry*? *The Quintessence of Prose and Poetry* is a book that embraces the quintessence of the prose and poetry of the excellent writers of the Tang Dynasty." It covers roughly the same scope as *Choice Blossoms of Literature*. Zhou Bida thought Yao Xuan "selected and explained one-tenth of *Choice Blossoms of Literature* and called it *The Quintessence of the Tang Prose and Poetry*." (*Notes on the Beginning of Compiling Choice Blossoms of Literature*) *The Synoptic Catalogue of the Complete Library of the Four Treasuries* also inherited this view, which, however, is not entirely correct. In *The Quintessence of the Tang Prose and Poetry*, there are works that cannot be found in *Choice Blossoms of Literature*, and in the preface, Yao Xuan said clearly: "I read all anthologies and collections available, and after appreciating and studying them, I selected the quintessential works from them." This should be credible. The relation between *The Quintessence of the Tang Prose and Poetry* and *Choice Blossoms of Literature* is not like the relation between *The Reading Text of the Ming Prose* and *The Sea of the Ming Prose*. *The Sea of the Ming Prose* is a big book (in 600 volumes) compiled by Huang Zongxi of the Qing Dynasty, and reduced to a 62-volume *The Reading Text of the Ming Prose* under his son's request in consideration of its size and accessibility. *The Quintessence of the Tang Prose and Poetry* is by no means the simplified version of *Choice Blossoms of Literature*, but an anthology with the compiler's own ideas.

The unique criteria for the selection of *The Quintessence of the Tang Prose and Poetry* are "to choose the works in elegant and dignified styles, not those in elaborate and ornamental styles. Therefore, the superfluous and lengthy ones are ignored." ("The Preface") In retrospect of the history of literary development, Yao Xuan reiterated the orthodox position of *The Book of Poetry*, reproached depreciatingly the works of Qu Yuan and Song Yu, and took even less consideration of the literature of the Liang, Chen and following dynasties. As for the Tang Dynasty, he recommended highly Han Yu's① practice of classical prose as "superbly extraordinary". Consequently, the majority of the prose in *The Quintessence of the Tang Prose and Poetry* is in the classical style, and few pieces of parallel prose are selected. The same is true for poems and rhapsodies: None of the poems in early modern style that was reaching its perfection in the Tang Dynasty was included. This is a real challenge to our expectation. Let's see some examples: The layout of *The Quintessence of the Tang Prose and Poetry* is just like that of *The Anthology of Poetry and Prose* and *Choice Blossoms of Literature*. The book in a total of 100 volumes was divided by genres into 16 categories: ancient rhapsodies, poems, hymns, comments, reports/memorials/letters/suggestions to the emperor, essays, suggestions, ancient essays, tablet-inscriptions, epigraphs, records, admonishment/exhortations, letters, prefaces, and recorded facts and accounts. The anthology selected 82 pieces of prose by Han Yu, scattered in 15 categories, and 58 pieces by Liu Zongyuan in 12 categories respectively. As for poems, the book selected over sixty poems by Li Bai, and few works were included for other famous poets. This is because both Han Yu and Liu Zongyuan were prose masters in the classical style in the Mid-Tang Prose Movement, and nine-tenth of Li Bai's poems are written in the classical style. They were the masters quite in accordance with the preferential criteria of Yao Xuan and

① Han Yu (768 – 824), courtesy name Tuizhi, a prominent writer, poet, and government official of the Tang Dynasty. Han Yu was an important Confucian intellectual who influenced later generations of Confucian thinkers, and led a reform in prose writing to return to a classical style that is simple, logical, and exact. He is considered one of China's finest prose writers.

accordingly enjoyed outstanding positions with more works selected in the book.

It is worth mentioning here that Yao Xuan had no prejudice against the poetry of the early modern style. On the contrary, he himself was an expert of it. It was recorded in *General Anthology of Poetry Talks* that Yao once composed a seven-syllable regular poem on flowers and fishing in the presence of the emperor. He did so well that he was awarded 100 *liang* of silver ingot. His preference for the prose and poetry in the classical style reflected his perseverance in his literary ideals. The movement of the classical prose was popular in the Mid-Tang Dynasty, but the parallel prose prevailed again in the late Tang and Five Dynasties, by which time the works of Han Yu and Liu Zongyuan received little attention. The collection of Han Yu in the early Song Dynasty, though basically complete, had many misprints and errors, and Liu Zongyuan's anthologies were rarely seen. That was a depressive scene. Yao Xuan had already engaged himself in the renaissance of the classical prose in opposition to the literary trend. In correspondence with the compilation of Han Yu and Liu Zongyuan's works by Mu Xiu, Yao Xuan compiled *The Quintessence of Tang Prose and Poetry* as a means, and thus became the forerunner of the innovation movement of prose and poetry in Northern Song Dynasty. *The Synoptic Catalogue of the Complete Library of the Four Treasuries* made a proper judgment on Yao Xuan's historical position and the situation Yao was faced with:

> No other dynasty ever enjoyed the prosperity of parallel prose and poetry as the Tang Dynasty did. However, decline followed the extreme prosperity as they faded into vulgar styles and became more disparate in the Tang Dynasty than in any other dynasty. Yao Xuan endeavored to terminate the trend, so he adopted the guides. Before the appearance of Ouyang Xiu[①] and Mei Yaochen, it is Yao Xuan

① Ouyang Xiu (1007 – 1072), courtesy name Yongshu and style name Old Drunkard, a statesman, historian, calligrapher, essayist and poet of the Northern Song Dynasty. He is regarded as one of the great masters of prose of the Tang and Song era. His poems are generally relaxed and humorous.

who resolutely initiated the correction of the malpractice of the Five Dynasties in correspondence with Mu Xiu and Liu Kai.

After Ouyang Xiu, Wang Anshi and Su Shi et. al appeared as great masters of the classical prose in the Northern Song Dynasty, the school of classical prose dominated the literary circle and its position could not be shaken. Needless to say, *The Quintessence of the Tang Prose and Poetry* made a great contribution to the movement and had a far-reaching influence in the history. Even later in the Qing Dynasty, Fei Yourong commented that this book excelled other anthologies in "appropriate judgment and discreet selection", "richness of the substance", "conciseness of knowledge" and "fulfillment of the aspiration". (*Postscript to the Collation of The Quintessence of the Tang Prose and Poetry*) Guo Lin even compiled a 26-volume *Supplements to The Quintessence of Tang Prose and Poetry*.

The following are some of the later anthologies similar to *The Quintessence of Tang Prose and Poetry*: *The Collection of the Song Prose as Mirrors* in 150 volumes by Lü Zuqian of the Song Dynasty, *The Collection of the Yuan Prose in Category* in 70 volumes by Su Tianjue of the Yuan Dynasty, *The Collection of the Best Ming Prose* in 98 volumes by Chen Banzheng of the Ming Dynasty and *Records of the Contemporary Prose* in 100 volumes by Yao Chun of the Qing Dynasty.

Chapter Two

Choice Blossoms of Literature and General Anthologies of Poetry and Prose in the Tang Dynasty

Choice Blossoms of Literature records about twenty thousand pieces of poetry and prose by two thousand and two hundred writers in total, nine tenths of which are works composed in the Tang Dynasty. Some scholars believed that it more or less resembled a general anthology of collections of poetry and prose of one dynasty in the later ages. (*A Study on Historical Documents of the History of the Tang Dynasty* by Huang Yongnian) In order to assemble the materials, the compilers, as mentioned above, included in it almost the complete works of Liu Zongyuan, Bai Juyi, Quan Deyu, Li Shangyin, Gu Yun, Luo Yin, etc. It is due to this conspicuous tendency at completeness that *Choice Blossoms of Literature* preserved a great volume of Tang's documents. Many general anthologies of prose and poetry in the later generations, such as *Records of Ancient Poems* by Feng Weina, *Records of Prose in the Past Ages* by Mei Dingzuo of the Ming Dynasty, *The Complete Collection of the Tang Prose* and *The Complete Collection of the Tang Poetry* of the early Qing Dynasty, had consulted and drawn materials from *Choice Blossoms of Literature*. *The Synoptic Catalogue of the Complete Library in the Four Treasuries* pointed out:

> The study on the Tang prose and poetry depended completely on the preservation of this book; it is really a sea of literary works.

Choice Blossoms of Literature is, to some extent, a very important part in the series of general anthologies of the Tang prose and poetry. Now we will investigate into the compilation of general anthologies of prose and poetry in the Tang Dynasty and enrich our knowledge about the status and value of *Choice Blossoms of Literature* in the history of general anthologies of literature.

1. The Contemporary Selections of the Tang Poetry

The Tang poetry is a part of the literature of the Tang Dynasty that has been profoundly and extensively influential. The people of the Tang Dynasty began to have an appreciative and proud attitude towards their own created poems at a very early time. There are about eighty to ninety selections of the Tang poetry to our knowledge. They are all the contemporary selections by the people of the Tang Dynasty. Rich and splendid as they are, these anthologies, whether seriously or carelessly edited, large or small in size, specified in one period or one region, or featuring one or more styles, reflected the enthusiasm of the people in the Tang Dynasty toward their contemporary poetry.

The two earlier anthologies of the Tang poems we now can see were both selected by the contemporaries in the Tianbao Period, and most poets selected were active in the Tianbao and Kaiyuan Periods, the most prosperous time of the empire. Therefore they were indeed "the contemporary selections". *Collection of the Prominent Poets of Rivers and Mountains*① was completed by Yin Fan② in the twelfth year (753) of the Tianbao Period, and *Collection of the Brilliant National Poets*③ by Rui Tingzhang④ over a year later. As we know, the An-Shi Rebellion broke out in the fifteenth year (756) of the Tianbao Period, and the fortunes of Tang Dynasty fell abruptly. These two books were completed at the turning point of the great change.

① *Collection of the Prominent Poets of Rivers and Mountains* is a collection of prime Tang poems.
② Yin Fan (years of birth and death unknown), a writer in the Tang Dynasty.
③ *Collection of the Brilliant National Poets* is a three-volume collection of Tang poems.
④ Rui Tingzhang (years of birth and death unknown), a writer in the Tang Dynasty.

Yin Fan as the compiler of *Collection of the Prominent Poets of Rivers and Mountains* devoted all his life to poetry compilation and remained in obscurity in his lifetime. Besides the collection, he also compiled *The Collection of Danyang*, which selected 18 poets such as Chu Guangxi et. al. in the Zhenjiang area. *Collection of the Prominent Poets of Rivers and Mountains* included 234 poems in two volumes by 24 poets: Li Bai, Wang Wei, Gao Shi, Cen Shen, Meng Haoran, Chu Guangxi, Wang Changling, et. al. Yin Fan proposed a well-known conclusion about the development and maturity of the Tang poetry: Good poems should integrate prosody with vigor. Naturally the standard he applied to the selection of poems concerned these two aspects: form and content. Although he proclaimed to select the excellent poems both in elegance and quality, it seems that he showed little enthusiasm for the newly matured early modern style that was in full blossom in his day. Most of the poems selected were in the classical style, and the regulated poems and quatrains are only in a small number. Later, Gao Bing in his well-known book *Collected Comments on the Tang Poetry* said that this book "favored only the classical style".

The special feature in *Collection of the Prominent Poets of Rivers and Mountains* is that every poet selected receives comments with cited sentences as evidence. Such a combination of selection and comment is a new pattern in the ancient general anthologies. Many comments Yin Fan made are very insightful and serve as the excellent generalization of the poetic development of the Tang Dynasty; therefore, his comments were cited repeatedly, for instance, the above mentioned "vigor", "prosody", etc.

Collection of the Brilliant National Poets is similar to *Collection of the Prominent Poets of Rivers and Mountains* in size with 220 poems in total, but the poets selected are greater in number than those of the latter, including 90 ranging from Li Qiao to Zu Yong. Apart from the first four poets of Li Qiao, Song Zhiwen, Du Shenyan and Shen Quanqi, the rest were all active in the Kaiyuan and Tianbao Periods. It seems that these two books happened to form a sharp contrast in that the latter focused on the classical style, while the former selected more five-syllable regulated poems, and quatrains the next, and few poems in the classical style. The latter paid more attention to vigor, whereas the former to prosody, color, and restrained elegance. Moreover, there is one standard for selection in *Collection of the Brilliant National Poets*: poems "can be matched to music", that is, they can be sung to the accompaniment of music. This naturally resulted in the preference to the regulated verses that were harmoniously rhymed. Therefore, *The Simplified Catalogue of the Complete Library of the Four Treasuries* commented that in the book "all the selected poems are quintessential and graceful", and it can be regarded as an appropriate exposition.

The Rebellion of An (Lushan) and Shi (Siming) brought profound impact on the psychology of the people in the Tang Dynasty. The optimism was replaced by pessimism and romanticism by realism. A powerful and prosperous society turned into ruins and debris in a twinkle, and people were in great sorrow and sadness, while the insightful men began to think about the reason. Yuan Jie[①] witnessed this great change and showed concern about people's lives. He even took part in the war in the An-Shi Rebellion. A year before he compiled *The Collection in a Suitcase*[②], he was introduced by Su Yuanming to Emperor Suzong of the Tang Dynasty who promoted him to an official post in Biyang. There he resisted Shi Siming's army, and defeated the enemy's attack. In the third year of the Qianyuan Period (760), Yuan Jie collected 24 poems by the seven poets — Shen Quanqi, Wang Jiyou, Yu Ti, Meng Yunqing, Zhang Biao, Zhao Weiming, and Yuan Jichuan — into the anthology of *The Collection in a Suitcase*. This is, as far as we know, the smallest general anthology of the Tang poetry, but never at any time negligible in influence. In his preface, Yuan Jie upheld the spirit of *The Book of Songs* as his goal, and opposed the contemporary trend of indulgence in prosody, imitation and description. All the poems in the anthology were five-syllable ones in the classical style, and just as the critics of the Qing Dynasty commented, they were "pure and simple, and free of superfluous ornament." (*The Synopses*) As we read the existing

① Yuan Jie (circa 723 – 772), courtesy name Cishan and style name Manlang or Aosou, a poet of the Tang Dynasty.

② *The Collection in a Suitcase* is a small but influential collection of the Tang poetry.

poems of these poets, we may discover that no poets except Meng Yunqing wrote the early modern regulated poems. It can be said that the poets of this school tried to express their real feelings in the classical poems, and were in opposition to the mainstream of the Tang poetry at that time. The unique presentation of *The Collection in a Suitcase* exhibited the quintessence of the five-syllable poems in the classical style. Later when Wang Anshi of the Song Dynasty edited *Selected Readings of 100 Tang Poets*, he included all the poems in *The Collection in a Suitcase*, which proves, in one way, that Yuan Jie's selection stood the test of time.

The Collection of the Talented Poets in the Restoration Era[1] is an influential contemporary anthology by Gao Zhongwu. It covers the poems written in the reigns of Emperors Suzong and Daizong of the Tang Dynasty, a time known as "the restoration era" after the suppression of the An-Shi Rebellion. It included 140 poems by 26 poets ranging from Qian Qi to Zhang Nanshi. Since the eight poems by Zheng Dang were lost in the Yuanyou Period of the Song Dynasty, only 132 poems were left when Chen Zhensun wrote his *Zhizhai Catalogue and Explanations*.

Like *The Collection of the Prominent Poets of Rivers and Mountains*, *The Collection of the Talented Poets in the Restoration Era* also attached comments to the poets selected and criticisms to the exemplary sentences. Just as Gao Zhongwu said, a lot of five-syllable poems were selected, while seven-syllable poems were few. In the five-syllable poems, the regulated poems prevail over the classical ones, and most of the exemplary sentences commented are indeed taken from the five-syllable regulated poems. The standards of selection, as Gao Zhongwu claimed, are "elegance" and "freshness". Most of the poems and sentences he selected are novel in description of scenery, lucid and elegant in diction, and well-balanced in couplets. These reflected the poetic trend of aesthetic tastes in the Dali Period of the middle Tang Dynasty, and were not the personal occasional preference of the selector. Qian Qi and Lang Shiyuan were highly

[1] *The Collection of the Talented Poets in the Restoration Era* is a collection of over 130 poems compiled in 756 – 779.

recommended in the anthology because they were good at writing five-syllable verses, especially the regulated ones. After the An-Shi Rebellion, the poets of the Dali Period lost the enthusiastic pride in the prime Tang Dynasty, and tended to be serene and harmonious to write fresh and flavorous poems of scenes, which were quite similar to the poetic style of Wang Wei in his late years. Wang is a poet of the prime Tang Dynasty. Gao Zhongwu showed enthusiastic admiration for him and respected him as the Master Poet; moreover, Gao perceived that after the death of Wang Wei, Qian Qi became dominant and his style was exactly "novel" and "refined". It can be said that *The Collection of the Talented Poets in the Restoration Era* is an anthology of the works of Qian Qi, et. al., geniuses of the Dali School. Their poems led a different trend in contrast with the realistic poems in *The Collection in a Suitcase*. A comparison between *The Collection of the Prominent Poets of Rivers and Mountains* and *The Collection of the Talented Poets in the Restoration Era* shows that they shared similarities and relevance in the combination of selection and comment, size, and compilation time (*The Collection of the Prominent Poets of Rivers and Mountains* ended in the twelfth year (753) of the Tianbao Period in the reign of Emperor Xuanzong, and *The Collection of the Talented Poets in the Restoration Era* began in the first year (756) of the Zhide Period in the reign of Emperor Suzong). However, *The Collection of the Prominent Poets of Rivers and Mountains* was earlier in time, so it embodied more poems in the classical style and favored the poems both in vigor and prosody with preference in vigor, while *The Collection of the Talented Poets in the Restoration Era* included a majority of five-syllable regulated poems, and favored the trend of lucid elegance and quiet mildness. This reflects the change of the poetic trends.

After it, there is *An Imperial Reader of the Poems* edited by Linghu Chu, which collected over 300 poems by 30 poets from Liu Fangping to Liang Huang, including the works basically in the reigns of Emperors Daizong and Dezong, and in the first year of the Yuanhe Period of Emperor Xianzong (approximately from 762 to 806). The anthology was originally edited under the edict of Emperor Xianzong for imperial reading, which was why it was named *Imperial Reader of the Poems*, or *The Collection*

Submitted for Imperial Reading. All the poems in it are the early modern regulated poems and story songs, but the classical poems are completely ignored. This reflected the trend of this period. *The Imperial Reader of Poems* has its own preference of taste: The critics of the Ming Dynasty thought they were "all bright colorful short poems" (in Hu Zhenheng's[①] word) and "chiefly slender and colorful expressions" (in Xu Xueyi's word). These comments pointed out their main character.

Yao He enjoyed as much esteem in poetic composition as Jia Dao did. He edited the anthology of poems as a famous poet and of course had his own brilliant judgments. The title of *The Collection of Superb Subtlety* itself indicates a quintessential anthology. It collected 100 poems (one was lost) written by 21 poets. Among them, only Wang Wei and Zu Yong are the poets in the prime Tang period, and the rest are all poets in the Dali Period: Geng Wei, Sikong Shu, Qian Qi, Lang Shiyuan, Huangfu Ran, Liu Changqing, Dai Shulun et al. had considerable poems recorded. Eight or nine out of ten poems selected are five-syllable regulated ones, and only two are classical poems. Now we can see that in fact the anthology is similar to *The Collection of the Talented Poets in the Restoration Era*, and it mainly is a collection of the talented poets of the Dali Period after Wang Wei. *The Collection of Superb Subtlety* had such a great influence that when Ji Yougong of the Song Dynasty compiled *Records of the Tang Poetry*, he would certainly mark out all the poems with annotations that Yao He had once selected.

Another distinctive feature of *The Collection of Superb Subtlety* is that all the poets, except four monks (Lingyi, Fazhen, Jiaoran and Qingjiang), were attached with a profile — his styled name, hometown, official positions, date of passing the civil examination, etc. The practice of attaching poets' profiles to an anthology began with Yao He in this book.

From the several anthologies above, we can discover that the time span between the compilers and the composers were growing gradually longer. *The Collection of the Prominent Poets of Rivers and Mountains*, *The*

① Hu Zhenheng (1569 – 1645), a book-collector and writer of the Ming Dynasty.

Collection in a Suitcase and *The Collection of the Talented Poets in the Restoration Era* can be regarded as the contemporary collections, while the completion of *The Collection of Superb Subtlety* is about 50 years after the death of Wang Wei. The longer the historical development of the Tang poetry is, the more historical, even panoramic the compilers' vistas are. The time span in anthology compilation, previously restricted within a period of time or a genre or a school, was expanded to some extent. For instance, *The Categorized Selection of the Tang Poetry* in 20 volumes by Gu Tao can be regarded as a large-sized anthology. A great part of this book has been lost, but from Gu Tao's preface preserved in *Choice Blossoms of Literature*, we learn that it "recorded up to 1,232 poems from the beginning of the Tang Dynasty to the present time". The several extant volumes of the book can be seen in the third part of *The Series of the Complete Library of the Four Treasuries*.

The selections of the Tang poems by the contemporaries reflected the poetic preference of the contemporaries, and are precious historical materials. It is truly regrettable that a large quantity of them has been lost. However, one contemporary anthology *Three Hundred Poems of the Tang Dynasty* is more fortunate than *The Categorized Selection of the Tang Poetry*. It was recovered in the 20th century, that is, *A Sequel to the Collection of Superb Subtlety* by Wei Zhuang①, the famous poet of the late Tang Dynasty. Here is the story: Professor Xia Chengtao is a distinguished scholar on lyrics and has written several chronicles on the lyricists of the Tang and Song Dynasties. In *The Chronicle of Wei Duanji* (Wei Zhuang), he mentioned *A Sequel to the Collection of Superb Subtlety* was scattered. When Semizu Sigumi of Kyoto University of Japan read this, he sent Xia a facsimile of the book preserved in Japan, so that it reappeared in its homeland.

A Sequel to The Collection of Superb Subtlety was edited by Wei Zhuang in the third year (900) of the Guanghua Period in the reign of Emperor Zhaozong of the Tang Dynasty, and it intentionally continued *The*

① Wei Zhuang (836? – 910), style name Duanyi, a poet in the late Tang Dynasty and the early Five Dynasties.

Collection of Superb Subtlety by Yao He. According to Wei Zhuang's preface, the anthology recorded 300 poems by 150 poets, but in the current version there are 297 poems by 142 poets. The earliest poet is Song Zhiwen of the early Tang Dynasty, and the latest poets are Luo Yin and others, Wei Zhuang's contemporaries. The selection concentrated on the middle and late Tang Dynasty. It is a general anthology that covers a wide range of years. Especially noteworthy is that it included the works of 10 monk poets such as Wuke, and 19 women poets such as Li Zhi, for the first time in its second volume. In *The Complete Collection of the Tang Poetry*, the poems by monks and women were put in separate volumes.

Like *The Collection of the Talented Poets of the Restoration Era* and *The Collection of Superb Subtlety*, the majority of *A Sequel to the Collection of Superb Subtlety* are poems of the modern style. This in one aspect reflected the dominant position of the modern regulated poems in the poetic circle. Moreover, in his own *Collection of Rinsing-Flower Poems*, all the poems were written in the early modern style, which can be regarded as the selector's personal aesthetic preference. The selection standard for *A Sequel to the Collection of Superb Subtlety*, as Wei Zhuang said in his own preface, is "to choose only lucid words and elegant sentences". Du Fu has the largest share in the selection (7 poems), and "lucid words and elegant sentences" happen to be the phrase Du Fu once used in *The Six Quatrains for Fun*. For other poets, such as Du Mu, Wen Tingyun, Jia Dao and Yao He, each has five poems selected. In a word, what *A Sequel to The Collection of Superb Subtlety* selected mainly are the poems of lyrical description of scenes in lucid and graceful expressions. It is an anthology with obvious preference. Wei Zhuang said in his own preface, "to leave the work of stressing on simplicity and eliminating decoration to the people in the later generations."

Wei Gu of the Five Dynasties edited *The Anthology of Literary Talents*, which is the largest extant general anthology of the Tang poetry compiled by a man of the Tang and Five Dynasties. The whole book consists of ten volumes, with 100 poems in one volume, and altogether there are 1,000 poems. In terms of styles, there are the classical, the early modern, and the mixed, story-song styles, and the regulated poems are in majority. The largest share of poems were written in the middle and late Tang Dynasty. The compiler explained in the preface that he edited the anthology simply because he was inspired by reading the poems of Li Bai, Du Fu, Yuan Zhen and Bai Juyi, but we find there is not a single poem by Du Fu in the present edition. Feng Shu of the Qing Dynasty defended Wei Gu with an excuse that it was because Wei Gu respected Du Fu too much to choose his poems. However, *The Synoptic Catalogue of the Complete Library of the Four Treasuries* pointed out clearly that the real reason was that the poetic style of Du Fu was not in accordance with the taste of *The Collection of the Literary Talents*. What it favored was undoubtedly the style of flowery diction and harmonious prosody. Let's see the actual selections: Although Li Bai was highly respected by the compiler, only 28 poems by Li Bai were chosen, while 57 poems by Yuan Zhen, 61 by Wen Tingyun, 40 by Li Shangyin, and 63 by Wei Zhuang were included in the anthology. Therefore, it can be seen that Wei Gu was interested in the flowery and beautiful style, and favored the works of feelings and complaints in the late Tang Dynasty.

2. The Premodern Anthologies of the Tang Poetry

The poets of the Song Dynasty followed immediately the poets of the Tang Dynasty. Facing the splendid achievements of the Tang poetry, they were bent on opening a new route of their own. However, the opening of the new route had to begin with a careful study of the Tang poetry. The study of the Tang poetry by the Song scholars was based on the compilation of various anthologies. In fact many individual anthologies of the Tang poetry were perfected in the collation of the Song scholars, and the most well-known ones were undoubtedly the collections of Du Fu and Han Yu. Their circulation owed much to the continuous work of collecting, revising and printing undergone by the scholars of the Song Dynasty. It was claimed that at that time there were 1,000 annotated versions of Du Fu's works and 500 of Han Yu's. The compilation of general anthologies, besides the individual collections, was thriving as well. As we have noticed in the previous chapter, *Choice Blossoms of Literature* contained 180 volumes of poems and could be regarded as the first general anthology of the Tang poetry compiled by the scholars of the Song Dynasty. Its greatest features are its high quantity and authenticity. Though there were only nine volumes of poems in Yao Xuan's *The Quintessence of the Tang Poetry and Prose*, they were all poems in the classical style and might be regarded as an insightful collection of the Tang poems in the classical style. The next one worth mentioning is *Selected Readings of 100 Tang Poets* in 20 volumes compiled by Wang Anshi.

There are over 1,200 poems composed by 104 poets in *Selected Readings of 100 Tang Poets*. Although it is big in size, it doesn't seem to have any particular purpose except for the obvious preference for the poems of the middle and late Tang Dynasty. With regard to its selection, it has incurred a lot of comments since its publication. Zhu Xi considered it a careless selection by Wang Anshi ("In reply to Gong Zhongzhi"); Yan Yu was very much discontented with the selected poems after the middle Tang Dynasty (*Canglang Poetic Talks*); Wang Shizhen claimed frankly that Wang Anshi's criteria of selection were beyond comprehension ("Postscript to *The Unabridged Edition of The Selected Readings of 100 Tang Poets* by Wang Anshi"); as for *The Synoptic Catalogue of the Complete Library of the Four Treasuries*, it simply said that the criteria for selection of the anthology "could not be understood at all". All these opinions resulted from one single fact: The anthology left out too many eminent poets in its selection. For example, it neglected "the four talents" of Wang Bo, Yang Jiong, Lu Zhaolin, and Luo Bingwang, as well as Shen Quanqi, Song Zhiwen, and Chen Zi'ang in the early Tang Dynasty; in the prime Tang Dynasty, it left out Li Bai, Du Fu, Wang Wei; in the middle Tang Dynasty, it missed out Han Yu, Liu Zongyuan, Yuan Zhen, Bai Juyi, Meng Jiao, Wei Yingwu, and Li He; and in the late Tang Dynasty, it missed out Li Shangyin, Du Mu, and Wen Tingyun. Just think about it: Without these poets, is there a prosperous scene of the Tang poetry? As for poets like Gao Shi, Cen Shen, Wang Jian, their poems saw a great deal of selection (almost 100 each), and no one knows why it was so unbalanced. This anthology was compiled in the Jiayou period of the Song Dynasty by Wang Anshi at the request of his colleague Song Minqiu, who provided more than 100 anthologies of the Tang poetry stored in his home as the source of selection. Someone guessed that the shortcoming of the book was due to the scarcity in Song Minqiu's collections, but Wang Shizhen argued that Song couldn't have been regarded as a bibliophile if his collections were inadequate. Another explanation was that Wang Anshi put stickers on the poems he chose for copying, but the copyists moved the stickers from the long poems to the short ones in their exhaustion of the endless transcription work. Wang Anshi did not check the copy, and the selection became a mess. This may be an excuse for the replacement of long poems with short ones, but not for the total absence of so many great writers. A better explanation was that the great poets had their personal anthologies, so only the lesser poets were included.

10,000 Quatrains of the Tang Poets, compiled by Hong Mai, a well-known scholar in the Southern Song Dynasty, is a general anthology of solely quatrains with a lot of mistakes and errors. There is a story about its compilation. Hong Mai compiled 5,400 quatrains of the Tang poets and presented it to Emperor Xiaozong in the Chunxi Period. When the emperor asked him the exact total number of the quatrains of the Tang Dynasty, Hong Mai answered without thinking: 10,000. Then the emperor ordered him to gather them all for him. This put Hong Mai in great trouble. After several years of arduous work, the book was finally completed in the third year (1192) of the Shaoxi Period. This anthology consists of 75 volumes of seven-syllable quatrains and 25 volumes of five-syllable quatrains, amounting to 100 volumes and 10,000 pieces (with an additional volume of six-syllable quatrains). Unfortunately only 91 volumes were left when it was included into *The Complete Library in the Four Treasuries* in the Qing Dynasty.

This voluminous book can be regarded as a general collection of the Tang quatrains from various individual anthologies, biographies, and even fiction. However, many problems arose in the course of making up a round number of 10,000. For example, it took in some quatrains of the Song poets, such as Li Jiuling, Guo Zhen, Teng Bai, Wang Chu, and so on. The strangest thing was that the quatrains by He Xun of the Southern Dynasties were included. Obviously it was a careless mistake in collation. If these mistakes were due to the compiler's carelessness, then splitting the regulated verses into quatrains was an obviously intentional operation to make up the number of 10,000. Early in the Southern Song Dynasty, Liu Kezhuang already pointed out in his *Houcun Poetic Talks* that Hong Mai gathered all kinds of books and had the quatrains copied, but without any critical examination, simply to make up the number. Later Zhao Huanguang and Huang Xiyuan of the Ming Dynasty revised and supplemented this book. Despite its many problems, *10,000 Quatrains of the Tang Poets* preserved many quatrains; for example, quite a few after the middle Tang Dynasty are absent in the individual anthologies we have now. Hu Zhenheng, an expert on the study of the Tang poetry in the Ming Dynasty, affirmed that "Hong Mai's contribution of research and collection cannot be denied."

10,000 Quatrains of the Tang Poets is, after all, a comprehensive and oversized book. Lin Qingzhi of the Song Dynasty once selected the better poems from it to make *Selected Quatrains of the Tang Poets* in 4 volumes, which contained 1,280 seven-syllable quatrains, 156 five-syllable quatrains and 15 six-syllable quatrains (Chen Zhensun: *Explanation to Zhizhai Catalogue*). However, it is lost now. In the Qing Dynasty, Wang Shizhen, great master of the Romantic Charm School, abridged it into *Selections of 10,000 Quatrains of the Tang Poets* in 7 volumes, which included 895 quatrains by 264 poets. The book was completed three years before his death, and could represent Wang Shizhen's literary ideas in his late years. The book has its own style, and was very popular for a time. Li Ciming praised that it collected "almost all famous quatrains and excellent sentences." (*Reading Notes of Yuemantang*).

The poetic style of the late Tang Dynasty prevailed from the early Northern Song Dynasty to the late Southern Song Dynasty. Zhao Shixiu, the "River-lake School" poet at the end of the Song Dynasty, also known as one of the "Four Lings of Yongjia", learned to compose poems from

Jia Dao and Yao He of the late Tang Dynasty. Their poetic style became naturally his criteria of selection when he compiled *The Collection of All Wonders*. The 76 poets selected ranged from Shen Quanqi of the early Tang Dynasty to Wang Zhenbai of the late Tang Dynasty. All the poems in the anthology are regulated ones, of which the greater part is the five-syllable regulated verses, and seven-syllable poems amount to only one-tenths. The fluent and graceful style prevails in this book. 23 poems by Liu Changqing were selected as the top contributor, whereas no more than ten poems were selected for each of the rest poets. However, no poems were selected from Jia Dao and Yao He, whom he admired most, for there is an anthology of *The Collection of Two Wonders* devoted solely to their works. This is much like the case of Wang Anshi's *Selected Readings of 100 Tang Poets*. Though Li Bai and Du Fu were not included in the book, there was a special anthology *Selected Works of Four Poets*, in which Li Bai was labeled as the fourth and Du Fu the first poets. *The Collection of All Wonders* was not published for a long time. Its circulation and transmission were achieved through the transcription of enthusiasts, which also proved its partiality for a particular style.

Another large general anthology of the Tang poems at the end of the Song Dynasty is entitled *Categorized Collection of the Tang Melody and Poetry*. Its compiler is Zhao Mengkui, a descendent of the eleventh generation of Emperor Taizu of the Song Dynasty. He was conferred on the title of would-be official in the same bulletin with Wen Tianxiang in the fourth year (1256) of the Baoyou Period of the Southern Song Dynasty. He categorized and compiled the poems from the anthologies stored in his home and works he collected from elsewhere into a voluminous book of 40,791 poems by 1,353 poets in 100 volumes, which approaches in size *The Complete Collection of the Tang Poetry* compiled in the Qing Dynasty. It is a pity that this anthology made through ten years of compilation was scattered gradually. Ye Wenzhuang of the Ming Dynasty only copied 27 volumes left (*Postscript to The Fragmented Version of Categorized Collection of the Tang Melody and Poetry*). Today there are only eleven volumes available — five in the categories of heaven, earth, mountains and rivers, and six of grass, trees, fish and insects. Many poems in the fragments are not found in other collections. If the anthology had been kept intact, it would have provided us with a great quantity of precious materials of the Tang poems.

In the Jin Dynasty, being confronted with the Southern Song Dynasty, the learning of the Tang poetry was quite different from that of the Southern Song Dynasty. People in the Southern Song Dynasty were especially fond of the five-syllable regulated poems of the late Tang Dynasty, whereas people of the Jin Dynasty liked the seven-syllable regulated poems of the Tang Dynasty. It has been said that *Advocacy of the Tang Poetry* compiled by Yuan Haowen selected solely the seven-syllable regulated poems of the Tang poets. The anthology has 596 poems by 96 poets in 10 volumes. But the chronological order for the poets is confused: The first poem is "Ascending the Tower of Liuzhou" by Liu Zongyuan, then the poems by Wang Wei, Li Bai, Gao Shi and Cen Shen were interspersed. Qian Qianyi believed the book was a casual record of Yuan Haowen's random reading and later went into circulation by transcription (Preface to *Advocacy of the Tang Poetry*). With regard to the contents, the book favored the poems of the late Tang Dynasty; for instance, it selected 31 poems by Xu Hun, 35 by Lu Guimeng, 22 by Pi Rixiu, 32 by Du Mu, 34 by Li Shangyin, 38 by Tan Yongzhi, and 19 by Wei Zhuang, whose selections are larger than others. Different from the slender and trivial style preferred by the poets of the River-lake school and the Four Lings of Yongjia of the Southern Song Dynasty, the poems in this anthology "on the whole are vigorous and magnanimous", as *The Synoptic Catalogue of The Complete Library of the Four Treasuries* commented. Even Xu Xueyi who was discontented with the book had to admit that "the delicate poems of the late Tang Dynasty amount to only one-tenth" (*The Origins, Genres and Styles of Poetry*); in other words, only a small number of poems selected were in the delicate style of the late Tang Dynasty.

The Yuan Dynasty did not see prosperity of its literature. In poetics, critics generally inherited the critical reflections of Yan Yu of the Southern Song Dynasty on the Song poems, and favored the styles of the Tang poetry. And in theory, they were no longer restricted to those of the late

Tang Dynasty, and gradually emphasized the styles of the prime Tang Dynasty. This trend was manifested in the anthology *The Voice of the Tang Dynasty*, compiled and commented by Yang Shihong. In his preface, Yang Shihong mentioned that many anthologies "represented the poems in the prime Tang Dynasty in brevity, but those in the late Tang Dynasty in detail", such as *The Collection of Superb Subtlety*, *A Sequel to The Collection of Superb Subtlety*, *The Collection of the Literary Talents*, *Selected Readings of 100 Tang Poets*, *10,000 Quatrains of the Tang Poets*, *Composition Methods of the Three Genres of the Tang Master Poets*, etc. Therefore, he selected more poems from the prime Tang Dynasty. There are, for example, 22 five-syllable regulated verses and 9 seven-syllable regulated verses by Wang Wei. In the layout, the anthology demonstrated its preference to the prime Tang Dynasty. *The Voice of the Tang Dynasty* is divided into three parts: "beginning of the voice" in 1 volume, "standard of the voice" in 6 volumes and "last of the voice" in 7 volumes. The "standard of the voice" referred mainly to the poems of the early and prime Tang Dynasty. It can be said that this anthology is the first to focus on the poems of the prime Tang Dynasty. This book, a result of 10 years of compilation, selected 1,343 poems by over 170 poets, and exerted a great influence on the studies of the Tang poetry. We will find that *Collected Comments on the Tang Poems* by Gao Bing of the early Ming Dynasty in fact "followed the guides of *The Voice of the Tang Dynasty* with some modifications," (*The Synoptic Catalogue of The Complete Library of the Four Treasuries*) but it is more compact and meticulous. It is undeniable that the basic theoretic tendencies, and the views on the relation between the standards and the changes of the poetry through the early, prime, middle and late Tang Dynasty in the two books are in conformity.

Collected Comments on the Tang Poems was compiled by Gao Bing, who was known as one of the "Ten Masters of Fujian". He expressed in the preface his discontent with *The Collection in a Suitcase*, *The Collection of the Prominent Poets of Rivers and Mountains*, *The Collection of the Literary Talents in the Restoration Era*, *Choice Blossoms of Literature* and *The Collected Poems of Music Bureau*, and believed, like Yang Shihong, that many anthologies presented the poetic development in the late Tang Dynasty in detail, but only briefly mentioned that in the prime Tang Dynasty. He praised only *The Voice of the Tang Dynasty*, which "can discriminate the beginning and the end of the development of the genres and styles and judge the orthodoxy and variation for the prosody." He developed the idea of *The Voice of the Tang Dynasty* into a new comprehensive system about the ranks, origins and variations of the Tang poetry.

The Collected Comments on the Tang Poetry in 90 volumes contained 5,769 poems by 620 poets, and later the 10-volume *Recollections* was added which included 954 poems by 61 poets. The book was arranged in seven genres of poems, including: five-syllable classical style, seven-syllable classical style, five-syllable quatrains, seven-syllable quatrains, five-syllable regulated style, five-syllable long regulated style, and seven-syllable regulated style. In each genre, there were subdivisions to evaluate the poems in different phases: proper beginning, standard, great masters, well-known masters, wings, successors, variations, reverberations, and bypaths. *The Voice of the Tang Dynasty* divided the Tang poems into three categories as "beginning voice", "standard voice" and "last voice" — corresponding roughly to the three stages of the early and prime, middle, and late Tang Dynasty. Gao Bing clearly divided the divisions of the Tang poetry into four phases: early, prime, middle and late. His "proper beginning" roughly refers to the early Tang Dynasty, "standard, great masters, well-known masters and wings" to the prime Tang Dynasty, "successors" to the middle Tang Dynasty, "variations, and last voice" to the late Tang Dynasty. The works by monks, Taoist priests and women were classified as "bypaths". What *The Collected Comments on the Tang Poetry* recommended most were the poets of the prime Tang Dynasty, such as Li Bai, Du Fu, Wang Wei, Meng Haoran, Cen Shen and Gao Shi. Considerable attention was paid to some poets of the middle Tang Dynasty as well, in view of the number of the poems selected from Liu Changqing, Qian Qi, and Wei Yingwu, for example. As for the powerful, fresh and delicate, leisurely and simple, and elegant styles, all were appreciated by Gao Bing.

The Collected Comments on the Tang Poetry exerted a great influence on the understanding of the development of the Tang poetry and the evaluation of the poets. Hu Yinglin said if one wanted to learn about the Tang poetry, the right way was to start with this book. The anthologies of the Tang poetry, according to Hu, "are complete up to *The Collected Comments on the Tang Poetry* of Gao Tingli (Gao Bing), and concise up to *The Standard Voice of the Tang Poetry*. To learn the Tang poetry, one must have an intimate knowledge of these two books so as not to go astray." (*Pond of Poetry*) The above-mentioned *The Standard Voice* refers to the 22-volume *The Standard Voice of the Tang Poetry*, a simplified version of *The Collected Comments on the Tang Poetry*, which is much more detailed than its unabridged version on the poetry of the prime Tang Dynasty.

The advocacy of the prime Tang poetry, first proposed by Yan Yu and later practiced and advocated by Gao Bing in his *The Collected Comments on the Tang Poetry*, made a great impact on the literary trends of the mid Ming Dynasty. *The Synoptic Catalogue of the Complete Library of the Four Treasuries* pointed out:

> Later Li Mengyang, He Jingming and others imitated the poems of the prime Tang Dynasty, which was called an abrupt rise, and its source actually started from here.

Most poetics of the Ming Dynasty expressed individual literary tastes. Li Panlong's *Selected Poems of the Tang Dynasty* was typical in this case to represent the literary taste for a time in the Ming Dynasty. This book was abridged by some later scholar from Li Panlong's *Ancient and Modern Poems after Deletion*, a book which included the poems from ancient times to the Tang Dynasty, skipped the works of the Song and Yuan Dynasties, and was followed immediately by the poems of the Ming Dynasty, thus illustrating Li Mengyang's view that "there is no poetry in the Song Dynasty". With regard to the part of the Tang poems only, i.e. as far as *Selected Poems of the Tang Dynasty* is concerned, it can fully reveal the selector's poetic tastes. Tu Long of the Ming Dynasty remarked: "The poems of the Tang Dynasty Li Yulin (Panlong) chose were all in a forceful style with sonorous rhymes, and were similar to the poems he composed himself." (*On Poetry and Prose*)

Li Chonghua of the Qing Dynasty also said: "Li Yulin is quite talented, but lacks some learning. His selections have not fully demonstrated the quintessence of the poets selected." (*Poetic Talks at Zhenyi Studio*) This reflects his preference in selection of poems.

The compilers of the Ming Dynasty in their selection of poems usually expressed their own preferences for literary genres and styles. In regard to this tendency, Tan Yuanchun at the end of the Ming Dynasty said very clearly: "In compiling anthologies, it is not that the later scholars selected the books by ancient people, but they adopted the approaches to write their own books." (Preface to *The Collection of Ancient Prose*) *The Convergence of Poems* co-edited by him and Zhong Xing is such an example.

The Convergence of Poems selected the poems from the ancient times to the Tang Dynasty: poems before the Tang Dynasty in 15 volumes and poems of the Tang Dynasty in 36 volumes, which were block-printed under the titles of *The Convergence of Ancient Poems* and *The Convergence of the Tang Poems* respectively. *The Convergence of Poems* was the fruit of some arduous work. Zhong Xing claimed that "nine-tenths of all my energy is devoted to *The Convergence of Poetry*." ("A Letter to Tan Youxia") *The Convergence of the Tang Poetry* consists of the poems of the early Tang Dynasty in 5 volumes, of the prime Tang Dynasty in 19 volumes, of the middle Tang Dynasty in 8 volumes, and of the late Tang Dynasty in 4 volumes, all attached with comments. Its main inclination is to propagate the poetic styles of "deliberation, strangeness, profundity and subtlety". Hence the poems selected are novel, and the well-known poems by great masters are usually excluded, such as Li Bai's "Hard Is the Road to Shu" and "Please Drink Wine". The major contributors, besides Li Bai and Du Fu, include Wang Wei, Meng Haoran, Chu Guangxi, Liu Changqing, Chang Jian, etc. All these indicated the aesthetic tastes of the compilers. The literary ideals of Zhong Xing and Tan Yuanchun, like those of the Gong'an School led by Yuan Hongdao, aim to express the natural feelings and oppose the restoration and imitation practice popular in the middle Ming Dynasty. Consequently *The Convergence of the Tang Poems* demonstrated the different literary inclination from Li Panlong's *The Selection of the Tang Poems*, and adapted itself to the trend of the late Ming Dynasty. Therefore, for a time it became very influential. It was said that almost every home kept one copy of it and revered it as much as *The Book of Poetry* abridged by Kong Zi. But as soon as it went out of fashion, *The Convergence of the Tang Poetry* was neglected by most people.

Still there was a similar selection whose selectors "in fact wrote their own books when selecting the poems by ancient people" (Zhong Xing: *A Letter to Cai Jingfu*) — Wang Shizhen's *A Collection of Samadhi of the Tang Master Poets* in the Qing Dynasty. This is a selection of the prime Tang poems, collecting over 480 poems by 43 poets beginning with Wang Wei, and obviously it has its own preference. Wang Shizhen said in his preface: He selected the poems in three volumes because he was indulgent in reading the poems written in the Kaiyuan and Tianbao Periods, and had "his own understanding" of the poetics of Sikong Tu and Yan Yu. These poems are the embodiment of Wang Shizhen's poetic concepts of "charm" and "wittiness" to some extent. Li Bai and Du Fu were excluded, as they were accounted for in *The Selected Readings of 100 Tang Poets* by Wang Anshi, while Wang Wei and Meng Haoran became the head poets in the selection. The book "focused mainly on harmony, simplicity and profundity", and "is the descendant of Wang Wei, but not the successor of Li Bai and Du Fu". (Weng Fanggang: *Examples of Samadhi of Seven-syllable Poems*)

Shen Deqian, on the contrary, respected Li Bai and Du Fu as great masters in his discussion of the prime Tang poetry. In the title of his book *Different Choices of the Tang Poems*, the phrase "different choices" was picked directly from Du Fu's poem in the "Six Quatrains for Fun". *Different Choices of the Tang Poems* in 22 volumes collected approximately 2,000 Tang poems, and covered a relatively wide scope with rational and balanced evaluation. It has long been valued by readers and circulated extensively. In the preface to the book, Shen Deqian mentioned Wang Shizhen's *The Collection of Samadhi of the Tang Master Poets*, and thought that although his selection manifested the charm of the Tang poetry, the aspect of grandiosity was not touched upon. Therefore, his *Different Choices of the Tang Poems* included the poems of different kinds of genres, and became a more comprehensive and widely accepted anthology. As we all know that for over two hundred years the most popular anthology of the Tang poems is *Three Hundred Poems of the Tang Dynasty* compiled by a hermit of Hengtang. It is actually based on *Different Choices of the Tang Poems* as its source materials, as more than two-thirds of the 300 poems of the Tang Dynasty are identical. This reveals in one aspect the great influence of *Different Choices of the Tang Poems*.

When many special anthologies reflecting the poetics of the compilers were popular in the Ming and Qing Dynasties, the general anthologies attempting to accumulate all poems of the Tang Dynasty began to grow. Apart from the series of *The Collection of 100 Tang Poets* by Zhu Jing of the Ming Dynasty and *The Collection of 100 Tang Famous Poets* by Xi Qiyu of the Qing Dynasty, the corpus of the Tang poetry was finished by the joint efforts of the scholars of quite a few generations: from the sizable general anthologies such as *The Complete Voice of the Tang Dynasty* in 1,033 volumes by Hu Zhenheng, *The Records of the Tang Poetry* in 170 volumes by Wu Guan, *The Categorized Collection of the Tang Poetry* in 200 volumes by Zhang Zhixiang, *Collected Poems of the Four Tang Periods* in 190 volumes by Wu Mianxue, and *Shicang Selected Readings of the Tang Poetry* in 110 volumes by Cao Xuequan in the Ming Dynasty, to *The Tang Poetry* in 717 volumes by Ji Zhenyi, and *The Complete Collection of the Tang Poetry* in 900 volumes by Peng Dingqiu of the Qing Dynasty.

The Records of the Tang Poetry in 170 volumes was compiled and block-printed by Wu Guan of the Ming Dynasty. He had printed Feng Weina's *The Records of the Ancient Poems* which was a big anthology in 156 volumes and included the poems from the ancient times to the Chen and Sui Dynasties. At that time, a man named Huang Qingfu had the intention to continue *The Records of the Ancient Poems* and started his work on the early Tang Dynasty. He died when 16 volumes were finished. His manuscripts were discovered by Lu Bi, Xie Bi, Yu Tichu et al., who encouraged the wealthy Wu Guan to continue the compilation. After the sections of the early Tang Dynasty in 60 volumes and the prime Tang Dynasty in 110 volumes were finished, the board of the compilers was dissolved.

Therefore, *The Records of the Tang Poetry* is actually a half-done general anthology of the Tang poems.

The Categorized Collection of the Tang Poetry and *The Categorized Collection of the Ancient Poetry* are two chronologically connected books and edited by Zhang Zhixiang. The 200-volume book is arranged in 36 categories: astronomy, geography, emperors and kings, officialdom, ceremony, civil and military officials, personage, residence, utensils, handicraft and techniques, grass and trees, insects and fish, etc. Zhang Zhixiang intended to collect all the poems of the Tang Dynasty indiscriminately within his reach and listed them in corresponding categories. But grouping the poems by category was out of date and did not work well in the compilation of a general anthology of the poems of an era.

The Complete Collection of the Tang Voice by Hu Zhenheng is another important general anthology of the Tang poetry in a great size of 1,000 odd volumes, and is regarded as the biggest general anthology compiled by an individual. It was divided into ten parts and arranged in the sequence of Heavenly Stems of *jia*, *yi*, *bing*, *ding*, *wu*, *ji*, *geng*, *xin*, *ren*, and *gui*, i.e. from one to ten, and aimed to accumulate all poems available of the Tang and Five Dynasties, and then arrange them in chronological order. In the tenth part of *gui* were recorded the criticisms and comments on the Tang poetry. We know that *The Records of the Ancient Poems* compiled by Feng Weina is also attached with 12 volumes of poetic comments by the previous critics. The tenth part of *gui* may be the most popular part of the whole book. Wang Shizhen, the leader of Qing poetic circle, had read it. The rest parts were never printed in full length due to their huge size. The first to be printed in the reign of Emperor Kangxi was the fifth part of *wu* in 201 volumes and *The Supplement* in 64 volumes. At that time Feng Ban and Feng Shu advocated the Xikun style① and attacked the Song poetry. The style of the late Tang poems prevailed at the time. The fifth part of *wu* contained all the poems of the late Tang Dynasty, while the *Supplement*

① The Xikun Style, a poetic style popularized by Yang Yi (974 – 1020) et. al. in their chant-and-reply, is characterized by delicate diction but weak thought.

contained the poems of the Southern Tang Dynasty and the Wu-Yue Kingdom. Those poems were in accordance with the trend, so they were printed first. On the printed copies, they were numbered Volumes 553 to 817 — those were their serial numbers in the whole book. It showed that the book was planned to be printed in full length. However, later the first four parts and the sixth and seventh parts were printed and rarely went in circulation. The complete book was kept in the imperial library and was very helpful to the later compilation of *The Complete Collection of the Tang Poetry*. Now the printed copies and the supplementary manuscripts are combined as the complete version and preserved in the Palace Museum, Beijing.

The most famous general anthology of the Tang's poetry in the Qing Dynasty is *The Complete Collection of the Tang Poetry*. It is also the most fundamental book so far for us to learn about the general outlook of the Tang's poetry. The compilation of *The Complete Collection of the Tang Poetry* in fact owes much to the two books compiled by the scholars of the Ming Dynasty, i.e. *The Records of the Tang Poetry* and *The Complete Collection of the Tang Voice*.

The Complete Collection of the Tang Poetry contained over 49,400 poems by 2,800 odd poets in 900 volumes. The poems of the emperors, empresses and imperial concubines were listed at the beginning of the book. Other poets were listed in chronological order. In the last part there were the poems of monks, Daoists, foreigners, young ladies of note, immortals, ghosts and monsters. The new lyrics were also included as an appendix. All poets were followed by their profiles, and some poems had annotations as the reference for the different wording. *The Complete Collection of the Tang Poetry* has some problems, such as wrong inclusion and repetition of poems, mistakes in the annotations and profiles, etc., which have been revised by Kewa Yomusiro of Japan, Wang Zhongmin, Sun Wang, Tong Yangnian, Chen Shangjun of China. Anyway, *The Complete Collection of the Tang Poetry* has made a great contribution to the history of Chinese literature. Its most outstanding merit is undoubtedly its "completeness", to gather the literary documents of one era for easy access. *The Synoptic Catalogue of the Complete*

Library of the Four Treasuries commented:

> Such an anthology presents clearly the origin and development, the beginning and end, and the standard and variations of the Tang poetry. Since the appearance of general anthology, there has never been such a quintessential and comprehensive general anthology like *The Complete Collection of the Tang Poetry*.

Generally speaking, this comment is appropriate.

The block printing of *The Complete Collection of the Tang Poetry* was supervised by Cao Yin, grandfather of Cao Xueqin who wrote the novel *The Dream of Red Mansions*. It was recorded that this sizable, beautifully bound book was finished at a surprising speed in one year and a half. We learn now that *The Complete Collection of the Tang Poetry* was in fact a final work of compilation of different anthologies of the Tang poetry in the Ming and Qing Dynasties. It is a synthesis of the academic achievements of several generations of scholars, and was not merely the result of the efforts of Peng Dingqiu and several academicians of the imperial academy of the Qing Dynasty. *The Synoptic Catalogue of the Complete Library of the Four Treasuries* mentioned that the basis for the compilation of *The Complete Collection of the Tang Poetry* was *The Complete Collection of the Tang Voice* by Hu Zhenheng and *The Collected Poems of the Whole Tang Dynasty* preserved in the imperial library. The former has been introduced above, and as for the latter, it was not until 1930s that it was confirmed to be *The Poems of the Tang Dynasty* edited by Ji Zhenyi, a native of Yixing, and a famous bibliophile in the early Qing Dynasty. In the preface of *About the Compilation of The Poems of the Tang Dynasty*, he professed that "(I) chose 42,931 poems by 1,895 poets; it took me 10 years, from the 3rd to the 12th years in the reign of Emperor Kangxi." The 10-year arduous work had its own basis:

> Minister Qian of Changshu once attempted to collect all the poems of the Tang Dynasty on the basis of *The Records of the Tang*

> *Poetry*. Although he was devoted to the cause and could do it, he did not complete it. No one in the south of the great river had any idea of such a book. When I got the manuscripts from Zunwang, the clan grandson of the minister, more than half of the book was missing. I revised them into a book of 717 volumes. (*About the Compilation of The Poems of the Tang Dynasty*)

That is to say, *The Poems of the Tang Dynasty* compiled by Ji Zhenyi was actually based on the incomplete manuscripts compiled by Qian Qianyi, a master in the poetic circle at the turn of the Ming and Qing Dynasties. According to Qian Qianyi's letter, the part of the early and prime Tang Dynasty in Qian Qianyi's general anthology was compiled mainly on the basis of *The Records of the Tang Poetry*. We have mentioned previously that *The Records of the Tang Poetry* consists of only the parts of the early and prime Tang Dynasty. Those two parts, through the work of Qian Qianyi and Ji Zhenyi, were finally embodied in *The Complete Collection of the Tang Poetry*. The block-printing of these two parts was the quickest in the entire book and finished within only about half a year. As to the poems of the middle and late Tang Dynasty, *The Complete Collection of the Tang Poetry* had more revisions and supplements in comparison with Ji Zhenyi's *The Poems of the Tang Dynasty*. Those revisions and supplements must have made good use of Cao Yin's collections (he once bought from Xu Qianxue dozens of anthologies of the Tang poetry printed in the Song Dynasty) and other collected books, in which Hu Zhenheng's *The Complete Collection of the Tang Voice* played an important role. For example, the anthology compiled by Yin Yaopan was not included in Ji Zhenyi's *The Poems of the Tang Dynasty*, but it was transferred to *The Complete Collection of the Tang Poetry* directly from *The Complete Collection of the Tang Voice*. Besides, many fragments of poems embodied in *The Complete Collection of the Tang Voice* were also transferred to *The Complete Collection of the Tang Poetry*. Therefore, *The Complete Collection of the Tang Poetry* is actually the final achievement of the joint efforts on the compilation of the general anthologies of the Tang poetry by scholars in the Ming and Qing Dynasties. The important figures to be honored should include Wu Guan, Hu Zhenheng, Qian Qianyi, Ji Zhenyi, and Cao Yin and Peng Dingqiu as well.

We have surveyed the compilation of general anthologies of the Tang poetry in different dynasties. The anthologies compiled by the scholars of the Tang Dynasty were mostly guided by certain literary concepts and each was in a distinct line of succession. The size of the anthologies began to grow in the Song and Yuan Dynasties; generally the poems of the late Tang Dynasty were favored, and this trend was also reflected in the compilation of anthologies. In the Ming and Qing Dynasties, people had a broader view and were able to understand a complete and comprehensive picture of the Tang poetry. Of the two kinds of collections, one was to uphold a literary concept, and another to accumulate all the poems of the Tang Dynasty; both had some success. Hu Zhenheng labeled these two inclinations as "selectors" and "collectors". *Choice Blossoms of Literature* contained many complete individual anthologies. Therefore, Hu Zhenheng put it and *The Records of the Tang Poems* in the group of "collectors", while *Selected Readings of 100 Tang Poets, The Quintessence of the Tang Prose and Poetry*, *Advocacy for the Tang Poetry*, *The Collection of the Tang Voice*, *The Collected Comments on the Tang Poems* and *Selected Poems of the Tang Dynasty* were grouped into "selectors". There were so many collectors because "many poems of the Tang Dynasty were missing in later ages." (*The Ten Parts of the Tang Voice*) It can be seen that *Choice Blossoms of Literature* (here referring specifically to the section of poetry) aimed at accumulating and therefore preserving the documents, and therefore played an important part in the compilation of general anthologies of the Tang poetry in the Song Dynasty and in the later periods.

3. Brief Introduction to the General Anthologies of the Tang Prose

The compilation of the Tang prose is not as successful as that of the Tang poetry. Only a few of the general anthologies of the prose of the Tang Dynasty are well-known, yet they are no less influential than the popular general anthologies of the Tang poetry.

There is no doubt that the classical prose Han Yu, Liu Zongyuan and others propagated and practiced had the greatest influence on the later generations in the prose of the Tang Dynasty. Although their efforts were frustrated for a time in the late Tang Dynasty, the several great prose masters of the Northern Song Dynasty succeeded to their cause and developed the classical prose to success. We have mentioned that Yao Xuan abandoned the parallel prose, recommended and respected the prose works of Han Yu and Liu Zongyuan. This is the precursor of the reform movement of prose and poetry in the Northern Song Dynasty. Later, a great scholar Lü Zuqian compiled *The Cruxes of the Classical Prose*. He also succeeded to the literary concepts of this school; in his collection he selected all the works of the classical prose masters of the Tang and Song Dynasties, and included over sixty pieces of the prose of the seven masters: Han Yu, Liu Zongyuan, Ouyang Xiu, Zeng Gong, Su Xun, Su Shi, Zhang Lei. It was said that at the end of the Song Dynasty, Xie Bingde compiled *The Model Essays* in seven volumes, in which there were 69 essays by 15 writers from the Han to Song Dynasties, and half of the essays were written by Han Yu — this obviously recommended and promoted the classical prose of the Tang Dynasty. At the beginning of the Ming Dynasty, Zhu You compiled *A New Selection of Essays by Six Masters*, in which he replaced Zhang Lei with Wang Anshi, and combined Su Xun, Su Shi and Su Zhe into one volume, to expand the group into eight together with Han Yu, Liu Zongyuan, Ouyang Xiu and Zeng Gong. *The Collection of Essays* in 64 volumes by Tang Shunzhi collected the essays by genres from the Zhou Dynasty to the Song Dynasty, in which only the works of above-mentioned eight masters in the Tang and Song Dynasties were included. Mao Kun① worshipped Tang Shunzhi in literary criticism. When he compiled the prose of these eight persons in 164 volumes, he directly entitled the anthology *The Prose Collection of Eight Masters in the Tang and Song Dynasties*.

① Mao Kun (1512 – 1601), courtesy name Shunfu and style name Lumen, an essayist and book-collector of the Ming Dynasty.

Since then, the term of "the eight masters of the Tang and Song Dynasties" was known to everyone all over the country. Mao Kun'a anthology was attached with comments and had an extensive influence. *The Synoptic Catalogue of the Complete Library of the Four Treasuries* commented: "Its selection is well-balanced between complexity and simplicity. Although the comments are not insightful, they are good enough to serve as a guide for beginners. For one or two hundred years, it was chanted and recited by common people." Later *The Complete Prose of 10 Masters in the Tang and Song Dynasties* by Chu Xin of the Qing Dynasty followed the pattern of Mao Kun's anthology, and added to the eight masters Li Ao and Sun Qiao of the Tang Dynasty. *The Quintessence of the Prose in the Tang and Song Dynasties* in 58 volumes endorsed by Emperor Qianlong of the Qing Dynasty is the revised edition of Chu Xin's anthology, supplemented with collations, comments and textual research.

With regard to all the anthologies mentioned above, as the classical prose of the Tang and Song Dynasties is in one line of succession, the essays of Han Yu, Liu Zongyuan, Ouyang Xiu, Wang Anshi, Zeng Gong, and three Sus were usually assembled in one book, and the Tang prose cannot be separated from the Song prose for its widespread influence. This is quite different from the divergence in styles of the poems between the Tang and Song Dynasties. In the later ages, the divergent styles often prevailed one after another, so each of the poetic collections and anthologies often could form a system by itself. As to a huge collection of the prose of the Tang Dynasty to embody all genres and all schools, the top on the list must be *The Complete Collection of the Prose of the Tang Dynasty*.

The compilation of *The Complete Collection of the Prose of the Tang Dynasty* lasted five years and a half in the reign of Emperor Jiaqing of the Qing Dynasty. Like *The Complete Collection of the Poetry of the Tang Dynasty*, it was a national cultural program under the imperial edict. Emperor Jiaqing found the manuscript of *The Complete Collection of the Prose of the Tang Dynasty* preserved in the palace and deemed it imperfect, so he ordered his officials to revise it. This manuscript proved to be the unfinished book compiled by Chen Bangyan, a native of Haining, in the reigns of

Emperors Yongzheng and Qianlong. It consisted of 16 cases, each case embodying 10 volumes. It included 10,000 plus several thousand essays by over 1,700 writers, which amount to three-fourths of the present version of *The Complete Collection of the Prose of the Tang Dynasty*. It was, however, a book without careful choice, and all its collections were ordinary versions; the individual anthologies were often based on the bookshop editions as the sources, which had many misprints and errors. The compilers of *The Complete Collection of the Prose of the Tang Dynasty* included Xu Song, an expert of the Tang history, and Chen Hongchi, who later composed *The Records on The Complete Collection of the Prose of the Tang Dynasty*. Based on Chen Bangyan's *The Complete Collection of the Prose of the Tang Dynasty*, they adopted with reference different anthologies embodied in *The Complete Library of the Four Treasuries*, different category books such as *The Great Canon of Yongle*, general anthologies such as *Choice Blossoms of Literature*, *The Quintessence of the Tang Prose and Poetry*, local records, stone inscriptions, and the Taoist and Buddhist canons, to complete *The Complete Collection of the Prose of the Tang Dynasty*, a 1,000-volume general anthology of the Tang prose, covering 20,025 essays by 3,035 writers of the Tang and Five Dynasties. Upon its completion, the book was sent to Yangzhou for collation and printing. The book obtained a better quality after the proofreading by Sun Xingyan and Gu Qianli, both distinguished scholars at that time. *The Complete Collection of the Prose of the Tang Dynasty* is better than *The Complete Collection of the Poetry of the Tang Dynasty* in terms of compilation and collation, and well deserves its fame as the general corpus of the prose of the Tang Dynasty.

Let's return to *Choice Blossoms of Literature*. Its aim is to accumulate literary documents. Most of its genres belong to the category of prose. In the "Guide" to *The Complete Collection of the Prose of the Tang Dynasty*, we may find that "the classification of genres and the order of exposition of the book are still modeled after *Choice Blossoms of Literature*". It shows that there are relevant connections and similarities in the layout between the two books. With regard to the similar functions of preserving literature, the best example is the anthology of the Tang poet Li Shangyin. *Annotations to The Collected Works of Fannan* (Li Shangyin) in the Qing Dynasty was in fact copied from *Choice Blossoms of Literature*. The present version in *The Complete Collection of the Prose of the Tang Dynasty* has over 200 essays more than *The Collected Works of Fannan*, and they were collected from *The Great Canon of Yongle* stored in the closely guarded imperial library. Based on these, Qian Zhenlun and Qian Zhenchang wrote notes and comments for *The Supplement to the Collected Works of Fannan*. The preservation of Li Shangyin's anthologies is indebted to both *Choice Blossoms of Literature* and *The Complete Collection of the Prose of the Tang Dynasty*.

One more thing needs to be explained. After *Choice Blossoms of Literature* and *The Quintessence of the Tang Prose and Poetry*, general anthologies of the poetry and prose of the Tang Dynasty were no longer made. It can be seen from the compilation of different anthologies of the poetry and prose of the Tang Dynasty that *The Complete Collection of the Poetry of the Tang Dynasty* and *The Complete Collection of the Prose of the Tang Dynasty* which aim to collect the documents of the entire dynasty are also separated clearly into poetry and prose.

Chapter Three

The Literary Documentary Value of *Choice Blossoms of Literature*

1. The Documentary Value of *Choice Blossoms of Literature*

The greatest contribution of *Choice Blossoms of Literature* in the study of literature and the literary history is its preservation of a great quantity of the literary historical materials of the Tang Dynasty. Many essays and poems in the book can be regarded as rediscovery after long disappearance, and many paragraphs and sentences provide the sources for collation and proofreading. The reason for the latter is because the compilation of *Choice Blossoms of Literature* was completed at the beginning of the Song Dynasty: Since it was still close to the Tang Dynasty, the selected essays and poems were naturally close to the original texts of the Tang Dynasty, while the present individual anthologies of the masters had been recarved and printed through ages, and there are usually mistakes and variations in characters and texts. Moreover, *Choice Blossoms of Literature* marked out all characters and texts with variances in the poems and essays, and readers can see the different versions of the same texts by the writers of the Tang Dynasty preserved in the Song Dynasty. Some works preserved the authors' own annotations, which were deleted in the present individual anthologies, such as the poems by Li Shangyin. These materials are extraordinarily valuable.

Rediscovery of what has been lost can be done with the help of *Choice Blossoms of Literature* simply because of its huge size and closeness to the end of the Tang Dynasty. At the beginning of the Song Dynasty, since all the individual anthologies were incomplete, "There were absolutely rare printed editions. The writings of Han Yu, Liu Zongyuan, Yuan Zhen, and Bai Juyi were not widely circulated; other anthologies of the famous scholars such as Chen Zi'ang, Zhang Yue, Zhang Jiuling and Li Ao were extremely rare in circulation." Right at this time, the scholars in compiling *Choice Blossoms of Literature* recorded and preserved a great quantity of writings, just as Zhou Bida pointed out: "As to Liu Zongyuan, Bai Juyi, Quan Deyu, Li Shangyin, Gu Yun, Luo Yi, et. al., their complete works might have been collected in the book." (*Notes on the Beginning of the Compilation of Choice Blossoms of Literature*) Such a work provided a great convenience for the use of the book. Let us just see some examples: There were over 300 collected works of the writers of the Tang Dynasty in *The Bibliography of Classics and Books* of *The New History of the Tang Dynasty*, but only 76 collected works left in the Qing Dynasty in *The Complete Library of the Four Treasuries*; besides, the collections mentioned previously of Li Shangyin, Li Yong, Li Hua, Xiao Yingshi, et. al. were all completed with materials mainly supplemented from *Choice Blossoms of Literature* (cf. the synopsis of each collection in *The Synoptic Catalogue of The Complete Library of the Four Treasuries*). Moreover, the different collections that were circulated in different ages again can usually be supplemented with *Choice Blossoms of Literature*. For examples, all kinds of catalogues in the Song Dynasty recorded 30 volumes for the collection of Zhang Yue of the early Tang Dynasty, but there were only 25 volumes in its block-print in the reign of Emperor Jiajing of the Ming Dynasty. Nowhere could the 30-volume collection be found when the compilation of *The Complete Library of the Four Treasuries* started in the Qing Dynasty. Then 61 pieces of hymn, exhortation, memorial, memorial to the emperor, written complaint, political discourse, question and answer, preface, report, letter, unsealed official letter, tablet inscription, in-tomb tablet inscription, brief biography of a diseased person, etc. were collected from *Choice Blossoms of Literature* and *The Quintessence of the Prose of the Tang Dynasty*. *The Synoptic Catalogue of The Complete Library of the Four Treasuries* listed three memorials absent from Dugu Ji's *The Collected Works of Piling* in 20 volumes: *A Memorial to*

Resign from the Post of Weizhou Governor on Behalf of General Dugu, *A Memorial to Resign from the Post of Runzhou Envoy for Mr. Cui*, and *A Memorial to Plead for Suspension of Official Post for Serving Parents on Behalf of Mayor Yu of the Capital*. In the reign of Emperor Qianlong, Zhao Huaiyu again emended *A Memorial to Thank for the Imperial Edict and Bestowal of Winter Clothes*, and *A Memorial to Plead for Absence from the Expedition on Behalf of Minister Guo of the Secretariat* in his collated edition. All these were found in *Choice Blossoms of Literature*. There are still many such scattered single pieces that can supplement the individual collections; even if *The Complete Collection of the Prose of the Tang Dynasty* and *The Complete Collection of the Poetry of the Tang Dynasty* had been supplemented from the sources *Choice Blossoms of Literature* provided, there still exist gaps and omissions, which also verifies the historical value of the abundant literary materials of *Choice Blossoms of Literature*.

Of course, *Choice Blossoms of Literature* is not completely free of mistakes, and many of the mistakes had been discovered in the different ages. In case of Li Bai's "Sun Rises at the Southeast Corner" (in volume 193), Peng Shuxia et. al. argued in his interlinear note that "there is no poem by that name in Li Bai's anthology, and in *The Collected Poems of Music Bureau* (edited by Guo Maoqian), it is attributed to Yin Mou." There are six memorials written by Li Yong in *Choice Blossoms of Literature*, but Peng Shuxia identified one of them *A Memorial to Congratulate on the Remittal* as written by Li Jifu in his *Differentiation and Rectification of Choice Blossoms of Literature*. Again two *Memorials to Congratulate on the Remittal* under the name of Dugu Ji concerned the events in the Xingyuan Period (784) of Emperor Dezong, but Dugu Ji died earlier in the Dali Period of Emperor Daizong, so it is certain that he is not the author.

Sometimes obviously imbalanced and inadequate selections can be found in *Choice Blossoms of Literature*. For example, Du Fu's representative works of "historical poems" — "Three Officials", "Three Partings", and "Thoughts on Historical Sites in Five Poems" — and Li Bai's well-known short poems such as "Mount Skyland Ascended in a Dream", "Leaving Baidi Town at Dawn" and "Seeing Meng Haoran off to Guangling" are excluded in *Choice Blossoms of Literature* as well. Though many articles of Liu Zongyuan can be found in *Choice Blossoms of Literature*, he had only one poem listed in the anthology. In contrast, as many as 130 poems by Song Zhiwen are included. There were totally 150 pieces of prose in Li Shangyin's anthology when it was reedited from *Choice Blossoms of Literature* in the Qing Dynasty, but 200 more were added to it from *The Great Canon of Yongle* in the process of compiling *The Complete Collection of the Prose of the Dynasty*. Therefore, what Zhou Bida claimed in "the whole collections might have been included in it" is not exact, for there is a great number of omissions.

Nevertheless, *Choice Blossoms of Literature* in the end preserved many historical materials of literature and these are very illuminating for us to understand the past events in the literary history. Let us just see one simple example here: In *Choice Blossoms of Literature*, "The Story of Everlasting Regret" by Chen Hong tells the love story between Emperor Xuanzong of the Tang Dynasty and Imperial Concubine Yang. At the end of the story, it noted that both *The Story of the Song of Everlasting Regret* and *The Song of Everlasting Regret* were composed at the inspiration when Bai Juyi, Chen Hong and Wang Zhifu chatted about the story in an outing. What are the details after all? A different version of *The Story of the Song of the Everlasting Regret* attached to the story from *The Collection of Love Stories* tells us the main story teller is Wang Zhifu. This clarified the truth of how Bai Juyi's creation of "*The Song of the Everlasting Regret*" was triggered. Of course, the more immediate value of *Choice Blossoms of Literature* lies in its preservation of the voluminous literary works.

2. *The Collected Works of Fannan* and the Evolution of the Parallel Prose

The preservation of Li Shangyin's works in *Choice Blossoms of Literature* has been repeatedly used as a typical example to show how its storage of the literary historical materials of the Tang Dynasty is beneficial to the construction of the complete history of literature.

Li Shangyin had compiled his own parallel prose into two books: *Collected Works of Fannan I* and *Collected Works of Fannan II*, each in 20 volumes. These were both mentioned in *The Bibliography of Classics and Books* in *The New Book of the Tang Dynasty* and *The Bibliography of Classics and Books* in *The History of the Song Dynasty*. But these two books were long lost. According to what Li Shangyin himself said in the preface to the two books, there were 433 pieces of parallel prose in the first volume, and 400 — selected from 500 to 600 pieces — in the second one; altogether there were over 800 pieces. In the compilation of *Choice Blossoms of Literature*, Li Shangyin was a huge contributor. Just as Zhou Bida said, "their complete collections might have been all included." The Qing Dynasty proved to be a peak for the recollection of ancient books. Zhu Heling collected over 100 pieces of prose from *Choice Blossoms of Literature* and *The Quintessence of the Tang Prose and Poetry*, and Xu Jiong again supplemented some. Together with his elder brother Xu Shugu, they worked separately on annotations and comments on the 150 pieces of prose, and completed *The Annotations and Comments on the Collected Writings of Li Yishan*. This book was later included in *The Complete Library of the Four Treasuries*. Based on this book, Feng Hao made revisions, and because the majority of the pieces were written in parallel prose, he changed its title to *The Collected Works of Fannan*, which is almost the same title Li Shangyin decided himself. So the annotated book was named *The Comprehensive Annotations to the Collected Works of Fannan*, a greatly enriched collection of Li Shangyin's parallel prose. When being an official in Beijing, Qian Zhenlun collected 203 pieces of Li Shangyin's prose unaccounted for in the above books from Volumes 771 to 782 of *The Complete Collection of the Prose of the Tang Dynasty*. In the reign of Emperor Xianfeng, only after he returned home to annotate and comment on his new findings with his brother Qian Zhenchang, did he have access to the *Biography of Scholar Hu Shunong* written by Ruan Yuan and learned the source of his findings. (Hu Shunong, or Hu Jing, was one of the chief compilers of *The Complete Collection of the Prose of the Tang Dynasty*. It was recorded in *The Biographies of the Qing Dynasty* that he composed most of the writers' profiles of *The Complete Collection of the Prose of the Tang Dynasty.*) *The Biography of Hu Shunong* mentioned that he once collected over 400 pieces of Li Shangyin's works from *The Great Canon of Yongle*, but the number of the articles disagreed with the known fact. Therefore, Qian Zhenlun went to visit Hu Ciyao, son of Hu Shunong, and checked against the copy that Hu Ciyao recorded. He then learned the so-called 400 pieces had included the pieces taken from *Choice Blossoms of Literature*. That determined the exact number of Li Shangyin's articles we could gather out of *Choice Blossoms of Literature* and *The Great Canon of Yongle*. The book completed by the Qian brothers was named *The Supplement to The Collected Works of Fannan*.

Only through these articles can we have a clear and comprehensive understanding of Li Shangyin's position in the history of parallel prose. He is an important writer and could not be neglected in the historical development of parallel prose. Huang Kan in his late years delivered lectures in the seminars at Jinling University; besides Confucian classics and philology, he lectured on Li Shangyin's parallel prose. Huang Kan pointed out: "The parallel prose of Fannan inherited the tradition of the Six Dynasties, and his prosody were all harmonious and pioneered the Song styles. His style is vigorous and singularly lofty."

We know that the sinograms are monosyllabic and the structure, sound and meaning of a character are closely integrated. Therefore it is quite natural to form a couplet. In *The Confucian Analects*, it recorded a chant in the Spring and Autumn Period: "The past cannot be admonished against; the future still can be chased after." The opening sentences in *Lao Zi* are, "The Dao that can be spoken of is not the eternal Dao; the name that can ben named is not the eternal name." In *Xun Zi*, couplets were even composed intentionally: "I used to meditate all day, but that is much less than what I learned in a moment; I used to tiptoe to look afar, but there is much less view than what I saw at a height." These are all very good examples. Usually parallel structure is used to reason and give expression to emotions in order to intensify the mood, and parallel couplets often appear at such moments. For example, when Li Si sent a memorial to the First Emperor of the Qin Dynasty and suggested an extensive assembly of local talents throughout the empire, he wrote the following famous sentences: "Mount Tai does not decline any soil, and it can become tall; rivers and seas do not choose any small stream, and they can become deep." On the basis of symmetrical couplet sentences, such an evolution witnessed refinement and elegance of diction, even harmony of prosody; couplets dominated entire articles or essays, with single sentences interspersed between them, and the parallel prose gradually became matured. It developed through the efforts of Cai Yong at the end of the Eastern Han Dynasty, Cao Zhi and Lu Ji of the Wei and Jin Dynasties, Bao Zhao of the Song Dynasty of the Southern Dynasties, Jiang Yan of the Qi Dynasty, and reached a peak with the works of Xu Ling[①] and Yu Xin[②] of the Liang Dynasty.

Xu Ling and Yu Xin were both mature writers for they grew up in the atmosphere of the court literature in the Southern Dynasties. They treated literature as the object of recreation, thus devoted a great part of their energies to the writings. They not only paid great attention to the grace and beauty of diction, but also the tonal harmony and fluency as well. In the Qi and Liang Dynasties, Chinese writers had greatly increased their knowledge about tones and prosody of the Chinese language, and could distinguish finely the four tones, and the voiced and unvoiced sounds. When the new prosodic knowledge was applied to the poetry composition, new styles of poetry emerged. This is the first step of the development and perfection of the regulated poems in the Tang Dynasty. Xie Tiao was the most successful poet of the new style and was highly praised by Li Bai. Xie Tiao once said, "Good poems should be as smooth and tactful as a pellet." Xu Ling and Yu Xin absorbed the practical experience of prosody, and greatly improved their tonal use in their parallel prose. Xu Lian of the Qing Dynasty said in his well-known collection of the medieval parallel prose *The Collected Prose of the Six Dynasties*: "When the parallel prose developed to the times of Yu Xin, selected tones and choice diction reached the acme

① Xu Ling (507 – 583), courtesy name Xiaomu, a famous poet and writer.
② Yu Xin (513 – 581), courtesy name Zishan, a talented poet.

in his works." By saying so, Xu Lian referred to the profundity Yu Xin had achieved in both diction and prosody. Furthermore, the proper use of a large number of natural allusions can be found in Xu Ling and Yu Xin's parallel prose. For example, in Yu Xin's preface to "Rhapsody of Mourning for the South of the River", he exclaimed:

> When parting afar in the Song of Yan, the sorrow is too much to bear;
> See off by the old man of Chu, how sad I shed the streaming tears!

We know that Yu Xin was a native of the Southern Dynasties and served Prince Zhaoming at first, and later he was forced to settle in the Northern Dynasties when he went there as a diplomatic envoy. Though he became a high-ranking official there, he was heartbroken and longed for his homeland all his life. "Mourning for the South of the River" was written when he heard about the downfall of the Liang Dynasty. "Although there were expressions about dangers and hardships, mainly he expressed his grief and sorrow." The allusions used in the above two sentences express these connotations: One is his own sadness by borrowing the desolate tone of Cao Pi's "The Song of Yan", and another is his painful feeling in serving the two different emperors by referring to the story of Gong Sheng of the Han Dynasty. (Gong Sheng was living at the end of the Western Han Dynasty. When Wang Mang usurped the throne, he was summoned into the imperial court but thought he, having received the old emperor's favor, could not serve the new monarch with a different surname, and even would feel ashamed to meet his old emperor in the netherlands, so he fasted for 14 days and died in the end. An old man came to grieve over his death in extreme sorrow.) Yu Xin had a mixed feeling of remorse and shame in comparison with Gong Sheng to serve the two monarchs of different dynasties. These allusions are appropriately used and very suggestive.

The parallel prose was still popular in the Tang Dynasty. Wang Bo, Lu Zhaolin, Luo Binwang and Yang Jiong of the early Tang Dynasty were addressed as the "Four Masters". Their parallel prose is like a vast sea in magnanimity, full of vigor in manner, and splendid and magnificent in diction and expression. The feminine grace of the parallel prose in the previous dynasty was replaced by their masculine and splendid style. Such sentences as in Wang Bo's "Preface to Prince Teng's Pavilion", "The rosy clouds at sunset are dancing with a single pheasant, and the water in autumn merges in the same color with the sky", and "Old but more vigorous, will you change your weather-worn heart? Poor but in a stronger will, do not let fall your soaring aspiration", etc. are all famous quotes that have been chanted for generations. In the prime Tang Dynasty, Zhang Yue and Su Ting were granted the titles of the Duke of the Yan State and the Duke of the Xu State, and consequently their writings were praised as "written by the great masters of Yan and Xu". Their essays extricated themselves from the splendid pomposity of the Qi and Liang Dynasties, as returned to the solemnity and simplicity of the Han and Wei Dynasties, as relatively fewer allusions and past events were used. Moreover, a great part of Zhang and Su's essays are practically written in official work. Zhang Yue was the chief writer in the imperial court, and half of Su Ting's articles are also practically written on the order of the emperor. This is a phenomenon worth considering. It seems that most of the parallel prose should be the pure essays in emphasis of diction, colors, prosody, more allusions and events, but in fact in the Southern Dynasties, everything could be written in the parallel prose for depiction of scenes, narration of stories, and expression of feelings. Especially with Jiang Yan's efforts, there was a great increase of practical content in the parallel prose composition. Jiang Yan was also a chief writer in the court. He wrote all the imperial edicts, imperial mandates, imperial decrees, imperial orders, memorials to the emperor, letters to an noble, and reports in the parallel prose. More than a half of his 100 articles preserved in his collection are about the imperial affairs. In the later dynasties, through the efforts of the classical prose writers in the Tang and Song Dynasties, when the classical prose with single and free sentences became dominant in the literary circle, memorials and reports of the practical writings were still composed in the parallel prose. The masters of classical prose, Ouyang Xiu, Wang Anshi, Su Shi, for instance, also contributed excellent works in the parallel prose of imperial edicts, memorials and reports. Sima Guang was a master of classical prose. When Emperor Shenzong appointed him academician of the Imperial Academy to take charge of edict-writing, he declined the offer several times. However, when he submitted his "Memorial to Present *History as a Mirror for Governance*", he wrote it in the parallel prose to follow the fashion. In the middle Tang Dynasty, Lu Zhi wrote many touching imperial edicts. Lu Zhi's articles were very simple and touched the readers' hearts with their sincerity and honesty. The well-known "Imperial Amnesty for Change of the Year Title at the Heavenly Mandate" is a good example. After the rebellion of Zhu Ci was pacified, the amnesty was issued for the change of the year title of Xingyuan. In the edict, the emperor regretfully admitted his mistakes and criticized himself; what he said accorded with the reality reasonably. It is said that the unruly commanders and soldiers of different places were moved to tears at the time.

The master of parallel prose in the late Tang Dynasty was no other than Li Shangyin. Li Shangyin remained in depression all his life as he didn't see the fulfillment of his aspiration. He acted as a private assistant for a long period and hence had to write many practical articles naturally, such as memorials, reports, recountals and prefaces. But unlike the works of the "great masters of Yan and Xu" and even the writings of Lu Zhi, Li Shangyin's writing style indeed was close to that of the Qi and Liang Dynasties. Zhu Heling of the Qing Dynasty, who collected Li Shangyin's articles from *Choice Blossoms of Literature*, stated in his preface to *A New Collected Writings of Li Yishan*, "Yishan's parallel prose originated from Yu Xin, so his paragraphs manifest flashing brilliance, and his sentences reflect wonderful splendor." Qu Duizhi, a scholar of the modern times and a disciple of Wang Kaiyun, the last master of parallel prose in the Qing Dynasty, stated in his *General Introduction to Parallel Prose* that the poems of Li Shangyin are akin to that of Yu Xin, and his parallel prose to that of Xu Ling. In a word, Li Shangyin's prose stemmed from Xu and Yu's work. In fact, Li Shangyin himself had proclaimed in "The Preface to *The Collection of Fannan I*" that he was once totally absorbed in the writings of Ren Fang,

Fan Yun, Xu Ling and Yu Xin. His parallel prose was in delicate balance and filled with clever allusions, yet they were quite smooth and dynamic. He wove the simple sentences into the parallel construction to achieve a special effect of variety. The "Preface to *The Collected Works at the Imperial Orders of Prime Minister, Marshal and Duke of the Wei State, Huichang the First Grade Official*" (a famous essay to comment on the accomplishments of Li Deyu in his life) he wrote for Zheng Ya is a good example. The preface was revised by Zheng Ya himself who deleted most of the simple sentences, but it was believed that by doing so he had weakened the vigor of the article. Li Shangyin's special talent was due to his early study of the classical prose. He did not begin to learn to write parallel prose until he became a private advisor of Linghu Chu and had to learn how to write the memorials that were generally in the parallel form. He soon became a master of it with the help of Linghu Chu (see the Preface to *The Collection of Fannan I*). Li Shangyin said in the Preface to *The Collection of Fannan II* that such parallel prose was written in haste, "not his favorite style in his life", and did not deserve fame. It was because Li Shangyin had a solid background in the classical prose that his parallel prose possessed the vigor besides its splendid form. (This point was discussed in *General Introduction to Parallel Prose* by Qu Duizhi.) Therefore, Huang Kan praised Li Shangyin's prose for its "unique vigor".

Most of Li Shangyin's parallel prose, like that by Zhang Yue and Lu Zhi, had practical purposes. But he used the splendid words and harmonious prosody, precise and appropriate allusions, the ancient prosaic vigor, and the quintessence of the parallel prose of the Six Dynasties, to promote the parallel prose further to a new high level after the impact of the movement of the classical prose. To be specific, he "pioneered the style for the Song Dynasty".

Li Shangyin is a great figure who had exerted a strong influence on the men of letters at the beginning of the Song Dynasty. His poems became the direct source of the Xikun-style poetry represented by Yang Yi, et. al. This is a familiar fact in literary history. "The Xikun style" is actually applied to both prose and poetry. Zhao Yanwei stated in *The*

Miscellaneous Collection of Yunlu, "The prose of our dynasty follow the line of the Five Dynasties, and the articles are often written in parallel structure and splendid diction. Master Yang started the Xikun style." Obviously, prose is also included in the category. Yang Yi and others continued the tune and style of Li Shangyin and were very influential at a time. Ouyang Xiu recalled: "At the time, Yang Yi and Liu Yun's writings gained a wide currency. The learned men, who would rather imitate their styles in imperial examination composition, may succeed and win pride and honor." ("Postscript to the Old Version of Han Yu's Prose") The poetry and parallel prose of Li Shangyin are internally connected, so are the Xikun-style poetry and parallel prose of Yang Yi (Qian Zhongshu's words cited in Zhou Zhenfu's Preface to *The Selected Works of Li Shangyin*). Their relation of direct inheritance is quite obvious. It was said that at the time, an actor appeared as Li Shangyin in rags on the stage and claimed that it was the result of tearing and ripping, to reflect dramatically the fact that Li Shangyin became the target of plagiarism in the early Song Dynasty. This situation didn't change until another branch of parallel prose emerged. That is the school of the "great masters of Yan and Xu". The majority of those excellent writers were in charge of the composition of imperial edicts. For example, Xu Xuan was a scholar of the Southern Tang Dynasty into the Song Dynasty. *The Synoptic Catalogue of The Complete Library of the Four Treasuries* commented that "Xu Xuan's articles followed the line of Yan and Xu", and just like Xia Song, the Duke of the Ying State, "Xu Xuan writes elegantly and abundantly in diction, demonstrates the sublime and brilliant vigor, and bears the distinct marks of Yan and Xu." Later, Wang Gui, Song Xiang and his brother Song Qi all followed the style of Yan and Xu. Wang Zhi of the late Northern Song Dynasty wrote *Talks on Parallel Prose,* the first book on parallel prose. It recorded the opinion of his father Wang Su about the development of parallel prose in the early Song Dynasty: "Parallel prose flourished in the Song Dynasty since Yang Yi and Liu Yun, carrying the obvious traces of feebleness of the Five Dynasties. The traces were wiped out completely in the memorials of the Duke of the Ying State (Xia Song). Wang Gui and Yuan Jiang both learned the parallel prose from the Duke of Ying, and Wang Anshi did too, though his style is superb and subtle." As a matter of fact, it was Ouyang Xiu who reduced the influence of the Tang's parallel prose, especially of Li Shangyin's, by writing the parallel prose in the same way as writing the classical prose, although we have mentioned above that the influence of the classical prose had been suggested in Li Shangyin's effort to integrate the couplet texture of the parallel prose with single and free sentences.

The parallel prose declined after the Song Dynasty and did not revive until the Qing Dynasty, when it reached a new height. Naturally Li Shangyin's parallel prose, as an outstanding part of the tradition, could not be ignored. For example, *The Synoptic Catalogue of The Complete Library of the Four Treasuries* once regarded the writings of Wu Qi, a master of parallel prose with exquisite style at the beginning of the Qing Dynasty, as "the pursuit of Li Shangyin".

From the brief outline of Li Shangyin's value and influence in the development of the parallel prose, we can recognize his importance and essential influence. However, had his excellent writings not been preserved in such books as *Choice Blossoms of Literature*, the whole history of China literature, and especially the course of the development of the parallel prose, would have been incomplete and different.

Chapter Four

The Tang Poetry as a Model and the Trends of the Premodern Poems

The over 180 volumes of poetry in *Choice Blossoms of Literature* are said to have been compiled by Yang Huizhi, and most are of course the works of the Tang poets. The Tang Dynasty has been regarded as the golden age of Chinese poetry, and Lu Xun once remarked: "All the excellent poems have been created by the Tang Dynasty." By that time, all the classical genres and the regulated patterns of poems had reached the acme of maturity that there was no room left for the later poets to create any new patterns. All kinds of styles had been tried and splendidly demonstrated: graceful unrestrainedness, depressive solemnity, sighing cadence, vast profundity, free serenity, splendid fluency ... Again for instance, in the works of many poets like Li Bai, Du Fu, Wang Wei, Bai Juyi, Li Shangyin, etc., all the styles mentioned above can be found; and in addition, a kaleidoscope of life embodied in the poems is really too much for the eye to catch, such as: fierce battles in the borders, peaceful leisure in seclusion, delight of chant and reply of poems between friends, true depiction of personal mood, authentic record of the upheaval of the times ... The great achievements of the Tang poetry are not only an invaluable heritage and eternal model, but a heavy pressure and "anxiety of influence" as well to the people after the Tang Dynasty. Jiang Shiquan of the Qing Dynasty wrote sympathetically: "The Song poets living after the Tang Dynasty really have difficulty blazing a new trail." (*Poems in Defense of Poetry*) As the people of the Ming Dynasty highly praised the Tang poetry and belittled the Song's, "If someone's poems were said to be the poems of the Song Dynasty, it is the same as to revile him." (*Inquiry into Poetry* by Ye Xie①) The Song poets who lived immediately after the Tang poets would doubtlessly bear the heaviest pressure. As a matter of fact, it is not only the Song poets, but all poets after the Tang Dynasty who in composing poems have to face the giant shadows of the Tang poems. Since the Song Dynasty, all the appraisals on the Tang poetry and even various comments made on the Song poetry in comparison with the Tang poetry are actually meant to balance the relationship between their own poems and the influence of the Tang Poetry. We might not exaggerate by saying that the poetic tide of the later half of the ancient Chinese poetry has been rolling on in various efforts of avoiding or chasing, or inheriting or changing the Tang poems to create the new.

Choice Blossoms of Literature is the first large-sized comprehensive collection of the Tang literature after the Tang Dynasty, and its section of poems is also the first large-sized comprehensive collection of the Tang poetry. Although it may not be as characteristic as the various selected works of the Tang poetry we have introduced in the previous chapters with clear-cut stances and unique styles, nor as comprehensive as the later anthologies like *The Complete Collection of the Poetry of the Tang Dynasty*, we might take it as a milestone in our study of the various connections of the Tang poetry with the poems and their evolution in the later ages.

1. The Song Poetry: Its Initial Imitation of the Tang Poetry and Its Eventual Departure

The literary circles in the early Song Dynasty basically followed and imitated the writing styles of the Tang and Five Dynasties. Fang Hui of the Yuan Dynasty was an insightful poetic critic. He pointed out that there had been three different poetic trends in the early Song Dynasty: Bai (Juyi)'s Style, the Xikun style and the late Tang style. He also added that Li Fang,

① Ye Xie (1627 – 1703), courtesy name Xingqi and style name Yiqi, a poetic theorist in the early Qing Dynasty.

Xu Xuan, Wang Yucheng, et. al. were the representatives of Bai's style ("The Preface to the Poems to See Luo Shouke Off"). The so-called Bai's style refers to the poetic works in imitation of the poetic style of Bai Juyi, the great poet of the Tang Dynasty. Li Fang and Xu Xuan, as we know, are the compilers of the huge books of *Choice Blossoms of Literature*, etc.

Bai Juyi was a great poet in the middle Tang Dynasty, and his poems are easily understood and melodious. He wrote many poems in reply to Yuan Zhen and Liu Yuxi. The high-ranking officials in the early Song Dynasty frequently imitated the ways in which the Tang poets chanted and replied with poems. Even the Song emperors were fond of poetry. For instance, Emperor Taizong of the Song Dynasty often bestowed poems on his subjects. Therefore, we can imagine the lively atmosphere in chanting and replying of poems at that time. The poems of chanting and replying between Li Fang and Li Zhi were edited into a book entitled *The Collection of Poems and Replies between Two Lis* and Li Fang said clearly in his own preface:

> In the past Letian (Bai Juyi) and Mengde (Liu Yuxi) had their *Collection of Poems and Replies between Liu and Bai* widely circulated in the empire, which became well known. Who knows that our collection would not be copied and circulated?

This is obviously an imitation. In the collection of Xu Xuan, the poems of chant and reply makes up three-fourths of the whole book. Fang Hui commented: "His poems have the style of Bai Letian (Bai Juyi)." (*Quintessence of the Best Regulated Poems*, vol.16) Originally there were fifty volumes for Li Fang's collected works, most of which have been lost, but we might listen to what another great master of Bai's style, Wang Yucheng, who claimed: "One should know that all the poems in his collection seemed to have been composed by Master Bai." ("An Elegy to Prime Minister Sikong") Later *The History of the Song Dynasty* also mentioned: "Li Fang imitated Bai Juyi's essays and poems, and his works were especially easy to understand." Wang Yucheng was a poet of great historical significance. A Song poet Cai Juhou said of him:

> At the beginning of the Song Dynasty, in following the poetic trend of the Five Dynasties, the scholar-officials all imitated the poems of Bai Letian (Juyi), and Wang Huangzhou (Yucheng) became the head of the poetic circles for the time being. (*Cai Kuanfu Poetry Talks*)

Wang Yucheng was generally accepted as a capable poet in the imitation of the Bai's style. Another poet Lin Bu, who lived in seclusion at Hangzhou and took the plum-blossom as his wife and the crane as his son, praised Yucheng in his poems: "Free and unrestrained are the poems written in the Tang Dynasty only by Bai Juyi, and the poems with great ease in our Song Dynasty are composed by Huangzhou (Wang Yucheng)." ("On Reading *Wang Huangzhou's Collection of Poems*")

As a youth, Wang Yucheng was also fond of writing chant-reply and courtesy poems. Later, while compiling his own collected works, he cut away most of them, which indicated a change in his poetic inclination. He was a man of aspirations and cared about people's lives. He had been demoted three times in his official career, but in his poems and articles, we can frequently read about his earnestness in serving the country and concern for the people's sufferings. His learning of Bai Juyi began from poetic chant and reply on the pleasures of life and evolved into the reflection of the reality in the style of the New Music Bureau. In narrating the social affairs with simple and plain language, he often expressed his own emotions and views in a frank way. What was more important about Wang Yucheng is the change of learning from Bai Juyi to further learning from Du Fu. Here is an interesting story: When he was demoted for the first time to Shangzhou as an assistant commander of the local armed forces, he wrote a number of poems entitled "Miscellaneous Impressions on Spring at Home", of which some sentences were pointed out by his son to be similar to those of Du Fu, and he was asked to change them to avoid any suspicion of plagiarism. Contrary to being annoyed, Wang Yucheng was pleased to hear what his son said, and thought he could even coincide with Du Fu through his own efforts of poem writing. He was so excited that he couldn't help chanting a poem, "At first I took Bai Juyi as my model; how dare I expect Zimei (Du Fu) to be my guide!" The two sentences mean: "At first I followed the poetic style of Bai Juyi, but how dare I be so bold to set Du Fu as my example?" (See *Cai Kuanfu Poetry Talks*) Wang Yucheng had made an insightful appraisal of Du Fu's poetic studies: "*The Collected Poems of Zimei* has opened up for the public a new world." Such a comment was extremely appropriate. It can be said that Du Fu was the most respected poet of the Tang Dynasty in the eyes of the poets of the Song Dynasty, no matter how different their styles and their poetic conceptions might be; all the important poets of the Song Dynasty, such as Ouyang Xiu, Huang Tingjian and Lu You, held Du Fu in esteem. Wang Yucheng can be counted as the first one in this trend. Wu Zhizheng of the Qing Dynasty compiled *Selected Poems of the Song Dynasty*. Although he thought Wang Yucheng "had learned from the poems by Du Fu, but didn't attain his realm", he confirmed Wang's contribution in starting the style for the Song poetry to follow: "It's Yuanzhi (Wang Yucheng) alone who started the Song style, and paved the way for Ouyang Wenzhong to follow. Although the poems of Wenzhong were grander and deeper than those of Yuanzhi, Yuanzhi was indeed the trail blazer." This was because Wang Yucheng "modeled his works after Du Fu's poems when no one else did the same."

After the vogue of Bai's style, the late Tang style of poems became in fashion. Most of the poets in this group who imitated Jia Dao and Yao He of the late Tang Dynasty were basically not in office, and their representatives were Pan Lang, Wei Ye, the Nine Monks, Lin Bu and Kou Zhun. Of all the poets in this school, Kou Zhun was the only high-ranking official, and naturally the head and center of the group in poetic chant-reply. Jia Dao was respected because of Yao He's admiration, which had became a fashion in the late Tang Dynasty. For instance, Lu Yanrang learned Jia Dao's way of searching hard for the best word for the poems: "I chant a character appropriately, only after twisting and breaking several beards." Li Dong even counted the beads in his hand while chanting

"Jia Dao Buddha" (*The Biographies of the Tang Talents*). In the early Song Dynasty, the worship of Jia Dao shown by the poets of the late Tang style was by no means inferior. Pan Lang said in his poem "In Memory of Jia Dao": "A man can usually live to the limit of 100 years, but you should live as long as 1,000 years." ("In Memory of the Immortal, Jia Dao": "Although a man dies a natural death at 100, you, sir, should live a thousand years.") Their painstaking effort of poem composition was similar to that of Jia Dao. Pan Lang wrote in the Postscript to *The Collection of Poems*: "One volume of the poems took me 20 years, and I often forgot meals in the day and sleep at night," which was quite similar to Jia Dao's lines: "Two lines of poems were obtained in three years; once I chant them, tears stream down my cheeks." ("A Postscript to the Poem") Painstaking chanting of lines and repeated weighing of each word might result in some wonderful poems, but they invariably lacked a grand vision. Of the names of the Nine Monks, Ouyang Xiu could remember only one (later it was the historian Sima Guang who remembered them all). The most distinguished monk is Hui Chong, but someone jeered at him by saying that his best sentences had been plagiarized from the poems of Sikong Shu and Liu Changqing: "It's not you, brother, who often plagiarized from the ancient poets; it's their sentences that too often coincided with your lines, brother." (*Poetry Talks Continued by Duke of Wen* (Sima Guang)) As we know, Yao He's *The Collection of Superb Subtlety* recorded mostly poems from the poets in the Dali Period. At the beginning of the Song Dynasty, the poets of the late Tang style worshipped Yao He, and naturally respected the talents of that period. Even the most famous lines in Lin Bu's *Ode to the Plum Blossoms*, "Dappled shadows of plum blossoms hang aslant over clear, shallow creek; Secret fragrance wafts in the moonlit dusk," were exposed by Li Rihua of the Ming Dynasty as a plagiarism and alteration from *Ode to the Sweet-scented Osmanthus* by Jiang Wei, a poet of the Five Dynasties. (The original lines were: "Shadows of bamboo hang aslant over clear, shallow creek; Fragrance of osmanthus wafts in the moonlit dusk.") Ouyang Xiu also noted a story: Xu Dong was good at prose and poetry writing. One day he gathered some poet-monks and asked them to write poems, but words such as mountains, rivers, wind, cloud, bamboo, stone, flower, grass, snow, frost, star, moon, animals and birds, were not allowed to appear; as a result, all the monks found themselves at their wits' end, and had to lay down their brushes. Thus their limitation of poetic conception can be obviously seen.

The poems of the late Tang style are exquisite and mostly written in five-syllable regulated form, in opposition to the simplicity and plainness of Bai's style. This may also be a progress. Wei Ye first learned Bai's style when he was young, and later he devoted himself to the study of the poems of the late Tang style for he was in close contact with Kou Zhun. However, their approach was too narrow, slippery and desolate. They looked unavoidably constricted and inferior in comparison with the poets who learned from the poems of Li Shangyin of the late Tang Dynasty.

The poets who learned from the poems of Li Shangyin were basically the high-ranking officials and noble lords in office. Yang Yi and others assembled a number of poets in the palace of Emperor Zhenzong of the Song Dynasty to compile *Important Events Archived in the Imperial Library*; meanwhile, they wrote poems for chant and reply. Most of the poems were later collected and edited by Yang Yi into a book entitled *The Xikun Collection of Chant-Reply Poems* in 250 pieces written by 17 poets. The Collection marked another achievement of the poems of chant and reply in the early Song Dynasty, but the target style had turned from the straightforward plainness of Bai Juyi to the allusive elegance of Li Shangyin. Because of the collection, these poems were labeled the "Xikun style". The works of the three poets Yang Yi, Liu Yun and Qian Weiyan in *The Xikun Collection of Chant-Reply Poems* occupied four-fifths of the whole book and amounted to 202 poems; therefore, there is no doubt they are the representatives of the "Xikun style".

Yang Yi was upright and outspoken in disposition, and he was a loyal and kind official. Most of his collections have been lost and perhaps *The Xikun Collection of Chant-Reply Poems* could not embody his styles completely, for even Shi Jie, who violently attacked his style, had to admit "his works are characterized by vigor and power." (*The Record of the Imperial*

Edicts in the Dazhong Xiangfu Period) There is no doubt that Yang Yi was fond of the poetic style in the collection, and it also exerted a tremendous influence at that time. Yang Yi recalled how he had learned from the poems of Li Shangyin. When Emperor Taizong of the Song Dynasty was in power, Yang Yi obtained by chance a hundred odd poems written by Li Shangyin: "I liked them very much, and yet I failed to grasp their profundity." It was not until the reign of Emperor Zhenzong that he began to study and appreciate them in depth, and had a mind to absorb them; then he found, "It is as though I have cast off my old self and take on a new one." Besides, because of his love of the poems of Li Shangyin, he also liked Tang Yanqian, who imitated the poems of Li Shangyin in the late Tang Dynasty. Quite often he mentioned them both at the same time, and "praised and spread the poems of Li Shangyin and Tang Yanqian in the scholarly circles." (*Categorized Facts and Events of the Song Dynasty*, vol.34) We know that Li Shangyin at first learned from Du Fu, and later developed his own characteristic style. Yang Yi and others learned the poems of Li Shangyin, but showed little interest in the remote master Du Fu, and they went so far as to belittle Du's poems as "platitude of a villager". It is obvious that what he pursued was only the poetic techniques of Li Shangyin and Tang Yanqian in the late Tang Dynasty rather than their poetic spirit. Ye Mengde said in his comment on Yang Yi and Liu Yun: "They both like the poems of Tang Yanqian only for his exquisite allusions and appropriate couplets." (*Shilin Poetry Talks*) It pointed out this preference of theirs. Resplendency and symmetry of the language are the unique features of Li Shangyin's poems. The poets of the Xikun style inherited and developed them. As for the use of allusions, they even made intensified efforts on purpose. Fang Hui spoke of the common features of the Xikun style as follows:

> Generally speaking, when a thing is chanted in the Xikun style, it must be substantiated with a story, names of persons, time, and gold, jade, brocade and embroidery, etc.

The most typical poem is "Tears", in which all the allusions, ancient and modern, were piled up, and various heart-breaking affairs of all ages enumerated, but it obviously emphasized "things" over "emotions". The comment made by Zhang Biaochen was quite relevant:

> A superior poem is usually natural and implicit, and an inferior poem is usually broken and chiseled. The poems of the Xikun style by Yang Danian (Yang Yi) are not bad, but they were fabricated with too much affected work, just like the myth in which Chaos dies when his seven orifices are chiseled out in seven days. (*Shanhugou Poetry Talks*) (See *Zhuang Zi* Chapter 7).

A general idea of the three schools of poetry at the beginning of the Song Dynasty is that each upheld a certain poetic style of one school, or a poetic master of the Tang poetry, and pursued it deliberately to gain strength and momentum. It can be seen that at the beginning of the Song Dynasty, the poetry of the Tang Dynasty had already become an inalienable background for the development of poetics.

The emergence of the new patterns, or the unique qualities, of the Song poetry began with Ouyang Xiu, Mei Yaochen and Su Shunqin. Ye Mengde said: "The poems of Lord Ouyang Wenzhong (Ouyang Xiu) aimed to rectify the Xikun style, so he emphasized flavor and ethos, and his poetic language was thus easy and flowing." (*Shilin Poetry Talks*) As for the status of Mei Yaochen and Su Shunqin, Ye Xie of the Qing Dynasty stated most explicitly, "It was Mei Yaochen and Su Shunqin who pioneered the style of the Song poetry." (*Inquiry into Poetry*)

Mei Yaochen was the oldest among the Song poets and exerted certain influence on Ouyang Xiu, and the main style of his poems was characterized as "plainness". Ouyang Xiu said so in *Liuyi Poetry Talks*[①], and Mei Yaochen himself also explained in *Reading the Collection of Poems by Shao Buyi*: "No matter what poem it may be, ancient or modern, the hardest thing of all lies

① *Liuyi Poetry Talks*, written by Ouyang Xiu (1007 – 1072), is the first book to focus on the theoretical discussions of poetry-making.

in plain presentation." But the "Inscriptions on the Memorial Tablet" written for him by Ouyang Xiu seemed to put forward new points:

> He was fond of lucidness, elegance, idleness and plainness at the beginning, and later he sought for profundity, and occasionally chiseled for strangeness and exquisiteness, for he was always full of spirit and vigor; therefore, the older he was, the more vigorous his poems were.

That is to say, his poetic styles are varied. In his writings, we can find the names of many poets he admired, such as Tao Yuanming, Wang Wei, Li Bai, Du Fu, Wei Yingwu, Han Yu, Meng Jiao, and Li He. Apart from the argumentative and essayistic transformation of his poems which was related to the new trend of the Song poetry, his interest in strange and exotic things and objects might be as well related to the Song people's study of the middle Tang poetry. In the middle Tang Dynasty, besides the type of plain and clear poems written by Bai Juyi, there was another type of poems — peculiar, tough and eccentric, written in the classical style by Han Yu, Meng Jiao, et. al. Some poets of this type delighted in hunting for some odd and unsightly things to write about, toward which Mei Yaochen showed particular understanding. He wrote some poems about mosquitoes, lice and fleas, and had tea-drinking, hiccup, meals, diarrhoea, etc. put into poems. He also mentioned in his poems that Ouyang Xiu once compared himself to Han Yu and Mei Yaochen to Meng Jiao. It is clear that this type of poets were quite conscious of the poetic styles of Han Yu and Meng Jiao in the middle Tang Dynasty.

The poems of Su Shunqin were "plainer and more artistic" in comparison with those of Mei Yaochen, and even more embodied the bold and vigorous style (Wei Tai: *Poetry Talks in Seclusion at the Han River*). This reminded people of Li Bai (although Ouyang Xiu compared Su Shunqin to Zhang Ji), and Li Bai was the very poet Ouyang Xiu worshipped. He once compared Li Bai with Du Fu, and said: "Du Fu can only be a part of Li Bai, though a more refined and powerful part; as for Li Bai's genius and boldness, Du Fu cannot attain them." (*Comments on Poem Composition*) The people at that time also wrote: "Lord Ouyang (Ouyang Xiu) didn't like Du Fu's poems very much... However, he appreciated Li Bai so much that he was perhaps moved by Li Bai's elation and transcendence." (*Zhongshan Poetry Talks*) In his poem to Wang Anshi, Ouyang Xiu drew a conclusion of the accomplishments of the Tang poetry and prose with Li Bai and Han Yu: "Li Bai wrote three thousand beautiful poems, and Han Yu's articles have been passed on for two hundred years." ("To Wang Jiefu (Wang Anshi)") That was also the goal he wanted to pursue in the aspect of literary creation. In fact, Han Yu not only set an example of essay-writing for Ouyang Xiu, but had a great influence on his poetic creation. Shen Deqian of the Qing Dynasty also said: "Ouyang Xiu devoted himself to the study of Changli's (Han Yu) seven-syllable poems in the classical style." We know the seven-syllable poems in the classical style were perhaps what Ouyang Xiu was expert at. For example, "A Song to Wang Zhaojun (an imperial concubine) in Reply to Wang Jiefu", which Ouyang Xiu in a drunken boastful mood claimed that even Li Bai and Du Fu could hardly compose, is a poem of the seven-syllable classical style. An important point that Ouyang Xiu learned from Han Yu was that he composed the poems in the way of essay writing; that is, he introduced the ways of syntax and text organization of ancient Chinese prose into poem-composition to produce an essayistic effect. Fang Dongshu once pointed out: "His poetic organization and structure solely adopted the method of ancient Chinese prose." (*Humble Opinions from Zhaomei*) This was a more internalized approach in comparison with the use of various poetic sentence patterns interspersed with the prosaic syntax. Essayistic and argumentative transformation was a remarkable feature of the Song poetry and a result of inheriting one line of the Tang poetry and expanding it.

Wang Anshi was an influential figure in the political history of the Song Dynasty and also occupied an important position in the literary history. His early poetic works were relatively crude, as Ye Mengde commented: "He was confident with aspirations; therefore, his poems expressed explicitly what they aimed at with little implication ... They just spoke in a straightforward way what he had in mind." (*Shilin Poetry Talks*) He cited this example: "A spray of red flower blooms among the thousands of exuberant green branches; / There is no need of many spring scenes to attract people." However, some of Wang's poems about daily affairs and politics read like documents with rhymes, and there is no need for further comment about that. Wang Anshi began to change his poetic style when he was a colleague of Song Cidao, from whom he borrowed various collected works of the Tang poets, read them repeatedly, and absorbed their essence until he compiled *Selected Readings of 100 Tang Poets*. By the time he was old and retired to seclusion at Jiangning, he had reached the "sublime" realm in poem-writing, and there was a world of difference from his early works. (*Notes after the Departure of Guests*) By then, the argumentativeness in his poems had been washed away, and analogies and images reappeared to embody the splendidness of the Tang poetry. Though some people criticized him, "His one hundred poems could not match one of any late Tang poets" (*Tingzhai Poetry Talks*), "Having not yet cast off the bad habit of the Song poets" (the comment by Li Dongyang), no one could deny the fact that his poems were similar to the Tang poetry. Literary creation had its own unique features. In his natural mature style was revealed his tempered and drilled spirit, just as Wang Anshi himself said in his poem: "It is the most unique and precipitous, though it looks quite common; It seems easy to succeed, but it entails arduous efforts." Wang Anshi was an erudite scholar, and was quite familiar with classical poems and the works of the previous poets. He initiated the practice of collecting sentences from the poems of the previous poets into new poems of "collected sentences", and we should know that how many excellent sentences of the previous poems he bore in mind. Owing to his familiarity with the previous creative works, from time to time he altered some lines of the predecessors consciously or unconsciously as his own poems. For instance, in the poem "The Northern Hill", the line "Being seated long I found more petals shed nearby" came from Wang Wei of the Tang Dynasty, "I found more shed petals when I sat here long." To show off his gift, he requested the antitheses to be precise and the allusions to be well-matched, for example, using translated

Sanskrit word to match translated Sanskrit word, Aranyaka (阿兰若) to match Stupa (窣堵波), the allusion in *The Book of the Han Dynasty* to match that in the same book, etc. His weighing of words was also well known; for instance, the verb "green" in "The spring breeze greens again the shores of the South" had been fixed after a dozen of replacement, while Li Bai of the Tang poet in fact already had such a sentence: "The east breeze already greens again the grass at Yingzhou." Possibly it was his knowledge that added luster to his poem. Wang Anshi's emphasis on talent and learning, stress on practice, fondness of altering the verses of the predecessors and even his argumentativeness all actually carried forward the styles of the Tang poetry, initiated the style of the Song poetry, and pioneered the school of the Jiangxi poets. The remarks of Huang Tingjian proved it: "I obtained the syntax of ancient poetry from the old man Banshan (Wang Anshi)." (*Guanlin Poetry Talks*)

Su Shi was a literary giant in the Northern Song Dynasty as well as in the whole Chinese literary history. He was a disciple of Ouyang Xiu, and finally he completed the task of establishing the style of the Song poetry. Yan Yu reckoned: "Dongpo (Su Shi) and Shan'gu (Huang Tingjian) began to write poems with their own ideas and changed the style of the Tang poets." (*Canglang Poetry Talks*) His gift was so great and his knowledge so rich that he could express with his powerful brush whatever he wanted to. As far as several special features of the Song poetry are concerned, Su Shi was able to demonstrate them to perfection with few flaws. For instance, he might express comments and reasons in his poem "Inscription on the Xiling Cliffs":

> It is a ridge viewed in face, and a peak from the side,
> Near or far, high or low, never is there a same sight.
> We cannot know the true face of the Lu Mountains,
> Simply because we are ourselves in the Mountains.

Far from being dull and dry, the poem became famous for its delight in reasoning. Ji Yun of the Qing Dynasty commented: "His poems involve direct philosophical consideration with wonderful freedom, but without the abstractness of philosophy." And again, to demonstrate his talent and knowledge in the poems, Su Shi was well-versed in classics, histories, philosophical books and literary collections, and different stories and novels, miscellanies, Buddhist scriptures and Daoist books. Hu Zai believed: "Dongpo was expert at using allusions. The allusions he used were easily understood as well as appropriate." (*Talks of a Reclusive Fisherman at the Tiao Stream*) Zhao Yi also said: "Su Shi was brimming with talent, and whatever he wrote seemed bursting with vitality; he read wide enough to be able to write with all ease and facility, so that everything can be expressed at his will." (*Oubei Poetry Talks*) And again, Su Shi was adept at breaking free from the limitations of literary genres to combine various ways of expression. In his creation of lyrics, he based his writing on the method of poem composition, which introduced a new channel for the development of lyrics; whereas in poem creation, he followed Han Yu's way of writing with prosaic techniques, so that his poems seemed surging forward, enthusiastic and uninhibited. "What was hidden would surely be expressed, and no emotions were too difficult to be exposed. That is why Su Shi has been considered a literary giant after Li Bai and Du Fu." (*Oubei Poetry Talks*).

Su Shi endeavored to absorb all the poetic heritage of the previous ages, of which the Tang poets were certainly an important part he devoted himself to. He once praised Li Bai and Du Fu of "transcendence of all ages", and Han Yu of "unrestrainedness and distinct peculiarity", and he repeatedly recommended Tao Yuanming, Wei Yingwu, Liu Zongyuan, et. al. for their poems which were simple and indifferent, but profound in implication. In his late years he always kept the poetry anthology of Tao Yuanming and Liu Zongyuan at hand, and read them frequently with admiration. Besides, he also learned from the poems of Bai Juyi. Qian Zhongshu in his *Selected Song Poetry with Annotations* listed Su Shi, Wang Yucheng and Zhang Lei of the Northern Song Dynasty as three famous poets of Bai's style. In fact, some ancient critic had already commented that Su Shi had the boldness of vision to learn from various famous poets in order to create his own excellent poems: "With his marvelous talent, Lord Su excelled all others, ancient and modern. Observing his will and intention, we may find that he attempted to embrace all the strong points of Li Bai, Du Fu, Han Yu and Bai Juyi." (*Zhenyi Studio Poetry Talks*) Su Shi composed poems by dint of his gift, which was indeed unlikely for everyone to learn. His knowledge, intelligence and disposition merged together through his talent. If he were a person with no gift or little gift, he could hardly have embraced so much emotion, intelligence and knowledge, but would only choose to grasp one aspect to develop. Huang Tingjian, a student of Su Shi, had possibly the most followers in the poetic circles of the Northern and Southern Song Dynasties; even the greatest Song poets after him — Lu You for instance — were shrouded under his giant shadow. Therefore, he and his tutor were listed together as Su-Huang. Of course, they both were gifted and learned, but comparatively speaking, Su Shi was a talent, while Huang Tingjian was a learned scholar. After generalizing the differences between Su Shi and Huang Tingjian, Liu Kezhuang at the end of the Song Dynasty said: "After the Yuanyou Period emerged a large number of poets here and there, whose poems might be categorized within the two styles of Huang Tingjian or Su Shi: one was marked with rich implications but poor rhythm, and the other featured fine diction but lacked emotions." (*Houcun Poetry Talks*)

Huang Tingjian read quite extensively. His two fathers-in-law Sun Jue and Xie Shihou were both erudite scholars, and his father Huang Shu learned the poems sedulously from Du Fu and Han Yu. He himself demonstrated a series of feasible ways to compose poems in the respects of diction, syntax and even refinement of meanings. As a consequence, he pointed out a route for the later poets to follow and had a greater influence than Su Shi. After all, it is easier to acquire knowledge than talent. Of all these methods, the most popular was: "Touch iron and turn it into gold", i.e. skilful changes of poetic lines or meanings of the previous poems into original poetic lines. This is inheritance with transformation on the one hand, and on the other, it is a way of composing poems with peculiar language, difficult rhymes and rare allusions. Later, Zhang Jie criticized him: "He knew only how to compose poems with peculiar language, but not with common language." (*Suihantang Poetry Talks*) The latter aspect seemed somehow similar to the Russian formalist literary concept of "strangeness" in the early 20th century, i.e. to create on purpose a kind of fresh and uncommon feeling. The poetics of Huang Tingjian exerted an extremely great influence at that time. For instance, Chen Shidao had at first learned the classical prose from Zeng Gong, and Su Shi once intended to accept him as his student, but Chen Shidao declined. Nevertheless, he took a different attitude toward Huang Tingjian and said in a letter in reply to Qin Guan:

> When I began to learn poem writing, I had no one to teach me. However, I liked it very much since childhood. I do not feel tired about it even when I am old, and I have written about a thousand poems. As soon as I met Huang Yuzhang (Tingjian), I burned them all to learn after him. As for my poems, they were all under the imitations of the poems of Yuzhang.

It can be seen that the poets worshipped Huang Tingjian at the time.

In fact, the poetics of Huang Tingjian took form and developed with his own characteristics under the pressure of the works of his predecessors. His poems are representative of the style of the Song poetry. Similar to the Song poetry in a state of "anxiety of influence" toward the Tang poetry, his poems were also the products of the typical "anxiety of influence". In order to change the poetic lines of the predecessors into new poems, he had to use rare allusions and difficult rhymes the predecessors had not tried to use. All these efforts indicated his ingenuity from those predecessors, and meanwhile laid bare the pressure of the literary heritage he had to endure. Even Su Shi's talent was also a pressure to urge him to acquire knowledge with strenuous efforts. Wang Ruoxu once said: "If there was no pressure from Dongpo, Huang Tingjian might not necessarily be what he is now." (*Hunan Poetry Talks*) It is somewhat suggestive that Huang Tingjian tried hard to distinguish his poems from those of his predecessors, especially those of the Tang poets, but the ways and channels he learned and developed were all derived from the Tang poets, among whom Du Fu and Han Yu exerted the greatest influence on him. In his comment on the poetry and prose of the Tang Dynasty, he praised: "Not a word of the poems by Master Du (Du Fu) or the articles by Tuizhi (Han Yu) is without the source." ("A letter in Reply to Hong Jufu") He thought that he had learned the quintessence of Du Fu's poetry, and even Zhang Jie who had criticized him seriously had to admit some of his poems "have reached the level of Zimei (Du Fu)". His language was jerky and peculiar, for his poetic composition with "peculiar language" might as well inherit and carry forward Han Yu's advocacy that "All the hackneyed words and trite expressions should be discarded".

Huang Tingjian's poetics was easy for the learners to practice because it laid stress on the feasible techniques, such as diction, syntax, prosody and sections and chapters; therefore, it was also quite influential. Lü Benzhong once drew a diagram "*The Genealogy of the Poets of the Jiangxi School*" at the end of the Northern Song Dynasty, in which he listed twenty-five poets like Huang Tingjian and Chen Shidao; many of them received direct instructions from Huang Tingjian, and still more learned indirectly from him. In the preface Lü Benzhong pointed out:

> It is not until the appearance of Yuzhang (Huang Tingjian) that the poetry began to be popular, thanks to his devotion to invigorating it. Later, the learners made concerted efforts of chant and reply to elucidate and practice the poetic essences to the full; therefore, here are recorded the names of the poets called the Jiangxi School, and its source and courses originated from Yuzhang.

Huang Tingjian was confirmed as the initiator and master of this poetic school. The reason for the name of "the Jiangxi Poetic School" is that Huang Tingjian was born in Jiangxi, not that all the poets came from Jiangxi. The main characteristic of this school is that its poets basically shared the same poetic concepts and the same interests rather than the same locality. Later, Yang Wanli explained it clearly: "The school of the Jiangxi poets was characterized by their poems in the Jiangxi style, and not that all the poets came from Jiangxi." ("The Preface to *The Poems of the Jiangxi School*")

The definition of the Jiangxi School in the Southern Song Dynasty changed from time to time and was expanded. At first, Lü Benzhong was in the list; later Liu Kezhuang thought Yang Wanli should also be included in the school; Yan Yu held that Chen Yuyi "ought to belong to the Jiangxi School with only small differences"; and finally Fang Hui concluded it with "one founder and three masters", i.e. Du Fu as the founder, Huang Tingjian, Chen Shiyun and Chen Yuyi as the masters, and Lu You, Fan Chengda, et. al. were all included in the school as well. Thus, almost all the poets from the late Northern Song to the Southern Song Dynasties were included within the Jiangxi School.

When a good proposition was practiced by countless people, malpractice would be inevitable; when it reached the extreme, there would be all kinds of odd phenomena. The poets of the Jiangxi School stressed on knowledge, as well as on using peculiar language and difficult rhythm and rhymes to the extreme; as a result, abstruse writings and clumsy rhymes emerged now and then. In fact, Huang Tingjian once criticized Wang Guanfu's poems as "fond of peculiar language, which is certainly a defect in poem writing", and "especially riddled with ornateness". After Lü Benzhong crossed the river to the Southern Song Dynasty, he tried hard to reform the Jiangxi Poetic School, and thought those who imitated the poems of Huang Tingjian were so rigid with the rules and norms in composing poems and certainly ran counter to the original intention of Huang Tingjian (*Comments on Poetry with Zeng Jifu*). Huang Tingjian had possibly sought to reach the realm of freedom through rules and norms, instead of being confined therewithin. He said again and again: "The excellence of Zimei's (Du Fu) poems lay in naturalness." (*Record of Daya Hall*) "A poem completed naturally without ornament can be regarded as a good poem." (*The Second Letter in Reply to Wang Guanfu*) It is in this spirit of Huang Tingjian that Lü Benzhong advocated "flexibility and rules".

> "Flexibility and rules" means that all the rules are stipulated, but the poet can still transcend the rules; everything is changeable but they do not violate any rule. Although this way has definite rules, it is not restricted within the definite rules; and although it is not restricted within the definite rules, certainly it has the definite rules ... Xie Xuanhui (Xie Tiao) once said: "A good poem is natural, mellow and round as a ball." This is a real understanding of flexibility and rules.

That is to say, poem-writing should have changes on the basis of observing techniques and rules, and create new meanings without restriction of the rules to demonstrate flexibility. He quoted the words of Xie Tiao, a poet of the Southern Dynasties, to express his expectation that poems should be fluent and lively, and not abstruse and clumsy. Zeng Ji was a good friend of Lü Benzhong in the study of poetics and once praised Lü's poems: "They are smooth as golden balls, and agile as a fleeting hare." (*Reading Lü Juren's Old Poems*) It can be seen that Lü Benzhong's theoretic reformation and his poetic creation complemented each other.

The importance of Lü Benzhong in the poetic history of the Song Dynasty reflected a change of poetic theories, while in practice Chen Yuyi demonstrated an outstanding achievement. The poems of Chen Yuyi were separated into two phases with his move to the Southern Song Dynasty as a dividing line. The style of his poems in the second phase changed into "simple and concise without elaboration, and firm and vigorous without delicacy and exquisiteness". (*Houcun Poetry Talks*) His early poems were also modeled after the poems of Huang Tingjian and Chen Shidao, but later his poetic inclination, together with his life and the fortune of the country, changed altogether. *The Synoptic Catalogue of the Complete Library in the Four Treasuries* commented: "Although he started by imitating the poems of Yuzhang (Huang Tingjian), he was extremely talented, and adept at changes. His style is vigorous, and his thinking is insightful and sincere; therefore, he could alone be able to blaze a new trail of his own." Obviously in the poetic attitude, it is not merely an imitation of the poems of Huang Tingjian. He once said: "Although a man should read extensively, he should be discreet not to be fond of using allusions." (Preface to the Second Volume of *The Poems after Refusing All Visitors*) He advocated explicitly learning from Du Fu and breaking through the Song poetic patterns of Huang Tingjian, and even Su Shi: "One should know what both Su Shi and Huang Tingjian had not done, and then he could get a touch of Master Du." (Preface to *Collected Poems of Jianzhai*) His study of Du Fu's poems was closely related with his personal experience in the political upheaval at the turn of the Northern and Southern Song Dynasties, which is similar to Du Fu's experience in the rebellion of An Lushan in the Tang Dynasty. In his poems the poet's feelings of experience and worries about the country were combined into one; he carried on directly Du Fu's spirit, and even altered some poetic lines of Du Fu's as his own. Chen Yuyi in his study of the Tang poets did not confine his study to Du Fu alone, but extended to the lucidness and plainness of Wei Yingwu and Liu Zongyuan. Chen Yan, an early modern scholar and an expert of the Song poetry, said in *Records of the Best Song Poems*: "The Song poets rarely learned from Wei Yingwu and Liu Zongyuan; if any, it was Jianzhai (Chen Yuyi), who learned best." This can be the evidence of how Chen Yuyi learned from Wei Yingwu and Liu Zongyuan.

Now let's review the poetic circles of the Northern Song Dynasty: At first Ouyang Xiu, Su Shunqin, and Mei Yaocheng attempted to establish a new style of poetry; in the middle, Su Shi rose vigorously with his talent, and Wang Anshi developed his own original style; Huang Tingjian synthesized various styles of the Song poets, and established the Jiangxi Poetic School, which exerted such an extensive influence that by then the Song poetry had become independent from the shadow of the Tang poetry, and the Song style was established. Nevertheless, this Song style actually developed along the way initiated by the Tang poets Du Fu, Han Yu and others. At the turn of the two Song Dynasties, the poetics of the Jiangxi School had undergone changes and developed into different styles. Fang Hui described them as follows:

> Master Du Fu is the champion of the Tang poets, and Huang Tingjian and Chen Shidao the champions of the Song poets. Both Huang Tingjian and Chen Shidao learned from the poems of Du Fu. The one who carried on the spirits of Huang Tingjian and Chen Shidao to propagate stirring pathos was Chen Jianzhai (Chen Yuyi), the one whose poems reflected smoothness and fluency was Lü Juren (Lü Benzhong), and the one whose poems displayed freshness and elegance was Zeng Chashan (Zeng Ji).

They all worshipped Du Fu, the sage-poet of the Tang Dynasty; each attained his perfection, like different tributaries coming out of the same source. Nevertheless, the poet who exerted the greatest influence on the poetic circles of the Southern Song Dynasty is the last one, Zeng Ji.

At the end of the Northern Song Dynasty, Zeng Ji made friends with the poets of the Jiangxi School, such as Lü Benzhong and Xu Fu, and also respected Han Yu as his teacher. He learned poetics from Lü Benzhong, propagated repeatedly his "flexibility and rules", and carried forward and developed the improved poetic style within the Jiangxi School. Lu You, a great poet of the early Southern Song Dynasty, was Zeng Ji's student when young; so was Xiao Dezao. Yang Wanli was also influenced by him. It was through Zeng Ji that these great poets established profound relation with the Jiangxi style, though they all went beyond the school later and created their own unique styles.

The deficiency of the Jiangxi School became increasingly conspicuous during the social upheaval and the changes of cultural trends at the turn of the two Song Dynasties. You Mao, a well-known poet at the time, had said: "The poems of the Jiangxi School could not be fine and smooth like those of Fan Chengda, straightforward like those of Yang Wanli, lofty and antique like those of Xiao Dezao, and elegant and pleasing like those of Lu You, so why must one take pains to study it?" This is naturally reasonable. What You Mao said just implied a breakthrough of the Jiangxi poetic style by the restoration poets; on the other hand, no one could deny that they all learned poem writing from the Jiangxi poetics, and it was on this basis that they treaded the paths of their own. Take You Mao himself as an example: He learned poems from Wang Yingchen, who followed Lü Benzhong. Take Xiao Dezao as another example: He once said, "Poems cannot be written without reading widely, or be written with reliance only on books." (*Face-to-face Dialogue at Night* vol.2) He indeed learned poems from Zeng Ji, and Yang Wanli also appreciated his "exquisite techniques". (Preface to *The Excerpts from Qianyan*) It can be seen that he had endeavored to write poems, but Qian Zhongshu thought: "His poems appears laborious, because he sought peculiarity and strangeness in diction and sentence structure." (*Selected Song Poetry with Annotations*) Therefore the habit of the Jiangxi style has not been completely eliminated from his poems.

Lu You was the greatest poet at the beginning of the Southern Song Dynasty. He learned poems from Zeng Ji at 18, and this influence lasted to his late years. However, his military career in his middle age greatly expanded his poetic vision, and he realized, "If you really want to learn poem-writing, efforts should be made beyond the poems." In his late years, he lived reclusively in his native town, and his poems tended to be plain and natural, that is, "A poem is basically a natural gift, as one perfect sentence can be obtained by chance." These views were right in opposition to the Jiangxi School's emphasis on books and knowledge. From the changes in the poems of Lu You's early, middle and later years, we can see the obvious influence of his realistic life on his poetic creation. But on the other hand, that Lu You was able to break through the restrictions of the Jiangxi School was inseparable from his personal talent and his study in many aspects of the poets of the previous ages. His unrestrained and romantic disposition enabled him to learn the lucidness and freshness of the Jiangxi style without imitating its slenderness and toughness, and to express the splendor of the Jiangxi style without using its difficult and affected language. With regard to the tradition of the poetics, he not only learned from Huang Tingjian, Lü Benzhong and Zeng Ji, but also learned from Mei Yaochen and Su Shi; he not only followed the Song poets, but read widely the works of the Tang poets. He said of himself that at 17 or 18, he was "most familiar with the poems of Mojie (Wang Wei)" (Postscript to *The Collection of Prime Minister Wang* (Wang Wei)), and again "absolutely love *Collected Poems of Cen Jiazhou* (Cen Shen)" (Postscript to *Collected Poems of Cen Jiazhou*), because Cen Shen's powerful poems about the frontier life struck a sympathetic chord in Lu You, a man with military backgrounds. As for Li Bai and Du Fu, they were surely the great poets Lu You adored, for he often mentioned them in his poems. His patriotic enthusiasm can be said to have inherited the tradition from Du Fu's concern about the country and people. As a result, people in the later ages liked to mention them in the same breath. Emperor Xiaozong of the Southern Song Dynasty once asked Zhou Bida: "Is there any poet today like Li Bai of the Tang Dynasty?" Zhou Bida answered, "Lu You." Henceforth, people called Lu You "Li Bai Jr." Lu You also cherished the poems of Tao Yuanming and said: "In poems, I admired Yuanming." (*On Reading the Poems of Tao Yuanming*) "In learning poem-writing, one should follow Tao Yuanming." (*Self-exhortation*) Some of his poems depicting rustic life and simple and honest folk custom embodied the style of Tao Yuanming. It is because of his extensive knowledge and wide absorption of others that Lu You was able to promote his own poetic conception and go beyond the confines of the Jiangxi style.

Fan Chengda was another great poet in the early Southern Song Dynasty, and we are still not clear from whom he learned to compose poems, but he was obviously nurtured in the poetic atmosphere of the Jiangxi style. Ji Yun, an erudite and well-informed scholar of the Qing Dynasty, praised his poems as "the excellent ones of the Jiangxi School", and in *The Synoptic Catalogue of The Complete Library of the Four Treasuries*, he was considered to have learned the poems from the middle and late Tang poets when he was young, because he made the footnotes himself for some of his poems as "imitation of Wang Jian", "imitation of Li He", which indicated his goal. Later, he began to study the poetic methods of Su Shi and Huang Tingjian, and developed a style of his own. Reading the poems of Fan Chengda, we can find his poems of idyllic life most characteristic. Some of his poems imitated those of Tao Yuanming, and some the New Music Bureau of Bai Juyi and Wang Jian in describing the hard life of people. Fan Chengda was perhaps one of the special poets at that time that chiefly adhered to the style of the Tang poetry and also embraced the style of the Jiangxi School.

Different from Fan Chengda, Yang Wanli came from the Jiangxi School but got rid of the trammels of the Jiangxi style through the study of the late Tang poetry, and reached the free realm of creation. That was a typical course of change. In his early poems of about 1,000 in total, Yang Wanli learned from the poems of the Jiangxi School, and later he burnt them all in his dissatisfaction with them. However, this did not mean his complete denial of the poetics of the Jiangxi School. In his late years, he still expressed his appreciation of Huang Tingjian in the Preface to *Chengzhai Poetry Talks*. Liu Kezhuang also thought Yang Wanli had truly put into practice Lü Benzhong's theory of the "flexibility and rules", and his poems were "smooth and fluent as a round ball". (General Preface to *Comments on the Jiangxi Poetic School*) All these showed the deep influence of the Jiangxi style on him. After that, he focused his study on the five-syllable regulated poems of Chen Shidao and the quatrains of Wang Anshi. That was a step upstream. Yang Wanli treasured the quatrains of Wang Anshi so much that he was fascinated with them, and a line of his poems reads: "The quatrains of Banshan (Wang Anshi) serve as my breakfast." (*On Reading Poems*) The poems of Wang Anshi in his late years were perfectly refined, and Yan Yu commented in *Canglang Poetry Talks*: "The quatrains of Master Wang (Wang Anshi) were the best of his poems; some excellent ones excelled those of Su (Su Shi), Huang (Huang Tingjian) and Chen (Chen Shidao)." His quatrains imitated from time to time the Tang poems. Yang Wanli also thought that it was not easy to write good quatrains, and "The late Tang poets and Jiefu (Wang Anshi) were adept at quatrains." (*Chengzhai Poetry Talks*) Therefore, it is natural for Yang Wanli to trace back from Wang Anshi to the late Tang poets. In his Preface to *Collected Poems of Jingxi* he recalled his own course of poetic learning: Immediately after he learned from Wang Anshi's "seven-syllable quatrains", he studied "the quatrains of the Tang poets". In the Tang poetry, Yang Wanli seemed to favor the late Tang poems. He said: "The poetry became flourishing in the prime Tang Dynasty, and by the late Tang Dynasty, it became perfectly refined." (The Preface to *Collected Poems of Secretary Huang*) When he recommended and appreciated the poems of Lu Guimeng, a late Tang poet, he also said: "With whom can I share his unusual flavor? The poems today are similar to those of the late Tang poets." (*On Reading Lize Series*) Yang Wanli's preference started a practice for the late Southern Song poets to follow the patterns of the late Tang poetry. Therefore, Yang Wanli learned poems first from the Jiangxi School and Wang Anshi, and then from the late Tang poets; gradually he got rid of the trammels of the patterns of the Jiangxi School. After all, he was still imitating others. He said himself: "The more I studied, the bitter I felt, and the fewer poems I wrote." Finally, at 50 he became instantly enlightened: He cast away all the rules and standards of both the Tang and Song predecessors, and entered the period of free creation of his own to express his emotions poetically completely from his personal experiences of life and observation of the natural phenomena. The poems of Yang Wanli in his late years portrayed the emotions and things few poets observed, and reflected them with intricate variations. Just because of his thorough and penetrating expressions, the celebrated lyricist Jiang Kui said jokingly: "All the mountains and rivers seem shy to see you." Besides, Yang Wanli used spoken language and vernacular in his poems; therefore, they read humorous and lively. All these features established a unique style of his poems. As a result, in the late Southern Song Dynasty, it seemed that his followers were more numerous than those who studied the poems of Lu You. But is it true that Yang Wanli in his late years followed nobody in poem creation? It can at least be said that his poems were easy and popular. "They described the states of objects, and expressed human emotions in great details and intricate subtlety." (Zhou Bida's comment on his poems) Therefore, more or less, his poems were close to those of Bai Juyi. Yang Wanli also had a profound understanding of Bai Juyi's poems, with which Yang Wanli could even replace wine in dispelling worries and curing diseases:

With no drink on the festival I feel even more worried,

I did house cleaning to dispel my boredom in illness.
It happened that I read some poems of Bai Xiangshan;
All at once I feel there is neither boredom nor illness.

(*Stopping Drinking in Illness on the Dragon-Boat Festival*)

The development of the poetry of the Song Dynasty began with the imitation of the Tang poetry, and later it had always been a central problem to get rid of the latter's influence. The Jiangxi Poetic School finally accomplished the task. However, by the time of Yang Wanli, because his style was close to that of the Tang poetry, he was divorced from the Jiangxi Poetic School. After this, the restoration of the Tang poetry seemed to be inevitable. In this trend, the most prominent poets were called "Four Lings of Yongjia", i.e. Xu Zhao, Xu Ji, Zhao Shixiu and Weng Juan. Because there was a character of "ling" in the courtesy names or style names of the four poets and they were considered to be natives of Yongjia, they were called the "Four Lings of Yongjia". At first, they were not very popular, and later became increasingly well-known because of the promotion of the contemporary celebrated thinker Ye Shi. Ye Shi collected and edited five hundred poems of theirs into *Selected Poems of Four Lings*, which was popular for a time, thus the poems of the Tang Dynasty had the tendency to resume its popularity. What the Four Lings learned was the poems of the late Tang pattern, so Fang Hui said: "The Four Lings of Yongjia resumed the late Tang style of the Nine Monks." That is to say, they resumed the learning of the late Tang poems at the beginning of the Song Dynasty, but what they pursued was the poetic style of Jia Dao and Yao He of the late Tang Dynasty. As we have introduced previously, Zhao Shixiu selected and edited two hundred poems of Jia Dao and Yao He into *A Collection of Two Wonders*, which indicated the target of their imitation. Different from Yang Wanli's learning of the quatrains of the late Tang poetry, the Four Lings focused on the five-syllable regulated poems. Zhao Shixiu once said: "It was fortunate for me that each poem had only forty characters. In case there were more characters, I really did not know how to deal with them!"

They were so successful in imitating the poems of Jia Dao and Yao He that their poems read similar to the latter's, and someone said those poems could not be distinguished from each other if they were put into the collection of Jia Dao and Yao He. The poems of Jia Dao and Yao He were characterized by careful diction, purity and desolation, and so were the poems of the "Four Lings". Yan Yu spoke of their style in *Canglang Poetry Talks*: "The present-day Zhao Zizhi (Zhao Shixiu), Weng Lingshu (Weng Juan) and his like favored only the poems of Jia Dao and Yao He, and they somewhat resumed the pattern of purity and desolation." *The Synoptic Catalogue of the Complete Library of the Four Treasuries* commented that Zhao Shixiu and others "concentrated their efforts on sentence refinement, and the key was to weigh appropriate words." All these are pertinent comments. In the course of transforming the practice of poem-writing, the "Four Lings" played a significant role. Their goal to imitate the late Tang poetry was clear, and the characteristics of poetic pattern were prominent, which were enough for them to write poems of fresh and distinctive effect; meanwhile, they gave up the way of the Jiangxi School in writing poems on the basis of knowledge and books which emphasized "the sources for every word", so in order to "write poems with no books for reference" (Liu Kezhuang's remark), "They voiced their own minds with nothing to rely on." (*The Synoptic Catalogue of The Complete Library of the Four Treasuries*) Although their poetic conception was narrow, their poems after all were their own creation. This certainly had quite a strong influence on the literary circle under the circumstance of rejecting the Jiangxi School in the late Southern Song Dynasty. Yan Yu pointed out that most of the later poets "followed their pattern, and they claimed for a time their poems to be the voice of the Tang Dynasty." Liu Kezhuang was influenced heavily by the Four Lings in his early poems. Although he talked about his early poems critically later, he did not deny the point that "The Yongjia poets tried their best and could only just see the fence of the poems of Jia Dao and Yao He, and so are my own poems." (Preface to *Melon Garden Collection*)

Poetry talks in the Song Dynasty were quite popular, and by the end of the Southern Song Dynasty, there appeared a book entitled *Canglang Poetry Talks*, which is a comprehensive conclusion of the poetics of the Song Dynasty. However, it clearly rejected the Song poetry, especially the poems of the representative Jiangxi School. It is easy for us to pay attention to the theories of the works of poetics, but they are usually the products of the ideological trends of the times. If *Canglang Poetry Talks* was put into the background of "returning to the Tang poetry" in the middle and late periods of the Southern Song Dynasty, its poetic tendency would not appear distinctive.

First of all, Yan Yu also objected to the poetic style of the Jiangxi School. He seriously criticized the emphasis on philosophical speculation in the Song poetry and the stress on knowledge of the Jiangxi School, and drew a conclusion of its characteristics as "to compose poems with focus on refinement of words, on talent and knowledge, and on comments". In comparison and contrast with the Tang poems that stressed on images instead of philosophical speculation, he suggested: "Poem-writing entails different materials, and not books." His recipe for treatment was identical with the contemporary poets, i.e. to rectify the situation with the Tang poetry. However, this Tang poetry was not the late Tang poetry as the Four Lings and even Yang Wanli practiced, but the poems of the prime Tang Dynasty. Next, Yan Yu spared no efforts in recommending the poems of the prime Tang Dynasty among those supporters of the Tang poetry. "We should take the prime Tang poetry as our model. Although I might offend many poets of our time, I shall be as good as my words." Such a remark was no doubt directed against the followers of the Four Lings. Yan Yu's inheritance and initiative had profound historical significance. On the one hand, he identified himself with the poets who took an objection to the style of the Jiangxi School, and returned to the trend of the Tang poetry; on the other hand, he held high the banner of the prime Tang poetry to break through the limitation of the late Tang poetry. Later, the poets of the Ming Dynasty must have followed the example of Yan Yu to emphasize "Poem-writing must follow the example of the prime Tang Dynasty".

2. The Poetic Circles in the Jin, Yuan, Ming and Qing Dynasties: The Growth and Decline of the Tang and Song Poetry

The resurgence of the trend of the Tang poetry in the Song dynasty was a gradual course after the repeated debates in literary circles, whereas in the Jin Dynasty, confronting with the Southern Song Dynasty, the advocacy of the Tang poetry and the depreciation of the Song poetry seemed to have already become a vogue. In the North, the influence of Su Shi was greater than in the South. His poems and essays were even more highly appreciated for the free expression of talent and the unrestrainedness of any rules. The Song poets usually evaluated Su Shi and Huang Tingjian separately, and valued Su Shi over Huang Tingjian. The most characteristic critical comment came from Wang Ruoxu: The poems of Huang Tingjian "showed his knowledge as erudition, and transformed trite expressions as original, but his poems did not flow naturally from the bottom of his heart." It is on this very point that Su Shi was far superior to Huang Tingjian. In fact, such a comment can also be found in the Song poets, who connected Su Shi with Li Bai, and Huang Tingjian with Du Fu, so as to trace back to the two great poets of the Tang Dynasty; by doing so, they widened the path to follow the Tang poetry in order to rectify the malpractice of the Jiangxi Poetic School. For instance, Lü Benzhong said that the poems of Du Fu and Huang Tingjian manifested "rules and criteria" while the poems of Li Bai and Su Shi were "magnanimous", "without awkwardness and laboriousness", and the latter could make up for the former. (*Comments on Poetry with Zeng Jifu*) Similarly, Yang Wanli believed the poems of Su Shi and Li Bai were free and unrestrained, while the poems of Du Fu and Huang Tingjian attained the realm of freedom through rules and standards. (*Preface to the Poems of the Jiangxi School*) The poets of the Jin Dynasty respected the poems of the Tang Dynasty and began with a wide range of selection, instead of beginning with the late Tang poetry as Yang Wanli and the Four Lings of the Southern Song Dynasty did. Zhao Bingwen headed the literary circle for a time, and advocated "to study only the poems of the Tang Dynasty." ("A Record of Returning Home and Living in Seclusion" by Liu Qi) In his *Letter in Reply to Li Tianyun*, he affirmed that each of the poets such as Wei Yingwu, Wang Wei, Liu Zongyuan, Bai Juyi, Li Bai, Li He, Meng Jiao, Jia Dao, etc. had his own style. Zhao held in high esteem Du Fu for his synthetic accomplishments, and Han Yu for his transformation of poems into the essayistic form. It can be seen that he absorbed a wide range of knowledge. Wang Ruoxu was known for his discourse on essays and talks about poetry. According to Yuan Haowen, he "learned poems of Bai Letian (Bai Juyi)". We actually read his praise of Bai Juyi's poems, "describing emotions and interests with superb art and refreshing style." The reason for Wang Ruoxu to recommend the poems of Bai Juyi and Su Shi was that they were written naturally and different from those of Huang Tingjian, which were written with knowledge and in a strange and eccentric style. We may better understand why the critics of the Jin Dynasty depreciated the Song poetry if we consider the criticism of Yuan Haowen on the Jiangxi style in the Song Dynasty in his *Thirty Quatrains on Poetry*.

The people of the Yuan Dynasty rose in the north, and they went south to conquer the Jin and the Southern Song Dynasties in succession. Their culture was basically at a low level, and its literary circles upheld the main trend of thoughts in the conquered place. At that time, the poets of both the Jin and Southern Song Dynasties followed the poetics of the Tang Dynasty, so did the scholars of the Yuan Dynasty. They were not very much satisfied with the late Tang poems either. We know that Yan Yu was not satisfied with the "Four Lings" for their imitation of the late Tang poems, and adopted a critical attitude toward them, while Yuan Haowen in his *Quatrains on Poetry* showed dissatisfaction with Lu Tong, Li Shangyin, and Li He. Therefore, the scholars in the early Yuan Dynasty just carried forward this general practice of the late period of the Jin and Southern Song Dynasties to study the poems of the prime Tang Dynasty instead of the poems of the late Tang Dynasty. By the middle Yuan Dynasty, the poetic circles also demanded, in line with the growth of the Empire, the grand and refined poetic style, and the poets all advocated the peaceful and refined language in the prime Tang Dynasty. Yang Zai, Fan Peng and Jie Xisi were the representatives of the poetic circles at that time, and they, too, basically recommended the Tang poetry. Jie Xisi once said: "A learner of poems should follow the Tang poets." He regarded Li Bai, Wang Wei, Wei Yingwu, Liu Zongyuan, and Chu Guangxi as the orthodox poets of the Tang poetry, and Du Fu as the synthesizer. Such a classification was quite influential for the later judgment of the historical status of each poet. For instance, *The Collected Comments on the Tang Poetry* compiled by Gao Bing of the Ming Dynasty had Li Bai classified as "one of the orthodox poets", and Du Fu as "a great master". In view of the development of poetry, Du Fu initiated the poetic pattern for the Song poetry, and naturally his poems were not so pure as the poems of the Tang style. Fan Peng also named Li Bai, Du Fu, Han Yu, Wei Yingwu, Wang Wei, Meng Jiao, and Li Shangyin as the representatives of the six different styles of poetics, and these were basically the great poets in the prime and middle Tang Dynasty. Besides, we have introduced Yang Shihong's *The Voice of the Tang Dynasty*, which also took the prime Tang poetry as the main part. All these manifested that the Yuan poetic circles appreciated the poetic tendency of the prime Tang Dynasty.

The poetic tendency of the Ming Dynasty was, first of all, to inherit from the people at the end of the Song Dynasty and the Yuan Dynasty. Gao Bing's *Collected Comments on the Tang Poetry* as we have introduced previously divided the whole Tang poetry into the early, prime, middle and late stages with the prime Tang Dynasty as the center. On the one hand, it was the inheritance of the view of Yan Yu's *Canglang Poetry Talks* which highly recommended the prime Tang poetry; on the other hand, it was a direct inheritance and development of *The Voice of the Tang Dynasty* compiled by Yang Shihong of the Yuan Dynasty. Gao Bing stated explicitly in the general introduction that only Yang Shihong knew the mystery of the Tang poets. Lin Hong, also a representative of Fujian poets like Gao Bing, clearly held to following the prime Tang poems.

The poems of the Han and Wei Dynasties are vigorous and

> powerful, but not quintessential enough. The poems of the Jin Dynasty favored metaphysics, the poems of the Song Dynasty favored smoothness and clarity, and the poems of the Qi, Liang and the later Dynasties focused on pomposity rather than real effect; only the poets in the Tang Dynasty are the synthesizers. However, in the Zhenguan Period, poems were still modeled after the old patterns of the previous dynasties; in the Shenlong Period, poems began to change their usual tunes; and in the Kaiyuan and Tianbao Periods, prosody was highly developed. Learners should follow the poems of that period. (*Biographies of Literary Scholars*, *History of the Ming Dynasty*)

He obviously regarded the Tang poetry as the acme of perfection for all poems, and in the different stages of the Tang poetry, the poems of the prime Tang Dynasty the best. It should be noted that Lin Hong strongly believed the Tang poetry was "mature in prosody", that is, mature in poetic forms. We remember that when Yin Fan commented on the maturity of the poems of the Kaiyuan Period, he said: "Prosody and vigor became mature." (Preface to *Collection of the Prominent Poets of Rivers and Mountains*) Now they gave up the "vigor". This was the starting point for the poets of the Ming Dynasty to lay stress on the specific skills and the formal characteristics of poetry, and later Li Dongyang's "theory of poetic pattern" meant the same thing.

Lin Hong only studied the poems of the Tang poets, and can be regarded as an active practicer of his poetics. However, it seems that he learned enough but failed to create a new pattern of his own. Li Dongyang commented: "He did his utmost to imitate not only the diction and syntax, but the titles as well. When we open his collection, at the first sight, it looks like an old collection of poems; after a perusal of his poems, we cannot point out one of uniqueness and originality." (*Lutang Poetry Talks*) This was a common disease of indigestion of the ancient knowledge. We can find that at the beginning of the Ming Dynasty, these striking characteristics had appeared in the comments on poetry by the Ming scholars which emphasized the prime Tang Dynasty, the forms, and the imitation of the poems of the ancients.

The subsequent popular style of the Ming poetry was the Cabinet style. Yang Shiqi, Yang Rong and Yang Pu, known as "Three Yangs", headed the literary circle for several decades. They catered to the prosperous times of the early Ming Dynasty, and often wrote eulogistic poems mainly in peaceful and refined patterns. They also valued the poems of the Tang poets. However, they saw only the Tang poems "eulogizing for the prosperity of the country with harmonious, peaceful, simple and straightforward minds". ("Preface to *The Collected Poems of Yuxue Studio*") Obviously, these poems saw the world through the colored spectacles of "serving the present monarch with ancient knowledge".

It was Li Dongyang who inherited the Cabinet style and began to make some changes of it. He agreed completely with the tendency since Yan Yu to respect the prime Tang poems, and once said: "Yan Canglang's comments transcended secularity. He had his own attainments, and his repeated metaphorical explanations have no discreet remarks." (*Lutang Poetry Talks*) But Yan Yu stressed on the metaphysical aspects, such as "subtle enlightenment" and "interest", while Li Dongyang differentiated the poems from the aspects of poetic prosody and tones, and demanded an understanding of cadence in tones and harmonious tonal patterns in the use of words. For instance, he said: "The poets of the prime Tang Dynasty were expert at light-toned words ... melodiousness derives all from it." Such an exposition of the distinctive quality of the Tang poetry in terms of tones, words and sentences was naturally easy to learn, and therefore had a great influence. Thus he provided the feasible methods for the contemporary demand of learning the poems of the Tang Dynasty, and promoted the movement. Wang Shizhen once said, "Li Dongyang's relation with He Jingming and Li Mengyang, who advocated the poems of the prime Tang Dynasty, was just like the relation between Chen Sheng, who first rebelled against the Qin Dynasty, and Liu Bang (Emperor Gaozu of the Han Dynasty), who overthrew the Qin Dynasty and established the Han Dynasty." (*Random Remarks from the Literary Circle*) Simply put, Li Dongyang made the contribution of enlightenment.

In the middle Ming Dynasty, there emerged two groups of seven scholars in the literary circles. The literary trend of restoration of the ancient patterns was prevailing for a time among contemporary scholars, and a conclusion by the later scholars was, "For prose, the writings of the Qin and Han Dynasties are definite models, and for poetry, the compositions of the prime Tang Dynasty are definite models." (*Biographies of the Scholars of Literature* in *The History of the Ming Dynasty*) In regard to the scope of poetry, to be more exact, "All the poems after the middle Tang Dynasty are discarded." For example, Li Mengyang, one of the former seven scholars, shared his own experience of learning from the early modern regulated poems of the Tang Dynasty and the song-stories of Li Bai and Du Fu in his Preface to *The Collected Poems*; then he traced back to the poems of the Six Dynasties, the Wei and Jin Dynasties, the *Songs of the South* and rhapsodies, and the *Book of Poetry*, which indicated his source-tracing concept in learning the ancient poems and his discard of the poems after the prime Tang Dynasty. Wang Shizhen, the leader of the latter seven scholars, also said: "The slender melodies of the Qi and Liang Dynasties, and the changed styles of Li Bai and Du Fu are certainly models for study, while after the Zhenyuan Period of the Tang Dynasty, the collected poems can only be used to cover the pots of pickles." (*Random Remarks from the Literary Circles*) They both did the same in cutting off the evolution of the poetry after the middle Tang Dynasty, and regarded Li Bai and Du Fu of the prime Tang Dynasty, the poetic patterns of the Qi and Liang Dynasties, and even the poets of the Wei and Jin Dynasties as the objects of their learning. This was in fact the view first expressed by Yan Yu. He affirmed "following the poems of the prime Tang Dynasty", but did not exclude the Wei, Jin and Six Dynasties. He believed: "A learner should take the poets of the Han, Wei, Jin and the prime Tang as masters, and should not learn from the poems after the Kaiyuan and Tianbao Periods." This is right the attitude of cutting off the evolution after that time. As for the study of the poems before the prime Tang Dynasty, He Jingming said even more clearly:

> Jingming learned song-stories and early modern regulated poems from the two masters (i.e. Li Bai and Du Fu), and also included the poems of the other early and prime Tang poets. As for the classical poems, I surely only studied those of the Han and Wei Dynasties. (Preface to *The Collected Poems of Haisou*)

It turns out that he differentiated the poems of the Han and Wei Dynasties and the prime Tang Dynasty as study objects by the genres. Basically, they held that a learner of classical poems should trace back to the source. The classical poems as a genre began with the poems of the Han and Wei Dynasties, and the early modern regulated poems were perfected in the prime Tang Dynasty. Therefore, there was a distinction between the objects of study of the classical genre and that of the early modern regulated pattern. Later, *The Synoptic Catalogue of The Complete Library of the Four Treasuries* had a most understanding conclusion: "A learner of the classical poems must follow those of the Han and Wei Dynasties, and a learner of the poems of the early modern regulated pattern those of the prime Tang Dynasty. They simulated syntax and imitated diction, and they studied the poems of the ancient people with no digestion." The first sentence refers to the objects of their study, and the second sentence their method of study. "Imitation of diction" and "simulation of syntax" both indicate their efforts in the forms of language use. This is also the usual attitude in the Ming Dynasty: stressing the patterns and tunes in learning the poems of the ancient people. We have introduced above that Li Dongyang differentiated the poems of the Tang Dynasty from the poems of the Song Dynasty through different application of substantial and unsubstantial words. Li Mengyang expounded substantiality and unsubstantiality through the structure of sections and chapters, and combination of emotions and scenes: "Roughly the first part is loose, and the second part must be compact; one half is spacious, and another half must be fine; one solid substance must be matched with one insubstantial part, and the overlapping scenes must have two different meanings." (*The Second Letter in Reply to He Jingming*) Although such analysis was helpful for understanding the art of the Tang poetry, it after all focused only on writing skills.

The imitation in this way surely led to apparent harmony, and caused poems to lose vigor and vitality. Li Panlong, the leader of the latter seven scholars, was a good example of laying stress on tones. "In the imitation of the poems of the Music Bureau pattern, sometimes he only changed some words in the classical poems and then considered them his own creation." (*The Biographies of Literary Scholars* in *The History of the Ming Dynasty*) That was why Qian Qianyi criticized them: "All are tied up with each other in imitating and plagiarizing merely tones, words and sentences." (*Collected Poems of the Different Reigns*) The problem caused debates within the scholars on the return to the classical poetics. Li Mengyang and He Jingming, the chief leaders of the former seven scholars, held the same view of restoring the classical poetic patterns, but as for the concrete ways and methods of restoration and imitation of the classical poetic patterns, there were heated debates between them. Li Mengyang insisted on learning the classical poetic patterns without any change. He took calligraphy as an example and said: "All consider it fine to copy the calligraphy model as faithfully as possible, and why must one create a pattern on his own when he imitates a poem or an essay?" (*The Second Letter in Reply to He Jingming*) He Jingming, having seen the necessity and inevitability of the conversion and development of the poems, classical and modern, advocated a course from imitation to "ending with creation". He asked in reply: "If only likeness of imitation was fine, why should Li Bai, Du Fu and others become master poets after Cao Zhi, Ruan Ji, Lu Ji, etc.?" (*A Letter to Li Kongtong on Poetry*) In consideration of the complete restoration of the classical poetic patterns, the statement of Li Mengyang was naturally strict in logic, but the real restoration to the classical poetic patterns itself was problematic. It was impossible for Li Mengyang to answer the question put forth by He Jingming. Although Li Mengyang dared not say Li Bai and Du Fu should not become master poets, he did adopt the attitude of denying all the Song poets by saying "There is no poetry in the Song Dynasty." The brilliance of the Tang poetry became a necessary background for the poets of later generations in their creation, and the poets of the Song Dynasty tried hard to open up a path of their own under its shadow. Since then, people after the Tang and Song Dynasties regarded the disputes of superiority between the Tang poetry and the Song poetry not only as the contention between two different artistic tendencies, but also a stage of expression of different attitudes toward the historical heritage: The poets who advocated creation often took the Song poetry as a pretext, while the poets who valued the traditional poets frequently sighed for the insurmountability of the Tang poetry. Although Li Mengyang's remark "There is no poetry in the Song Dynasty" shocked the literary circle, it was by no means unreasonable. Li Panlong, one of the latter seven scholars, argued, "The poetry after the Tianbao Period of the Tang Dynasty are worthless for reading." (*The Biographies of Literary Scholars* in *The History of the Ming Dynasty*) His *Collected Ancient and Modern Poems after Deletion* recorded the Tang poems, which was immediately followed by the Ming poems. He really wiped the Song poems out of the history of poetry and prohibited their appearance on the stage. Such an extreme judgement was hardly convincing among people. Wang Shizhen, one of the latter seven scholars and once under Li Panlong's influence, at first also maintained: "A learner must follow the poems of the prime Tang Dynasty, and not read the poem collections after the Dali Period." (*The Biographies of Literary Scholars* in *The History of the Ming Dynasty*) In his late years, he admitted that many things could be learned from the poems of the Song and Yuan Dynasties.

The trend of thought in the Ming Dynasty to respect and promote the Tang poetry gradually declined owing to the gradual change of the literary views in restoring classical literature, especially the challenge of the new literary trend of thought in the late Ming Dynasty. This new literary trend of thought came from the literary concept of the Gong'an School with Yuan Hongdao as the leader, which advocated the free expression of mind. Yuan Hongdao advocated, "Voice the mind only, regardless of the rules and patterns," and particularly objected to the literary views of the restoration of the classical literature. He opposed directly the slogan "There is no poetry in the Song Dynasty", and insisted partially that "There is no poetry in the Tang Dynasty." (*A Letter to Zhang Youyu*) Of course, that was an ironic remark. In fact he had seen the times were changing, and each generation had its own literature. He listed the examples: The poetic rules changed and developed owing to the malpractice and drawbacks of the previous times. For instance, the poetry in the Six Dynasties was transformed in the early Tang Dynasty to smoothness and gracefulness, but the poems of the early Tang Dynasty were delicate and exquisite; therefore, the poems of the prime Tang Dynasty were magnificent; the poems of the middle Tang Dynasty tended to be realistic, so they were vulgar; and the poems in the late Tang Dynasty again turned peculiar, which led to narrowness, so the poems of the Song poets tended to be all-inclusive, like the rolling rivers. (Preface to *Collected Poems of Xuetao Pavilion*) Such an ever-changing historical concept was widely accepted among the people after the periods of the former and latter seven scholars. For example, Tu Long said: "Poetry changed and developed with the world." Hu Yingling also said: "The poetic patterns changed with the times." However, both Tu Long and Hu Yingling still continued the line of thought of the seven scholars to respect and promote the poems of the Tang Dynasty and to depreciate the poems of the Song Dynasty, but Yuan Hongdao stressed the new changes of poetry. He particularly objected to the imitation of words and sentences in the Classical Literary Restoration School and said:

> Poem-writing must be modelled after the poems of the prime Tang Dynasty; they copy and imitate, following closely just as shadow and echo. Whenever a sentence is found to be not alike, it was at once criticized as heresy ... Poem-writing must be modelled after the poems of the prime Tang Dynasty, but had poets of the prime Tang Dynasty imitated the poems of the Han and Wei Dynasty word by word? ... If the prime Tang poets followed closely the poems of the Han and Wei Dynasties, could there have been the prime Tang poetry today? (*Discourse on Xiaoxiu Poems*)

This was a criticism of the Classical Literary Restoration School, and also a correct understanding of the prime Tang poetry. The poetic views of

Yuan Hongdao inspired the general mood of the Song poetry, but a long accumulated habit was difficult to change, and the Tang poetry was still worshipped as the orthodox by the Ming poets. For instance, Zhong Xing and Tan Yuanchun, the heads of the Jingling School, rose from rectifying the superficiality and simplicity of the Gong'an School, and valued the Tang poetry as well. We have recommended one of their books *The Convergence of Poems*, in which the part of the Tang poetry still emphasized the poems of Wang Wei, Meng Haoran, and even Jia Dao of the late Tang period in the style of quietude, seclusion and peculiarity. Chen Zilong, known as the last great master poet of the Ming Dynasty, based his style on the restoration poetics of the seven scholars, though he transformed his poetic pattern after the demise of the Ming Dynasty, as he sighed for the time in the tones of sadness, desolation and vehemence. Wu Weiye praised his poems for "loftiness, elegance and majesty" (*Meicun Poetry Talks*), which was the very pattern of the seven scholars.

The great upheaval of political situations at the turn of the Ming and Qing Dynasties caused the changes in the poetic styles. Although the great masters like Huang Zongxi, Qian Qianyi and others conducted themselves in the world differently, they all paid attention to the Song poetry; particularly they respected Xie Ao, Wang Yuanliang, etc., the adherent poets of the Ming Dynasty. On the one hand, they shared the same sadness in the different dynasties, and on the other hand, they had the intention to widen up the narrow ways of imitating only the poetic pattern of the prime Tang Dynasty. Those poets at the turn of the Ming and Qing Dynasties did not exclude completely the poems of the Tang Dynasty, and considered it absurd to be restricted within the prime Tang Dynasty like the former and latter seven scholars of the Ming Dynasty. Huang Zongxi said:

> In the thousands of years, why must they demand the restriction to the Tang Dynasty? And in the hundreds of years of the Tang Dynasty, why must they demand the restriction to the prime Tang period? The prime Tang poems were certainly excellent, but they varied in different styles of serenity, unusualness, vigorousness, and

simplicity — which should people follow?

The comment was a very clear example. In his early years, Qian Qianyi had a great interest in the poems of the former and latter seven scholars. He claimed to have a "thorough command" of the works of Li Mengyang and Wang Shizhen, and worshipped Wang Shizhen's *Random Comments from Literary Circle* as infallible precepts. Later he became enlightened and burned up his works written before 37 or 38 years of age, but it is not deniable that he still upheld his stand of worshipping the Tang poetry; to be exact, Qian Qianyi was a great master of both the Tang and Song poetry, and ushered in a period in which the people of the Qing Dynasty valued the Song poetry.

The conversion of Qian Qianyi's poetic views was greatly influenced by Cheng Jiasui. According to Qian Qianyi, Cheng Jiasui commented on the poems from the early and prime Tang to the poets of the middle Tang like Qian Qi, Liu Changqing, Yuan Zhen, Bai Juyi, etc., and in his late years he studied the poets of the Song, Jin and Yuan Dynasties such as Lu You, Yuan Haowen, etc. "The scope of my study was basically the same as his." (*A Letter in Reply to Zunwang*) Obviously, he extended his study gradually from the Tang poets to the Song and Yuan poets. Hence, he broke away from the limitation of the former and latter seven scholars, turned to attack their poetics, and finally discarded them altogether. Qian Qianyi favored Li Dongyang of the Ming Dynasty, because Li's study covered Du Fu and Bai Juyi of the Tang Dynasty, Su Shi of the Song Dynasty, and Yu Ji of the Yuan Dynasty. This was also the way Qian Qianyi took later. Feng Ban, a town fellow of Qian Qianyi, said: "He often talked about the poems of the Song and Yuan Dynasties to rectify the prejudices of Wang Shizhen and Li Mengyang." (*Dunyin Miscellanies*) This shows the significance of Qian Qianyi's new views on poetry and his influence upon others.

However, such a practice was not extended in full, for the Tang poetry still held a dominant position at that time. In the Wuzhong area assembled the poets of the three rival poetic schools: the Yushan School headed by Qian Qianyi, the Yunjian School headed by Chen Zilong, and the

Loudong School headed by Wu Weiye. The latter two took the Tang poetry as the model, while the Yushan School diverted their attention to the Tang poetry as well when it was passed down to the brothers Feng Ban and Feng Shu. Qian Qianyi was endowed with the great ability to study the poems of the Tang and Song Dynasties, while many poets who followed him could only study the Song poets and thought it fresh and unusual. But the Feng brothers considered it entirely wrong. They believed it was natural to follow the prime Tang poems made in the Kaiyuan and Tianbao Periods: "Those with aspirations should do so, the same way as the Confucians are willing to study Duke Zhou and Kong Zi." But in the practical criticisms, they seemed to favor the poems of the late Tang Dynasty. The Feng brothers commented on *The Anthology of Literary Talents* in collaboration. Feng Shu again revised carefully *New Odes to the Jade Terrace*, which was compiled in the Liang Dynasty of the Southern Dynasties, recommended Wen Tingyun and Li Shangyin as the models of poem-composition, and promoted the Xikun style created by Yang Yi and others in imitation of the poems of Li Shangyin at the beginning of the Song Dynasty. All these objects for study were centered around Wen Tingyun and Li Shangyin of the late Tang Dynasty; from the early poems of the Qi and Liang Dynasties to the late poems of the Xikun style, they constituted a poetic tradition of grace and gorgeousness, and could be regarded as the extension of the late Tang poetic pattern at the beginning of the Qing Dynasty. This is a change to Qian Qianyi's theory. Qian Qianyi followed Li Shangyin, but was not fond of the poems of the Qi and Liang Dynasties. He held a different attitude from the Feng brothers who recommended the Xikun style as an orthodox poetic tradition. The literary tendency of the Feng brothers was influential in the early Qing Dynasty; He Chang, Wu Qiao, etc. were their followers. He Chang in his *Zaijiuyuan Poetry Talks* "commented only briefly on the poems of the early and prime Tang Dynasty, but elaborated in detail on the poems of the middle and late Tang Dynasty", and he also commented in detail on the gains and losses of the Song poetry. In a word, he still held a depreciative attitude toward the Song poetry, and in the end, he valued the Tang poetry. That is the same case as the Feng brothers praising the Song poets such as Su Shi: When making a general comparison between the Tang poetry and the Song and Yuan poetry, they would not hesitate to compare them to the beauty "Xishi" and the ugly "old rustic woman". One point worth noting is that He Chang in his comments on the Song poetry always chose the poems in the similar or the same styles as the Tang poetry; as to the distinctive style of the Song poetry of "poem-writing in the essayistic approach" as well as comments, etc., he never hesitated to deny them. This quite resembled the selections of the Ming poets such as *Collected Poems in the Literary Garden of the Song Dynasty* by Li Gun and *Shicang Selected Poems of the Past Ages* by Cao Xuequan in worshipping the Tang poems in the Ming Dynasty. An advocator of the Song poetry in the Qing Dynasty, Wu Zhizhen criticized their partiality in his Preface to *The Selected Poems of the Song Dynasty*: "They only selected the poems that were distant from the Song style but close to the Tang style ... If the selection of the Song poems was done in this way, it would not in the end be close to the Tang style, but the poems of the Song poets had already not existed." Therefore, they were fundamentally worshippers of the Tang poems. Wu Qiao favored the poems of Feng Ban and He Chang, so in his *Weilu Poetry Talks*, he frequently quoted the comments from *Dunyin Miscellanies* and *Zaijiuyuan Poetry Talks*. His favorite poet was Li Shangyin, but he did not like the poems of the Xikun style as Feng Ban did. The line of poetic criticism received a response from Zhao Zhixin, who was Wang Shizhen's nephew-in-law but objected to Wang's ideas vehemently. Zhao Zhixin worshipped the late Tang poetry. He read Feng Ban's books and said: "I like his works very much. After I learned them, I would no longer read books written by anyone else." He once looked everywhere for Wu Qiao's *Weilu Poetry Talks* and thought "his comments on poetry are quite appropriate."

Wu Weiye was a great poet at the turn of the Ming and Qing Dynasties. Though he did not write poetic criticisms, his inclination was quite clear. Like Chen Zilong, he accepted the thoughts of the literary restoration trend of the Ming Dynasty and worshipped the Tang poetry. He once said that Wang Shizhen "devoted himself to the study of the poems of the prime

Tang Dynasty", and "could be considered a master of poetics". As for the orthodoxy of poetry, "Is there any other one except for the poems of the Kaiyuan and Dali Period?" In the aspect of poetic creation, Wu Weiye also followed the tradition of the Tang poetry. *The Synoptic Catalogue of The Complete Library of the Four Treasuries* praised his poems, "In prosody, he followed the four masters (the four masters of the early Tang Dynasty), but his charm was profound; in narration, his poems were similar to those of Xiangshan (Bai Juyi), but his style is brilliant." His rich and beautiful language, and vague and remote emotions displayed definitely the charms of the Tang poems.

On the whole, the general trend in the early Qing Dynasty still emphasized the poetics of the Tang Dynasty, though the poets across the dynasty such as Huang Zongxi and Qian Qianyi widened their poetic vision and studied the poems of the Song and Yuan Dynasties. Such a situation did not change at all until the early reign of Emperor Kangxi when the poems of the Song poetry prevailed for a time, but the influence of the Tang voice was still strong. After a period of conflict and reconciliation between the advocators of the Tang poetry and the advocators of the Song poetry, the former still occupied the dominant position. We may understand this if we see the head poets in the poetic circle such as Wang Shizhen and Shen Deqian were all worshippers of the poems of the Tang Dynasty from the reigns of Emperor Kangxi to Emperor Qianlong. Or we may understand the situation if we see that among "the six master poets of the new dynasty", namely Shi Runzhang, Song Wan, Zhu Yizun, Wang Shizhen, Zhao Zhixin and Zha Shenxing, the first five were all advocators of the Tang poetry.

Shi Runzhang and Song Wan enjoyed equal popularity, and they were known as "Shi of the south and Song of the north" at the time. Shi Runzhang was born in a family of Principlist philosophers, and his poetics were heavily ingrained in Confucian thought. He laid stress on traditional poetic analogy and association, advocated implication, and held that the knowledge should not be piled up in poems "just as the eye would not allow a grain of gold dust". Such a view means that he naturally held a critical attitude toward the Song poetry. He once pointed out that the Song scholars annotated Du Fu's poems with the guiding concept "Every word has its source", drew far-fetched analogies, made strained interpretations, and "reduced" all the merits of the poems of Du Fu. In his mind, the excellent poets were Tao Yuanming, Wang Wei, Li Bai, Wei Yingwu, etc., whose poems were natural and easy to understood, while the poems of Han Yu, Meng Jiao, Li He and Jia Dao in the Han and Meng group belonged to "a different tone," and even Du Fu was also considered the "modulated tone" of the Tang poetry because of his "depression and fantasy" and "soul-stirring ambience." We know both Du Fu and Han Yu were the poets who initiated the new styles for the poems of the Song Dynasty. In the following we shall mention Ye Xie who embraced the study of the poems of the Tang and Song Dynasties. He paid particular attention to the study of Han Yu, and held that "Han Yu was the pioneer of the new prospect for the Song poets like Su Shuqin, Mei Yaochen, Ouyang Xiu, Wang Anshi and Huang Tingjian." Tian Wen, a representative of the advocators of the Song poetry, regarded Han Yu as an important link between Du Fu and the Song poetry. "No one has imitated Shaoling (Du Fu) as well as Changli (Han Yu)", "Master Ouyang Xiu rose in the Song Dynasty, inherited directly the poetics of Du Fu and Han Yu, and continued their development."

Song Wan in his early years studied the literary restoration thought of the Ming Dynasty, and held an affirmative attitude toward the former and latter seven scholars. He compared the former seven scholars to Chen Zi'ang, Shen Quanqi, and Song Zhiwen, and the latter seven scholars to Gao Shi, Cen Shen, Wang Wei and Meng Haoran. He also highly recommended Chen Zilong, etc. of the Yunjian School, who identified themselves with the literary concepts of the two groups of seven scholars. Therefore, in his poetic criticism, he worshipped the Tang poetry and strictly distinguished the early, prime, middle and late stages of the Tang Dynasty, for the stress on the poems of the early and prime Tang Dynasty was the continuation of the standard concept of the literary restoration in the Ming Dynasty. It was not until his late years that he changed his mind:

On one hand, "I became fond in sadness of reading the late Tang poems", and on the other hand, "I was astonished to find wonderful sentences in the poems of Lu Fangweng (Lu You)." His vision was greatly widened, and this also indicated the gradual growth of the poems of the Song Dynasty.

Ye Xie was the tutor of Shen Deqian. His *Inquiry into Poetry* was an excellent theoretical book on poetics, and was not merely well-known for the witty comments. He held an ever-changing concept in regard to the historical development of poetry, and expounded the changes of poetry from the perspective of constant replacement; therefore, he did not restrict his comments within the poems of one dynasty and one style. In his mind, it was not worth arguing for superiority between the Tang poetry and the Song poetry. What he emphasized was the master poets at the critical moments in the transformation of the history of poetry, and this included three master poets Du Fu, Han Yu and Su Shi. Du Fu embraced both the antique simplicity of the Han and Wei poetry, and the beauty and richness of the Six Dynasties, but "there is not one word or sentence from the poems of the previous poets"; Han Yu represented the critical transformation of poetry and prose, ancient and present, in the middle Tang Dynasty for he "rose particularly as the Father" — this "Father" means the initiator of the Song poetry; as for Su Shi, "his poetic realm was unprecedented in all the times, ancient and present", for he could write essays with playing, laughing, anger and weeping as materials and describe everything in the world under his brush, so he was really "a great change after Han Yu". Ye Xie held that change was a common phenomenon like the change of four seasons. There is no need at all to discuss the superiority in terms of change; can spring, summer, autumn and winter be differentiated as superior or inferior? It is naturally unreasonable to depreciate the poems of the Song Dynasty. He regarded the poetic development from the remote ancient times to the Song Dynasty as a continuum: *The Book of Poetry* was the root of a tree, the poems of the Han Dynasty were the sprouts, the poems of the Jian'an Period were the twigs, the poems of the Six Dynasties were branches and leaves, the poems of the Tang Dynasty were the exuberant foliage, and the poems of the Song

Dynasty were just like flowers at the top of the tree. Obviously, he affirmed definitely the achievements of the poems of the Song Dynasty, and had a far-reaching insight of breaking free from the restriction of the times.

As a matter of fact, the advocators of the poems of the Song Dynasty were usually sensible or embraced the study of both the Tang poetry and the Song poetry. Qian Qianyi, as we have mentioned previously, did not lay stress merely on the poems of the Song and Yuan Dynasties and ignored the poems of the Tang Dynasty. Huang Zongxi also regarded the Song poetry as the development and transformation of the Tang poetry: "It is only the people of the Song Dynasty who learned the Tang poetry best." The above-mentioned comments of Ye Xie and Tian Wen about Du Fu and Han Yu opening up a new route for the development of the Song poetry meant the same idea. At that time, many scholars who advocated the Song poetry were related to Huang Zongxi. For instance, Lü Liuliang and Wu Zhizhen were followers of Huang Zongxi. Wu Zhizhen compiled *The Selected Poems of the Song Dynasty*, which helped the spread of the Song poems. He said in the preface: "The Song poetry changed from the Tang poetry ... and preserved only its spirit."

The trend of advocating the poems of the Song Dynasty prevailed in the first years of the reign of Emperor Kangxi in two different tendencies: One was to respect Su Shi as the representative with the poetic features of free demonstration of talent and unrestrained grace, and the other was to worship Huang Tingjian as the representative with the poetic features of refinement in diction and syntax. Qian Qianyi of the early Qing Dynasty once devoted himself to the study of the early Tang poetic pattern for a time. He began to pay attention to the poets of the Song and Yuan Dynasties such as Su Shi, Lu You and Yuan Haowen, but rejected Huang Tingjian considerably. He said in *A Brief Guide to Annotations on the Poems of Du Fu*: "Since the Song Dynasty, a learner of the poems of Du Fu at the same time was quite familiar with the poems of Huang Luzhi (Huang Tingjian) ... They just thought that the unrestrained vigorous poems, unusual sentences and peculiar expressions were the legacy of the poems of Du Fu, but these were actually his 'side door and small lane'." This group of poets also frequently learned from Lu You, Fan Chengda, Yang Wanli, etc. Shen Deqian said: "The poetics of Qian Qianyi have been spread all over the country, and lasted so long that every household knows Wuguan (Lu You) and Zhineng (Fan Chengda)." One of the six masters in the early Qing Dynasty, Zha Shenxing, also belongs to this group. He took Huang Zongxi as his tutor, but showed great interest in Su Shi. He devoted his whole life to supplementing, correcting and annotating the poems of Su Shi, and wrote *The Supplements to and Annotations on the Poems of Su Shi* in fifty volumes. Therefore, he learned the merits of the poems of Su Shi and studied the style of the poems of Lu You, before becoming a top poet then. Song Luo at an early time bought an incomplete copy of the poems of Su Shi annotated by Shi Yuanzhi in Suzhou. He supplemented and collated the book, and had it printed for circulation. This led to *The Supplements and Annotations* by Zha Shenxing, who was also a worshipper of Su Shi. According to Wang Shizhen, Zha Shenxing once drew the portrait of Su Shi and stood by his side, obviously holding him in deep respect. Another line of worshipping Huang Tingjian began with Huang Zongxi. One sentence of his poem read: "The poetic ancestor of my family is Huang Luzhi." He also called the Jiangxi Poetic School "the assembly of the Song poets". Later, his disciple Wu Zhizhen called Huang Tingjian "the ancestor of the Song poetry family" in *Collected Poems of the Song Dynasty*. This poetic pattern of following Huang Tingjian's style of slenderness, sturdiness and vigor had a direct influence on the movement of the Song poetry at the end of the Qing Dynasty.

The supporters of the Tang poetry often complained about the prevailing practice in favor of the Song poetry for a time. Zhu Yizun said in his Preface to *The Collected Poems Joint-carved by Envoys Ye and Li*: "When critics comment on poems today, they are often bored with the poems of the Tang Dynasty and turn to talk about the poetic schools of the Song Dynasty. The learned scholars follow Su Shi and Huang Tingjian, and the common people just follow Yang Tingxiu (Yang Wanli). In their poems, howls and clamors were regarded as unusual expressions, while slangs and colloquialisms were held as the orthodox." He was especially dissatisfied with the poems of Lu You and Yang Wanli of the Southern Song Dynasty. He said: "The poems of Huang Tingjian were choppy, the poems of Lu You were easy and familiar, and the poems of Yang Wanli after the change became vulgar and slangy; all turn to imitate the poems of Yang Wanli and not Huang Tingjian." (Postscript to *The Collection of Jiannan*) Zhu Yizun is a scholar and a poet. Weng Fanggang praised him, "His temperament matches his knowledge." Therefore, his poems demonstrated his erudition, splendor of diction, use of rare allusions and difficult rhymes. Zha Shenxing of the Song Poetry School praised him of "weighing his words and sentences with care", and "feeling ashamed to follow the vulgar trend of the easy and simple poems in the pattern of the Song Dynasty." (Preface to *The Book-Sunning Pavilion Collection*) Therefore, it is understandable that he was dissatisfied with the colloquial and easy poems of Lu You and Yang Wanli. Then it seems that Zhu Yizun should have some favorable feeling toward Huang Tingjian who wrote poems with knowledge, but it was not completely so. He once criticized Yan Yu who rejected the Jiangxi School most vehemently:

> The poets today were empty-headed and shallow. All started with the hint in Yan Yiqing (Yan Yu)'s sentence "Poem writing should draw materials other than knowledge." Can a learner write poems without knowledge?

In fact, the reason for such a seemingly paradoxical phenomenon was that Zhu Yizun followed firmly the traditional Confucian poetics and demanded refinement and implication in poem-writing. The poems of the Song Dynasty were not as natural and implicit as the poems of the Tang Dynasty, and they were either like fresh cusps of leaves, or easy and vulgar, so naturally Zhu Yizun could not feel satisfied with them. However, theory was one thing, and creation another; Zhu Yizun in poem writing stressed knowledge and appropriate use of allusions, and his poems always read like the works of the Song poets. Song Luo of the Song Poetry School said of him: "In his poetic comments, he was quite dissatisfied with Fuweng

(Huang Tingjian), but the jerkiness and sturdiness of his poems are right the poetic characters of Fuweng." Hong Liangji in favor of "the theory of temperament" also said that his poems in late years "followed the poems of the Northern Song poets".

Wang Shizhen was the head of the contemporary poetic circle, and his theory of "spiritual charm" became fashionable for a time. In his narration, he said that the poetic comments of the three critics were most enlightening: Zhong Rong's *Grades of Poetry*, Yan Yu's *Canglang Poetry Talks*, and Xu Zhenqing's *Records of the Talks on Poetry*. There is no need to talk about the first book. The latter two books both favored the poems of the Tang Dynasty, mainly the prime Tang poems. Thus we can see where Wang Shizhen showed his interest in. However, in his idea, the prime Tang poems were not the poems that the former and latter seven scholars in the Ming Dynasty supported in the patterns of loftiness, elegance and magnificence, but were mainly the poems of Wang Wei and Meng Haoran in the patterns of detachedness, simplicity, implication and naturalness. Wu Qiao in supporting the late Tang poems once satirized Wang Shizhen as a "delicate Li Panlong", meaning he favored a different line of the Tang poems. Zhao Zhixin exposed his intention and said: "He particularly disliked Shaoling (Du Fu). Although he dared not attack Du Fu openly, he often quoted the remarks of 'the Villager' Yang Danian as his comments." *Collection of Poetic Samadhi of the Tang Poets* compiled by Wang Shizhen in his late years, as we have mentioned previously, is undeniable evidence that he favored the poems of Wang Wei and Meng Haoran.

Wang Shizhen's course of poetic study, according to his own introduction, underwent two changes. He first cherished the Tang voice, later liked the freshness of the Song poetry, and finally went back to the Tang poetry for purity, remoteness and plainness. From that we may see the powerful influence of the Song poetry in the reign of Emperor Kangxi and its final return to obscurity.

The reigns of Emperors Qianlong and Jiaqing marked a conclusive period of the poetics of the Qing Dynasty. Three poetic schools of the pattern, the temperament and the texture took shape with Shen

Deqian, Yuan Mei and Weng Fanggang respectively as representatives. As to the advocacy of the poems of the Tang or Song Dynasties, they all demonstrated the trend from the Tang poetry to the Song poetry.

Shen Deqian was the disciple of Ye Xie, who once posted his poems to Wang Shizhen, and Wang set a high value on his poems. Shen Deqian was always deeply grateful to Wang Shizhen, and when he headed the poetic circle, he upheld the banner of advocating the poems of the prime Tang Dynasty. Zhu Tingzhen in his *Xiaoyuan Poetry Talks* commented on Shen Deqian, "His school followed Yuyang (Wang Shizhen)," which should not be considered wrong. The reason for Shen Deqian's favoring the poems of the Tang Dynasty was his insistence in the traditional poetics that poetry should be kind, sincere and implicit. "The poems of the Tang Dynasty are natural and implicit, while the poems of the Song Dynasty, explicit." (*A Guide to Differentiation of the Poems of the Qing Dynasty*) In that logic, naturally the poems of the Tang Dynasty were better than the poems of the Song Dynasty. However, there were obvious differences between Shen Deqian and Wang Shizhen: Wang Shizhen valued the poems of Wang Wei and Meng Haoran, while Shen Deqian appreciated the poems of Li Bai and Du Fu who boasted mighty strength and vastness like "huge whales in the blue seas". That is why he affirmed the poems of Li Mengyang and He Jingming of the Ming Dynasty to a great extent. Zhu Tingzhen was also somewhat insightful to say that he adopted the poetic comments from time to time of the seven scholars of the Ming Dynasty and even Chen Zilong.

Contrary to Shen Deqian, Yuan Mei advocated the theory of "temperament". He regarded poetry as a tool to give expression to one's personality and emotions, and thought it should not be judged for superiority in the light of the times, ancient or modern. He criticized the advocators of the poems of the prime Tang Dynasty for knowing only imitation, like a puppet performance, while "the advocators of the Song poetry purposefully tread the deserted trail, and it is like a beggar moving his home." Both routes were undesirable. He bitterly depreciated the former and latter seven scholars, also in opposition to Shen Deqian's comments. In a word, he aimed to break down the limitation of worshipping the poems of the Tang Dynasty, and to embrace the poems of both the Tang and Song Dynasties. He said: "The best learners of the poems of the Tang Dynasty are the people of the Song and Yuan Dynasties, and the worst learners are the the seven scholars of the Ming Dynasty." The reason is that the poets of the Ming Dynasty focused their attention only on studying poetic forms, but the poets of the Song Dynasty learned the poems of the Tang Dynasty and transformed them in the same way as the learners of the Tang Dynasty learned the poems of the Han and Wei Dynasties and made different changes of them. Similar to Yuan Mei, Zhao Yi who upheld the theory of talent and temperament did not emphasize the poems of any one dynasty but had a wide vision. He listed in his *Oubei Poetry Talks* ten poets of Li Bai, Du Fu, Han Yu, Bai Juyi, Su Shi, Lu You, Yuan Haowen, Gao Qi, Wu Weiye and Zha Shenxing, which included not only the poets of the Song and Yuan Dynasties, but the poets of the Ming and Qing Dynasties.

Like Yuan Mei, Weng Fanggang intended to embrace both the poems of the Tang and Song Dynasties, but his starting point was contrary to that of Yuan Mei. In emphasizing temperament, Yuan Mei traced back to Yang Wanli, inherited Yuan Hongdao, and absorbed directly the spirit of free expression of the people of the Song Dynasty, while Weng Fanggang, in light of stressing the substantiality of the style of study in the Qing Dynasty, sought and chose the poems compatible with the pattern of the Song Dynasty to comment on. He believed, "The poems of the Song Dynasty became increasingly meticulous," "The subtle realm of the Tang poems is in emptiness, while the subtle realm of the Song poems is in substantiality." Therefore, the poems of the Song Dynasty suited his intention for he wanted to rectify the unconventional freedom of Wang Shizhen's theory of "spiritual charm" with "meticulosity". That is the reason why he advocated it with great effort. Yao Nai① as a fellow scholar of Weng Fanggang also embraced both the poems of the Tang and Song

① Yao Nai (1731 – 1815), courtesy name Jichuan or Menggu and style name Master Xibao, a well-known scholar and essayist of the Qing Dynasty. He was one of the founders of the Tongcheng School.

Dynasties in his poetic creation, though he was not so outstanding in the theoretic creation. His uncle Yao Fan praised the poems of Huang Tingjian as "splendid sentences with metaphysical ideas", "towering arrogance" and "unusualness". Yao Nai accepted Yao Fan's views, and his students such as Fang Dongshu and Mei Zengliang both worshipped Huang Tingjian in their comments on poetry. So the tendency of advocating the poems of the Song Dynasty rose gradually, and became the main trend unexpectedly in the early modern poetic circles.

Chen Yan said in his Preface to *Collected Early Modern Poems* that Qi Wenrui and Lord Zeng Wenzheng (Zeng Guofan) were the heads of the poetic circles during the reigns of Emperors Daoguang and Xianfeng. We know Qi Wenrui was the son-in-law of Chen Yongguang, the disciple of Yao Nai, and to Yao Nai, Qi Wenrui was his grand student. According to Chen Yan, he learned from the poems of Du Fu, Han Yu, Su Shi and Huang Tingjian. Zeng Guofan had close ties with Mei Zengliang, and was on friendly terms with He Shaoji and Zheng Zhen. They both were the disciples of Chen Enze, who advocated the Song poetry, especially the poems of Huang Tingjian, and Zeng Guofan treasured Huang's poems as well. Shi Shan said in *Wangyunlou Poetry Talks*:

> Prime Minister Zeng Guofan treasured Huang Tingjian's poems, and his poems resembled Huang's too. As a result, the poetic trend changed in the south and north of the Great River, and the value of Huang's poems rose up to an exorbitant price for a copy.

Zeng Guofan in his important political position called on the public to study the Song poetry, which all at once became a fashion.

But the people who worshipped the poems of the Song Dynasty often could not exclude the poems of the Tang Dynasty completely. The poets in the reigns of Emperors Daoguang, Xianfeng and Tongzhi learned the poems of Su Shi and Huang Tingjian, and meanwhile studied the poems of Du Fu and Han Yu of the Tang Dynasty, who initiated the poetic patterns of the Song Dynasty. In the reigns of Emperors Guangxu and Xuantong, the poets advocating the poems of the Song Dynasty as a new generation even suggested a theory of "Three Yuans" as the prosperous periods in the history of poetry, i.e. the Kaiyuan Period as a mark for the prime Tang, the Yuanhe Period for the middle Tang, and the Yuanyou Period as a mark for the beginning of the Song poetry; the poems of the Three Yuans were models for learners. We can see then the Tang poetry was indispensible for any poet.

Let us review the history of poetry since the middle ancient times. In the Song Dynasty, the Tang poetry was an unshakable reality, and the poets under the "anxiety of influence" did their best to blaze a new trail for themselves. In a positive point of view, they opened up a new realm of poetry, and in a negative point of view, it was right the result of the powerful pressure of the Tang poetry. In their evasion and change was disclosed the influence of the Tang poetry. After the Song and Yuan Dynasties, the Tang poetry and the mature Song poetry that developed in a distinctive path became a pair of models in mutual opposition and complementation, and determined the poetic route of the poets in the Ming and Qing Dynasties. As for the poets of the Ming Dynasty that opposed the poems of the Song Dynasty and advocated the poems of the Tang Dynasty, and the poems of the Qing Dynasty that developed in the repeated confrontations and reconciliations, they were all the products of the Tang and Song poetry. It is especially worth noting that people in advocating the poems of the Tang Dynasty were usually prone to cutting off the evolution of poetry after it, thus being narrowly restricted and strongly inclined to the classical literary restoration, while the people in advocating the poems of the Song Dynasty usually would not arbitrarily deny the achievements of the Tang poetry as well as the achievements of the poems of the Han and Wei Dynasties. Even if they devoted themselves to the study of one school or one poet of the Song Dynasty, in the poetic theories they always embraced both the Tang and Song poetry. The example for the former is the argument "There is no poetry in the Song Dynasty" in the concept of the classical literary restoration in the Ming Dynasty, and the examples for the latter are Qian Qianyi of the Qing

Dynasty who studied the poems from the Tang Dynasty down to the Song and Yuan Dynasties, Yuan Mei who only commented on the poems about their refinement and clumsiness without mentioning whether they were the poems of the Tang or Song Dynasties or the ancient or present times, and even Chen Yan and others who advocated the theory of "Three Yuans", etc. There are too many examples. All these can prove one thing: The Tang poetry is indeed the result of the golden age of the Chinese poetry, and it is a reality impossible to be outshined.

Chapter Five

The Influence of the Tang-Song Prose on the Premodern Literary Circles

1. The Tang-Song Classical Prose Movements as a Continuum

Choice Blossoms of Literature collected the writings of a variety of genres. While poems make up the largest part, the majority of the rest genres can all be considered as "prose" today. Therefore, it is appropriate to say *Choice Blossoms of Literature* is a general anthology of prose. The prose in *Choice Blossoms of Literature* mainly included the works of the scholars in the Tang Dynasty, and naturally there are many parallel essays, such as the essays of Li Shangyin, as we have mentioned in the previous chapter. Of course there are many famous essays, such as Han Yu's *A Reflection on Improving Learning*, *An Inquiry into the Way of Confucianism*, *An Inquiry into Human Nature*, *An Inquiry into Slander*, *A Reflection of Man*, *An Epitaph of Liu Zihou*, *The Tablet of Pacification of Huaixi*, *Preface to See off Meng Dongye*, *The Biography of Mao Ying*, *Preface to See off Li Yuan to Return to the Pan Valley*, *A Record of the Wall of the Office Hall of the Vice Magistrate of Liantian County*, *An Elegiac Address to My Nephew the Twelfth*, etc., and Liu Zongyuan's *Three Warnings*, *A Reflection about Heaven*, *The Insect of Fuban*, *The Biography of Song Qing*, *The Legendary Boy Ou Ji*, *A Record of the Little Stone Pond*, *The Anecdotes of Marshal Duan*, etc. They remind us of an important classical prose movement in the Tang Dynasty, which renewed profoundly the prose tradition and pioneered the prose mainstream for the thousand years to come.

"The classical prose" was opposite to "the contemporary prose" which was a type of prevailing parallel prose for civil service examinations at that time. Unlike the parallel prose which demanded the same number of characters in sentences, opposite tones and rhymes, miscellaneous use of allusions with detailed rules, and splendid diction and expressions, the classical prose mainly used single sentences for relatively free narration of things and expression of emotions. The classical prose continued the unparallelized prose tradition in the pre-Qin and the Han Dynasty before the Wei, Jin, the Southern and Northern Dynasties.

Today when we talk about the changes of genres and styles of the prose, we tend to consider the topic from the aspect of literature itself. As a matter of fact, since prose laid more stress on practicality than poetry did, in the ancient times the prose style went beyond literature and became a serious problem of politics. Therefore, Han Yu combined his advocacy of the classical prose and his ambition of reinvigorating Confucianism into one. In the pioneer days of the classical prose movement, the conflict between the advocacy of the classical prose and that of the parallel prose had a clear political significance. When Yang Jian, Emperor Wendi of the Sui Dynasty, advocated thriftiness, Li E then submitted a memorial to express his strong dissatisfaction with the selection of talented persons by means of their literary abilities, and furthermore, he totally negated the style of flowery language of the Six Dynasties. At that time, even judicial measures had been taken against those who wrote official documents in the splendid parallel prose. Wang Tong, a great Confucian scholar at that time, also advocated that prose should be used to expound the Confucian doctrines and denounced the masters of the parallel prose Shen Yue, Xie Tiao, Xu Ling and Yu Xin. The rectification of the literary tendency in the Southern Dynasties had become a universal trend at the turn of the Sui and Tang Dynasties. The historians in the early Tang Dynasty also took a critical attitude to the literature of the Six Dynasties as they hoped to realize a compromise between the substantial content and the splendid language. At that time the eight historical books were being written: *The History of the Jin Dynasty*, *The History of the Liang Dynasty*, *The History of the Chen Dynasty*, *The History of the Northern Qi Dynasty*, *The History of the Zhou Dynasty*, *The History of the Southern Dynasties*, *The History of the Northern Dynasties* and *The History of the Sui Dynasty*. Although they manifested in different degrees the splendid pattern of the parallel prose, they had to use essayistic language in the narration, especially the simple and concise language used in *The History of the Liang Dynasty* and then *The History of the Chen Dynasty*. Therefore, Zhao Yi, the historian and poet of the Qing Dynasty, held that it was the father and son Yao Cha and Yao Silian who started to use "the classical prose" in writing *The History of the Liang Dynasty* and *The History of the Chen Dynasty* (*Reading Notes on the Twenty-Two Historical Books*).

It could not be denied, however, that parallel prose was still the most frequently used prose form in the early Tang Dynasty. Even Chen Zi'ang continued the old pattern, although he was an expert of poetry and advocated actively the literary restoration of the classical style of the Han and Wei Dynasties. His memorials, prefaces, etc. were written all the same in the style of parallel prose, while his theses, letters, etc. were written in somewhat prosaic style — simple, concise, and close to the classical style. As for the widely acknowledged pioneers of the classical prose movement in the Tang Dynasty, such as Xiao Yingshi, Li Hua, and Dugu Ji, most of their extant works are parallel prose (*Choice Blossoms of Literature* selected many of their essays). However, they expressed their clear inclination of classical prose restoration. For instance, in his comments on the past writers, Xiao Yingshi complained about the splendid language that Qu Yuan, Song Yu, Mei Cheng, Sima Xiangru, etc. used in their works, and made no comments on the writers of the Southern Dynasties, while the writers he most highly recommended were Jia Yi of the Han Dynasty and Chen Zi'ang of the Tang Dynasty. Obviously what he affirmed was the style of forceful language with substance used before the Southern Dynasties. Li Hua and Dugu Ji both paid attention to the prose of the Han Dynasty, and in their writings, they mixed couplets with single sentences and demonstrated their change of orientation. At this time, the most outstanding writer was Yuan Ji. All the extant essays of Yuan Ji, Li Hua and Dugu Ji are in the classical style. Zhang Xuecheng paid even more attention to Yuan Ji's historical position in the classical prose development: "People usually held that the prose of the Six Dynasties was in the splendid and graceful pattern. Changli (Han Yu) began to reinvigorate the prose after the decline of the eight dynasties. They do not know that fifty years before, Yuan Ji already studied the classical prose when no one in the country did." (Postscript to *The Collection of Yuan Cishan*)

Not long before Han Yu, a group of scholars also began to advocate the classical prose. Liu Mian was born in a historian family: His father Liu Fang was a historian official, and he himself was a historian official once for a time. As a historian official, he had experiences of writing in essayistic form, and at the same time he attached great importance to Confucianism; therefore, his goal of uniting literature with Confucianism can be considered as a guide to the literary concept of Han Yu. In his mind, the line of the orthodox had been passed down from the remote ages of Yao, Shun, Duke Zhou, Kong Zi, through Meng Zi, Xun Zi to Jia Yi, Dong Zhongshu of the Western Han Dynasty; as to Qu Yuan, Song Yu, Sima Xiangru, Yang Xiong, Cao Zhi, Lu Ji, etc., they were only men of letters that the superior men would not strive to be. The men of letters in the Southern Dynasties were even not worth mentioning at all. Different from Liu Mian who set store by Confucianism, Liang Su was a disciple of the Tiantai Sect and had acquired a profound and wide knowledge of Buddhism, but in writing, he adopted the essayistic form instead of the parallel style. Liang Su learned writing from Dugu Ji while Han Yu studied under Liang Su. From Dugu Ji through Liang Su to Han Yu, we may see faintly the clue of the classical prose movement. For instance, although Liang Su worshipped Buddhism and Han Yu set store by Confucianism in direct opposite orientations, Liang Su followed Dugu Ji and emphasized particularly the writings of the Han Dynasty; therefore, what he learned was wider than what Liu Mian had. He listed Jia Yi, Sima Qian and others as one line, and Mei Cheng, Sima Xiangru and Yang Xiong as another line, and he absorbed both. Han Yu stressed on the study of the prose of the Han Dynasty, and also drew knowledge from Sima Qian, Sima Xiangru and Yang Xiong, but he did not belittle the men of letters excessively as Liu Mian did.

On the basis of efforts made by literary writers of the previous dynasties, Han Yu stepped forward courageously, called for the classical prose movement, and demonstrated his outstanding creative works as examples; as a result, he could transform the literary trend of the time. One of the important reasons that his predecessors were unable to accomplish the great cause of transformation of the literary trend is that they could not create excellent works. For instance, Liu Mian sighed in his essay: "I have the will for the literary restoration of the classical prose, but I have not enough strength; my words are close to the Confucian way, but my language is not elegant." Han Yu was highly talented, unrestrained, and resourceful; moreover, he was tenacious and perseverant. Li Han recalled Han Yu's advocacy of the ancient prose restoration, "Many people at first felt surprised, later they jeered at him and rejected it, but he became even firmer in his will. Finally they were in accordance with him." (The Foreword to *The Collection of Master Changli*)

Both Han Yu's prose and his thought seemed to advocate the restoration of the classical prose to return to the realm of the pre-Qin and the Han Dynasty across the Six Dynasties. In his essay "A Reflection on Improving Learning", when he talked about the study of classics, history books and philosophical works, he listed *The Book of Poetry*, *The Book of History*, *The Zhou Book of Change*, *Zhuang Zi*, *The Song of the South*, and the works of Sima Qian, Sima Xiangru and Yang Xiong as his examples — it meant the same thing. But his literary slogans were: "All the trite expressions should be discarded," (*A Letter in Reply to Li Yi*) and "One should write his own words." (*The Epitaph of Fan Shaoshu of Nanyang*) As a matter of fact, similar to most pioneers in history known as the advocators for the classical prose restoration movement, he was in reality a creator and a pioneer of the new times instead of a reviver of old times. His classical prose was full of vigor, rich in content, prominent in personality and free in reasoning, narration and expression of his emotions; they were by no means mere imitations of the prose of the Qin and Han Dynasties, but a creation of an effective and practical new essayistic style since the middle ancient times. They, of course, were transformed from the prosaic style of the pre-Qin and the Han Dynasty, not from the parallel prose of the Six

Dynasties. This is what he meant by "classical prose restoration" — the creativity was his major contribution in the history of prose.

Liu Zongyuan was another great master in the classical prose movement of the Tang Dynasty. When young, he stressed merely on the graceful language in his writing. Later, he turned his attention to the classical prose that expounded Confucianism. He made remarkable achievements in his landscape essays, fables and even in biographies and sketches, all of which had proved to be successful in the classical prose style. His traditional study covered the scope approximately similar to that of Han Yu. For instance, in *The Letter in Reply to Wei Zhongli on Being a Teacher*, he listed *Five Classics*, *Meng Zi*, *Xun Zi*, *Zhuang Zi* and *Lao Zi*, *Discourses on the States*, *The Songs of the South*, and Sima Qian as examples. In addition, he covered a variety of fields: Liu Zongyuan was greatly influenced by Buddhism, so that he advocated the combination of Confucianism with Buddhism. Liu Zongyuan's literary style was different from Han Yu's. If we say the writings of Han Yu read grand and vigorous, then those of Liu Zongyuan sounded serious, clean and meticulous. Han Yu rejected flatly all the men of letters in the Six Dynasties, while according to Fang Bao of the Qing Dynasty, Liu Zongyuan's writings "were mixed into the tradition from various patterns of various scholars of the Zhou, Qin, Han, Wei and Six Dynasties." (Postscript to *The Collected Writings of Liu Zongyuan*) As a whole, Liu Zongyuan seemed to be more tolerant of different styles.

However, in the efforts to change the literary tide in the country, a flat denial is more effective than tolerance, so that the chief commander of the classical prose restoration movement was Han Yu, not Liu Zongyuan. Han Yu had undoubtedly exerted a much greater influence than Liu Zongyuan at that time. Liu Zongyuan did not have the unruly personality like Han Yu, or experienced various political frustrations and lived in the border areas; therefore, his disciples were much inferior to those of Han Yu. Among the disciples of Han Yu, there were the famous classical prose writers like Li Ao, Huangfu Shi and Fan Zongshi. Li Ao inherited the cause of Han Yu completely in the aspects of thought and prose.

Ouyang Xiu, the leader of the classical prose restoration movement of the Song Dynasty, listed Han Yu and Li Ao together in order to respect Li Ao as an orthodox master. However, what the followers of Han Yu tended to develop was his fresh and unusual style. Han Yu's writings were considered "peculiar and strange" at his time, which might be due to its dissimilarity to the civil service examination prose and its stress on rejection of all the trite expressions. By the time when Huangfu Shi became popular, he endeavored even more vigorously to advocate: "It is only novelty in idea that can be different from usualness." (*A Letter in Reply to Mr. Li*) Fan Zongshi's writings were known to be even more jerky and difficult to understand, and his several extant essays were known to be hard to punctuate. His writing style was considered at the time as the "obscure" style, for he strived for "unusualness" but went to the extreme. *The Supplements to the History of the Tang Dynasty* recorded: "After the Yuanhe Period, the prose learners followed Han Yu for his freshness and peculiarity, and Fan Zongshi for his esotericism and obscurity." Thus we can see the tendency of prose development.

After Han Yu, the classical prose restoration movement declined gradually, and the parallel prose prevailed in the late Tang Dynasty. At that time, only a few writers continued the classical prose writing and persevered in their efforts for the prose reformation in the middle Tang Dynasty. These people included Du Mu, Pi Rixiu, Lu Guimeng, and Luo Yin; the first was an eloquent orator and poet, while the rest three distinguished themselves for their brilliant essays. In addition, Liu Tui and Sun Qiao were the classical prose writers of the Han Yu School well-known for unusualness. Liu Tui's collected works were compiled with the selections taken from *Choice Blossoms of Literature* and other books in the late Ming Dynasty. *The Synoptic Catalogue of The Complete Library of the Four Treasuries* commented that his writings were a little easier to understand than those of Fan Zongshi, but a little more difficult and stranger than those of Sun Qiao. Sun Qiao was a disciple of the Han Yu School, and his tutor was Lai Wuze, who was the disciple of Huangfu Shi. His essays were strange, risky and full of uncertainty, on such topics as to catch a serpent bare-handed, or to mount on an unsaddled horse, kicking and jumping without stop. *The Synoptic Catalogue of The Complete Library of the Four Treasuries* commented on the writings of Sun Qiao as "striving for unusualness" instead of Han Yu's "naturalness and loftiness", which pointed out pertinently his pursuit in essay writing. Sun Qiao and his likes only learned one aspect of Han Yu's style of classical prose, so naturally they could not carry on his cause. On the whole, the classical prose in the Late Tang and Five Dynasties was on the decline.

The prose style in the Late Tang and Five Dynasties returned again to the parallel prose. The scholars at the beginning of the Song Dynasty came mostly from the Southern Tang and Later Shu Dynasties. Xu Xuan and others were adepts in the parallel prose with splendid language, and dominated the literary circles at that time. Opposite to this main current of parallel prose were Liu Kai and Wang Yucheng. Liu Kai made some contributions in his theoretic advocacy. When young, he admired Han Yu and Liu Zongyuan so much that he changed his own name as Jianyu (literally, to shoulder the burden of Han Yu) and Shaoyuan (literally, to succeed to the cause of Liu Zongyuan), both meaning he would shoulder the task to carry forward the tradition of the classical prose of the Tang Dynasty and succeed to its cause. It seemed that the people at the beginning of the Song Dynasty respected Han Yu mainly because he was in the line of Confucian orthodox figures such as Duke Zhou, Kong Zi, and Meng Zi; they viewed Han Yu in consideration of his reinvigoration of Confucianism, and further opposed the literary elegant style for its hindrance to the expression of Confucian doctrines. Therefore, they supported Han Yu's restoration of the classical prose. As a result, many could not write good prose, and their influence then could not extend. *The Synoptic Catalogue of the Complete Library of the Four Treasuries* made a comment on Liu Kai:

> In the Song Dynasty, it was Liu Kai who began to advocate the classical prose to change the trend of the parallel prose, but his writings are too obscure, and that is his weak point.

Relatively speaking, Wang Yucheng's classical prose was smooth, and he himself said that he would "learn the Six Classics of the remote times, and study the writings of Han Yu of the close time in order to make his sentences easy to say, and his meanings easy to understand." (*The Second Letter in Reply to Zhang Fu*) But he was not so extreme in attitude as Liu Kai. For instance, Liu Kai rejected the parallel prose completely. Wang Yucheng mixed the classical prose with the parallel prose in his writing, and although it was feasible and practical, the literary impact was not dramatic enough. Liu Kai and Wang Yucheng were not powerful enough to turn the main tide of the parallel prose. After their death, the Xikun parallel prose, which Yang Yi and others worked on by imitating the works of Li Shangyin, prevailed in the literary circles for a time.

The Xikun style, already mentioned in the previous chapter in the discussion of the development of poetry, is not only the trend of poetry at that time, but also that of prose. The exquisite diction, prosody and allusions formed its beauty, and thus it attracted countless men of letters. At that time, the classical prose school was still only a tributary of the literary circles. Zhang Jing, the disciple of Liu Kai, collected his master's manuscripts, inherited and carried forward Liu's theory. Mu Xiu spent several decades revising the collected works of Han Yu and Liu Zongyuan, and sold them openly in the Great Temple of the Xiang State, hoping some people might study them. On the whole, they were lonely, and people usually considered their works as absurd talks or confusing theories. Besides, Shi Jie attacked vehemently the prose of the Xikun style from the standpoint of Confucianism; however, he was not powerful enough to blaze a new trail. The works of these classical prose writers seemed still choppy and unsmooth in their practice. We may read a sentence written by Mu Xiu about a horse tramping a dog dead on the way: "A horse galloped away, when a yellow dog came under the hoofs and died," and realize at once that the true revival of the classical prose in the Song Dynasty had to wait for the appearance of Ouyang Xiu.

Ouyang Xiu was a man of importance to carry on the classical prose restoration movement initiated by Han Yu and Liu Zongyuan, but he started the prose reformation as an assistant secretary in the house of Qian Weiyan, the key figure of the Xikun style, where he made acquaintance of Yin Zhu, a friend of Mu Xiu. Yin Zhu's writings were profoundly influenced by the laconic and circumspect style of *The Spring and Autumn Annals*. One day Qian Weiyan asked the two to write an article for his newly completed twin osmanthus building. Ouyang Xiu wrote over a thousand words, while Yin Zhu only five hundred. That greatly suprised Ouyang Xiu and inspired him into writing the classical prose. (*A Record of Mr. Shao's Personal Experience*) Because of this background, in Ouyang Xiu's writings, the mixed sentence patterns of both parallel prose and classical prose forms can still be seen. He held a rather objective attitude toward the writers of the Xikun style, such as Yang Yi and others, and praised them for their "great writings and erudition", while he believed that Shi Jie, who did his utmost to depreciate the Xikun style, "had highly overestimated himself", and "could not be a model enough for the late-comers to follow." But Ouyang Xiu was after all a man eager to revive the classical prose, and the man he adored most was definitely Han Yu. When he was young, he obtained from a neighbor a copy of Han Yu's collected works in a broken trunk. On the first reading he only found it grand and erudite, and on the second reading, he took it whole-heartedly as his model. After he met Yin Zhu and started to write the classical prose, he collated *The Collected Works of Han Yu*. After that, the essays of Han Yu became gradually popular in the country. (*A Postscript to the Old Copy of The Collected Works of Han Yu*)

However, the choice of orientation was a problem in the inheritance of Han Yu's classical prose legacy. We have pointed out that in their study of the writings of Han Yu, the learners of the Tang Dynasty such as Huangfu Shi, Fan Zongshi and Sun Qiao emphasized one aspect of unusualness of Han Yu's prose and developed it to the extreme; therefore, they went sideways. As for the difference of personality between Han Yu and Ouyang Xiu, Ouyang Xiu would not inherit the aspect of unusualness and peculiarity, but favor natural simplicity. Han Yu demonstrated a masculine beauty, while in the remark of Yao Nai of the Qing Dynasty, Ouyang Xiu belonged to the feminine beauty. (*A Letter in Reply to Lu Jiefei*) In Su Xun's mind, the writing style of Ouyang Xiu was "leisurely and all-inclusive, moving back and forth in a hundred turns, and yet, everything is fluent and smooth without interruption ... and there is no sign of difficulty and laboriousness." That is to say, his writings were both tactful and winding, and fluent and easy to understand. Obviously his style was much different from that of Han Yu. It is because of the establishment of this flowing and easy style that the style of the Song prose could be distinguished from that of the Tang prose. The prose of the Tang Dynasty, especially the classical prose of Han Yu, still bore the fresh unusualness of the emergent classical prose, and was extraordinarily brilliant. Furthermore, the concept of "discardment of all the trite expressions" might as well cause the oddity of unusualness. All these seemed to have been dissolved in the Song prose, especially in the writings of Ouyang Xiu. It might be a vivid and reasonable contrast in the past that the Tang prose was like precipitous mountains, while the Song prose was like a wide stretch of flatland. The change began right with Ouyang Xiu.

The establishment of the fluent and easy style by Ouyang Xiu was realized through efforts and struggles. When the Xikun style died away, where should the classical prose go? The Imperial College style at the time provided another way out. At the Imperial College, Shi Jie and others were all scholar-officials with thorough knowledge of classics and the classical prose writers. The students were naturally dissatisfied with the splendor of the parallel prose, but they were bent on seeking after profundity and unusualness, thus their writings were peculiar and difficult to understand. In the second year of the Jiayou Period, when Ouyang Xiu presided over the imperial examination, he resolutely picked out the examination paper of Liu Ji, the most distinguished student of the Imperial College, corrected it in red ink and dismissed him. Thus, he dealt a serious blow to the Imperial College style. This imperial examination produced a significant impact, for those dismissed students went so far as to wait until Ouyang Xiu came out of the hall and held up his horse to stir trouble, but the writing style changed ever since. In another respect, through this examination Zeng Gong and the brothers Su Shi and Su Zhe were enrolled and formed a qualified reserve force for the classical prose restoration movement of the Northern Song Dynasty. These two respects enabled the fluent and easy style to become the basic tone of the prose of the Song Dynasty. It should be pointed out that the easiness of the prose of the Song Dynasty was not to write freely at a low level, but in the same plainness as the Song poetry; it is the easiness and fluency through repeated and hard improvement. Ouyang Xiu's famous essay *The Pavilion of the Old Tippler* at first opened with description of the surrounding mountains of Chuzhou with tens of characters, and finally they were reduced into five characters: "环滁皆山也。" (Literally: Surrounding Chuzhou were all mountains.) Someone in the Southern Song Dynasty read the original manuscript, and Zhu Xi could not help saying: "Master Ouyang also refined his essay repeatedly to subtlety."

Ouyang Xiu's discovery and promotion of the talents of younger generation was also the crucial factor for the success of the classical prose restoration movement with him as the head. For instance, Wang Anshi, Zeng Gong, the three Sus were all recommended by him, and some were his disciples. The five mentioned above plus himself were the six top masters of the Song prose and were universally accepted by people of later generations.

Zeng Gong had been addressed together with Ouyang Xiu by the people of the Ming and Qing Dynasties, and his writings were considered to have obtained the subtlety of the essays of Ouyang Xiu, for they were concise, rigorous, elegant and leisurely, and good at reasoning; moreover, they were regarded as the smoothest and most substantial in the prose of the six masters. Wang Anshi received comments and guidance of Ouyang Xiu on his essays through the recommendation of Zeng Gong. When Ouyang Xiu was demoted to Chuzhou, Zeng Gong went to ask for advice about his essays in the classical prose pattern, and he brought with him the articles of Wang Anshi for comment. Owing to Ouyang Xiu's appreciation, Wang Anshi's works became popular among the literati. Wang Anshi was a man of unique personality with political insight, and his writings were clear in thought, concise in conveyance, refined in style, vigorous in content, and good at political argumentation. His prose has a style of his own.

Su Xun, Su Shi and Su Zhe were well-known as the father and son writers in the history of Chinese literature. Their cultural education was completed at their hometown in Sichuan, far away from the cultural centres, through self-study and father-son teaching. Su Xun did not like the parallel prose, nor pursued an official career through the imperial examinations, but devoted himself to the study of the texts of *The Strategies of the Warring States*, and the Legalist and Confucian works of Han Fei, Meng Zi, etc. His writings were free and unrestrained with the features of a political strategist, and he claimed himself to be as eloquent as Jia Yi when he talked about the state affairs. He taught his young sons, Su Shi and Su Zhe, in accordance with these traditions. When writing the inscription for Su Shi's tomb tablet, Su Zhe said: "At first Su Xun liked the works of Jia Yi and Lu Zhi, and talked about how to pacify the country." Su Xun went to the capital with his two young sons to seek the guidiance of Ouyang Xiu, and won the praise of the latter; in the next year his two sons succeeded in the imperial examination and became would-be officials. Since then, they entered the mainstream of the classical prose restoration movement and became the elite writers of the literary circles, and Su Shi also became the leader of the literary circles after the death of Ouyang Xiu. Ouyang Xiu seemed to have predicted this. When Su Shi succeeded in the imperial examination and became a would-be official, Ouyang Xiu said to his son: "In thirty years no one will remember me!" However, Su Shi had always been grateful to his benefactor; he compared Ouyang Xiu to the "contemporary Han Yu", and gave his tutor an extremely high place in the history of literature. Ouyang Xiu was more fortunate than Han Yu, because he had a rare talented student Su Shi, who could carry forward his cause, while Han Yu had no such luck. Su Shi had a good command of writing: He wrote at his will whether it was to narrate things, to express emotions, or to make comments and arguments; he could freely write lengthy articles, sketches or reading notes, and his writings were all-inclusive in various genres. The realm of prose he pursued after was the further development along the orientation of easiness and fluency Ouyang Xiu had pointed out. His writings were smooth and natural, and had an unpredictable flow. When Su Shi talked about writing, he liked to compare it to water: "My writing is like inexhaustible springs, which gushes out the earth wherever it flows. On the level ground, it flows swiftly, and it is not difficult for it to go a thousand *li* a day; when it winds its way through stone mountains, it takes shape as it meets, and nothing can be predicted. What I can know about it is that it moves constantly as it should, and stops when it must stop." (*A Talk on Writing*) "It resembles floating clouds and flowing water ... textures of writing are all natural and its patterns are in great variety." (*A Letter in Reply to Xie Minshi*) Since Su Shi reached a new height of achievements in creation, established the new norms of the Song prose, and made it firm and unchangeable, the revival of the classical prose restoration movement that began with Han Yu and Liu Zongyuan gained its final success. Like Ouyang Xiu, Su Shi did his best to reward and promote the talents of the younger generation. Most of his students were excellent writers, and could continue to develop various aspects of his style. For instance, the comments of Chao Buzhi "surged forward in sweeping waves" (*The Synoptic Catalogue of The Complete Library in the Four Treasuries*), and the essays of Zhang Lei were easy and natural in hundreds of different postures (Ye Mengde: Preface to *The Collected Works of Zhang Wenqian*). All these are important factors for the development of the classical prose restoration movement.

At the end of the Northern Song Dynasty, the writings of Su Shi were banned owing to the struggle of the political parties, and seemed to have disappeared for a time. But after the Imperial Court of the Northern Song Dynasty was forced to cross the Yangtze River, the ban on Su Shi's writings was lifted, and soon his writings regained popularity and became a target of admiration by different walks of life; his style even became the model for the imperial examination. At that time, both the writings of Ouyang Xiu and Su Shi became the models for prose writing. For example, Chen Liang compiled twenty volumes of *Selected Readings of Ouyang Xiu*, and Lü Zuqian compiled 27 volumes of *Selected Works of Three Sus*. Lü

Zuqian was a Principlist, and at the same time emphasized literature. He compiled two volumes of *The Key to the Classical Prose*, including sixty-two essays from eight writers of Han Yu, Liu Zongyuan, Ouyang Xiu, Su Xun, Su Shi, Su Zhe, Zeng Gong, and Zhang Lei with annotations and comments. It was just an emphasis of the literary tradition of the classical prose restoration movement in the Tang and Song Dynasties. He stated explicitly in the introduction entitled *A Guide to Reading the Classical Prose*: "A learner of prose must read repeatedly Han Yu, Liu Zongyuan, Ouyang Xiu and Su Shi." All these embodied the emergence of the classical prose tradition. Zhu Xi, a master of Principlism, was deeply dissatisfied with the publication of *The Key to the Classical Prose*, because he insisted in the theory that Confucianism should precede prose-writing. But he could not refuse the influence of the prose reformation of the Northern Song Dynasty and said: "Dongpo's (Su Shi) writings are lucid and lively, and Su Sr. (Su Xun) vigorous and firm. They both had their excellence. With regard to the writings of Master Ouyang, Zeng Nanfeng (Zeng Gong) and Han Changli (Han Yu), how can they not be read!" Chen Liang, antagonistic in thought to Zhu Xi, and Chen Fuliang of the Zhedong School, took particularly Ouyang Xiu as their model (*An Occasional Talk in the Woods*). As for the mainstream of the writings of the Southern Song Dynasty, there were two lines: One was the different branches of the Principlist writings, and the other was the inheritance of the works of Ye Shi of the Zhedong School. Even if there are differences between their writings, both of them undoubtedly continued the classical prose tradition.

The Song Dynasty was an age of prosperous development of artistic criticism: There appeared a large number of books of poetry talks, and a few monographs were also published on the study of prose. Li Qiqing at the end of the Song Dynasty wrote a book in one volume entitled *The Essence of Writings*. He commented on the styles of the most representative writers of the Tang and Song Dynasties — Han Yu, Liu Zongyuan, Ouyang Xiu and Su Shi — in the classical prose movement: "The writings of Han Yu are like the vast sea, Liu Zongyuan the gurgling springs, Ouyang Xiu the quiet billows, and Su Shi the surging tides." He also traced the origin of the classical prose writers of the Song Dynasty back to the pre-Qin times and the Hans Dynasty, and pointed out that Su Shi learned the writings from *Zhuang Zi*, *The Strategies of the Warring States*, and *Records of the Historian*, while Zeng Gong studied Liu Xiang. So far as we know, Han Yu learned the classical prose through the ancient classics, history books and philosophical works, and followed the examples of the pre-Qin times and the Han Dynasty but rejected the writings of the Six Dynasties. The classical prose writers of the Song Dynasty studied the writings of Han Yu, and at the same time, they would certainly trace back to the pre-Qin times and the Han Dynasty. This comment of Li Qiqing pointed out clearly that the origin of the classical prose of the Song Dynasty went through Han Yu and Liu Zongyuan of the Tang Dynasty back to the pre-Qin times and the Han Dynasty.

2. A Debate on the Tang-Song Prose and the Qin-Han Prose, and Their Connection

The Yuan Dynasty boasted commendable dramas, loose tunes, and even poetry, but no noteworthy essays. Yao Sui and Yu Ji were considered two great masters at that time. When Huang Zongxi recalled the achievements of the prose of the Ming Dynasty, he even mentioned the two together with Han Yu of the Tang Dynasty, Ouyang Xiu and Su Shi of the Song Dynasty, and Yuan Haowen of the Jin Dynasty, and thought there had not been such great prose masters in the Ming Dynasty. Liu Guan, a Principlist and the tutor of Song Lian[①], was a famous writer at the beginning of the Ming Dynasty. He once praised Yao Sui after his death for "having wiped out the floating decadence and returned resolutely to the way of the classical prose". However, most of their articles were for practical use, such as tablet inscriptions, imperial decrees and edicts, etc.; although they are elegant and refined, they are not worth a comment in the

① Song Lian (1310 – 1381), courtesy name Jinglian and style name Qianxi, a statesman, historian and essayist of the Northern Song Dynasty. He is famous for his compilation of *The History of the Yuan Dynasty*.

eyes of the modern literary historians.

Song Lian should be considered a great literary master of the early Ming Dynasty. When he was seventeen years old or so, he began to learn to write classical prose; however, later he deeply regretted having indulged himself in the beauty of prose language, and upheld Principlism as the mainstream. His literary conception was actually a mixture of Principlism and the classical prose tradition since the Song Dynasty. When he presided over the compilation of *The History of the Yuan Dynasty*, he changed the practice of separate divisions of *The Confucians* and *The Literary Writers* since *The Book of the Later Han Dynasty* by Fan Ye, and combined them into *Biographies of Confucians and Scholars*, thus implying oneness or inseparability of writing and morality. He once said clearly in *The Preface to The Collected Works of Instructor Xu*: "There is not the way of Confucianism outside of prose, and there is not prose outside of the way of Confucianism." This concept of oneness of prose and the way of Confucianism is originally the tradition of the classical prose movement of the Tang and Song Dynasties. When Han Yu talked about the orthodoxy of Duke Zhou, Kong Zi and Meng Zi, he regarded implicitly himself as the successor, and Ouyang Xiu also shouldered the tasks of the classical prose restoration movement and the revival of the way of Confucianism as the common cause. Therefore, Han Yu and Ouyang Xiu became the scholars Song Lian accepted and respected. He thought their writings could connect the prose tradition from the ancient times, the Zhou, Qin and Han Dynasties. (The Preface to *The Collected Works of Zhang Cuiping*) Song Lian can be regarded as the leader of succeeding to the literary tradition of the classical prose movement. His student Fang Xiaoru was an even purer Confucian scholar in the cultivation of Confucianism in comparison with the erudite tutor. Fang Xiaoru did not value the prose of the Tang Dynasty, and thought there was only one essay *Inquiry of the Way of Confucianism* by Han Yu to be in conformity with the teachings of the ancient sage. Therefore, he selected it into his literary collection *The Orthodoxy of Prose* which laid great emphasis on morality and political cultivation. He thought all the poems after *The Book of Poetry* were worthless, and only Zhu Xi's poem *Thoughts on Reading the Book* was the only good poem that inherited the spirit of *The Book of Poetry*. It was very difficult for people to accept this extreme literary concept of Principlism, and it also indicated the negative pressure on the literature from Principlism at the beginning of the Ming Dynasty. Fang Xiaoru made criticisms on the superiority between the Tang and Song prose from his Principlist point of view, and said: "As far as only the prose was concerned, the Song writers had not surpassed those of the Tang Dynasty; but in regard to morality, the Song Dynasty was superior to the Tang Dynasty." (*Three Poems to Zhao Boqin*) This view is obviously opposite to the universal inclination of emphasizing the literature of the Tang Dynasty and depreciating the Song Dynasty in the literature of the Ming Dynasty.

It was Li Mengyang, an advocator of the classical literary restoration movement, who made a strong attack on the Song prose in opposition to the Principlist concept. He said: "The rise of Confucianism in the Song Dynasty leads to the decline of the classical prose." That is to say, the rise of Principlism caused all the men of letters under the heaven to seek moral conduct, and they only pursued the gilded loftiness, unlike the ancient people who exposed their true nature. The former seven scholars overlooked the prose of the Tang and Song Dynasties, which in fact implied a rebellion against the negative pressure of Confucianism on the literature since the Song Dynasty. Therefore, we should make a careful analysis of the advocacy of the classical literary restoration movement in the respect of prose writing. The advocators kept on saying: "A learner must follow the prose of the Qin and Han Dynasties." Li Mengyang said: "After the Western Capital (i.e. the Western Han Dynasty), the writers are not worth mentioning at all." (*On Learning*) Wang Shizhen said: "The writings of the Western Capital were substantial, while those of the Eastern Capital (i.e. the Eastern Han Dynasty) weak," (*Random Remarks from the Artistic Circles*) as if all the writings after the Western Han Dynasty could be discarded. However, Wang Shizhen recorded in *Random Remarks from the Artistic Circles* that Li Mengyang only "persuaded people not to read the prose after the Tang Dynasty". Wang Shizhen himself made a list of reading for others, which ranged from the pre-Qin times to the Tang Dynasty: "The six classics, *The Book of Rites*, *Meng Zi*, *Lao Zi*, *Zhuang Zi*, *Lie Zi*, *Xun Zi*, *Discourse on the Warring States*, *Zuo's Commentary* ... the writings after the two capitals (i.e. the Western and Eastern Han Dynasties) to the Six Dynasties, Han Yu and Liu Zongyuan — the learners should select the best and read them repeatedly until they can understand and recite them." He only said that the writings after the Han Dynasty should be selected, and did not say anything about discarding them all; however, he did not say a word about the Song Dynasty. The literary writers of the classical prose restoration school drew strictly the line of desirability between the Tang and Song Dynasties, which had deeper meanings. What they tended to talk about were the techniques, prosody, structure of the composition of poetry and prose. The debates between He Jingming and Li Mengyang were also about whether one should aim at vivid imitation or self-establishment. These different views to some extent went against the tradition of emphasizing both writings and the way of Confucianism since the classical prose movement of the Tang and Song Dynasties. They only focused their study on the artistic forms, and caused the reaction of the contemporary Tang-Song School.

The Tang-Song School refers to a group of writers like Wang Shenzhong and Tang Shunzhi who respected the classical prose of the Tang and Song Dynasties. Their rise and prosperity happened in a period between the former and latter seven scholars. Wang Shenzhong and Tang Shunzhi had been influenced before by the general practice of the times, and also learned the writings of the Qin and Han Dynasties advocated by Li Mengyang and others. Later they turned to develop a style of their own and advocated the classical prose of the Tang and Song Dynasties, especially the type of the writings in the Song Dynasty with Ouyang Xiu and Zeng Gong as representatives. *Biographies of the Literary Scholars* in *The History of the Ming Dynasty* recorded how Wang Shenzhong and Tang Shunzhi changed their viewpoints:

> Shenzhong devoted himself first to the study of the writings of

> the Qin and Han Dynasties, and said there would be nothing worth learning after the Eastern Capital (i.e. the Eastern Han Dynasty). Later when he became enlightened with the writing rules of Ouyang Xiu and Zeng Gong, he burned all his previous works, and concentrated himself in following the two prose masters, especially Zeng Gong. Shunzhi was not convinced at first, and after a long time he also changed his attitude to follow him.

Their change of orientation was also influenced by Confucianism. Wang Shenzhong at first did not read the writings after the Han Dynasty. After he got in touch with the Mindology of Wang Yangming, he again studied the works of the Confucian scholars of the Song Dynasty, paid attention to the inside meanings of Mind and Nature, and advocated that writings should be based on meanings. He criticized the literary writers of the classical prose restoration school for pursuing only the beauty of language in prose-writing: After they "copied three or five sentences from *Records of the Historian*, or *The History of the Han Dynasty*", they thought that they had learned the style of Sima Qian and Ban Gu. He particularly respected the writings of Zeng Gong, who "could understand the intention of the sage" and "thought everything only out of morality". (Preface to *The Collected Works of Zeng Nanfeng*) This was actually reaffirmation of the tradition of laying stress on both the writing and the way of Confucianism in the classical prose movement of the Tang and Song Dynasties. At the same time, in considering the combination of the writing and the way of Confucianism, Tang Shunzhi explained from the artistic perspective why a learner should study the writings of the Tang and Song Dynasties instead of the prose of the Qin and Han Dynasties. Tang Shunzhi was a great master of the eight-part essays, and knew thoroughly the structure of introduction, development, transition and conclusion of an article and its presentation of ideas. In his opinion, the excellent scheme of the writings of the pre-Han times and Han Dynasty existed tracelessly in the texts, while the prose of the Tang and Song Dynasties were marked with clear rules and regulations. Therefore, the latter was easier for a learner to follow, while the former, if mistaken as being without rules, was likely considered to be loose and irrelevant. (Preface to *The Collected Works of Vice Minister Dong Zhongfeng*) Therefore, the feasible way was naturally following the writings of the Tang and Song Dynasties, not that of the Qin and Han Dynasties. This was exactly what Gui Youguang did in practice: He began with his study of the prose of the Tang and Song Dynasties, and then traced back to the writings of the Qin and Han Dynasties.

What Gui Youguang faced at that time was the group of the latter seven scholars of Li Panlong, Wang Shizhen, et. al. who, a little later than Wang Shenzhong and Tang Shunzhi, opposed strongly their literary advocacy and reiterated the concepts of classical literary restoration of the former seven scholars. Gui Youguang, like Wang Shenzhong and Tang Shunzhi, emphasized the morality of writing, and expressed strong dissatisfaction at the practice then of the so-called "following the steps of the Qin and Han Dynasties" in order to "refine sentences" in prose writing. Gui Youguang valued the classical prose of the Tang and Song Dynasties, especially the writings of the Song Dynasty, and said: "The well-known prose masters of the Song and Yuan Dynasties were strong enough to match the writers of a thousand years ago." Later literary writers all considered that he, Ouyang Xiu and Zeng Gong were of the same kind. Qian Qianyi said: "He followed Ouyang Xiu and Zeng Gong closely." (*The Profiles of the Poets in The Collected Poems of the Different Reigns of the Ming Dynasty*) Gui Zhuang thought his writings "could match Ouyang Xiu and Zeng Gong." (Postscript to *The Complete Collection of Gui Youguang, Late Minister of the Imperial Stables and Carriage*) In fact, the classical prose writers of the Tang-Song School did not reject the writings of the Qin and Han Dynasties: Wang Shenzhong held that Ouyang Xiu and Zeng Gong were the best learners of Sima Qian and Ban Gu, and Gui Youguang liked the writings of Sima Qian, too. They both began their study from the classical prose of the Tang and Song Dynasties, and then traced back to the classical prose of the Qin and Han Dynasties. Such a literary system had a far-reaching influence on the classical prose of the Qing Dynasty. The classical prose of the Tongcheng School followed the examples of the eight great prose masters of the Tang and Song Dynasties, traced back to the source of the classical prose of the Qin and Han Dynasties, and prevailed in the whole literary circles of the Qing Dynasty for a time with Gui Youguang as a leader, who made the greatest achievements in literary creation among the writers of the Tang-Song School. If we can see that Fang Bao and Gui Youguang had an equally great interest in *The Records of the Historian* and made quite a number of comments on it, we know then they were in direct continuation. It was Fang Bao who saw clearly the capability of Gui Youguang in combining the study of the classical prose of the Qin-Han and the Tang-Song Dynasties together: "The writings of Zhenchuan (Gui Youguang) ... possibly his flavor and tone were obtained from Zichang (Sima Qian); therefore, he could learn the scheme of writing from Ouyang Xiu and Zeng Gong with little alteration of their forms." (Postscript to *The Collected Works of Zhenchuan*) The comment of *The Synoptic Catalogue of The Complete Library of the Four Treasuries* might be more objective than the words of Fang Bao who inherited the legacy of Gui Youguang: "Since the late Ming Dynasty, the scholars learned the classical prose from the writings of Han Yu, Liu Zongyuan, Ouyang Xiu and Su Shi, and traced all the way back to the Qin and Han Dynasties. Youguang made substantial contributions to this cause."

Gui Youguang won himself a historical place with his efforts. He and Wang Shizhen once attacked and slandered each other. But after Gui's death, Wang Shizhen, the leader of the latter seven scholars, acknowledged Gui's stand of connecting the study of the writings of the Qin and Han Dynasties with that of the Tang and Song Dynasties. He wrote: "After a thousand years, you followed the way of Han Yu and Ouyang Xiu. How can I take a different path from yours? For a long time, I feel regretful." The influence of the Tang-Song School existed not only on the prose of the Tongcheng School of the Qing Dynasty, but also held sway on the Gong'an School of the late Ming Dynasty. The Gong'an School also attacked the classical literary restoration concept, and considered that there were excellent poetry and prose in the Song and Yuan Dynasties. So it proposed to cast off the yoke and only express one's own soul. The Tang-

Song School, influenced by Wang Yangming's Mindology, had already manifested the signs. For instance, Tang Shunzhi claimed: "An article should be written with inspiration and present its true qualities." (*The Second Letter in Reply to the Magistrate Mao Lumen*)

The literary achievements of the Tang-Song School might not be great, but its position in the literary history as a link between the past and the future cannot be ignored. Because of *The Selected Writings of the Eight Great Prose Masters in the Tang and Song Dynasties* compiled by Mao Kun, the achievements of the classical prose movement of the Tang and Song Dynasties were known to everyone; because of Gui Youguang's combination of the classical prose development in the Qin and Han Dynasties and that of the Tang and Song Dynasties, the source and course were connected, and directly promoted the generation of its last fruit — the Tongcheng School.

At the turn of the Ming and Qing Dynasties, most of the great prose masters were the followers of the Tang-Song School. As we have introduced in the previous chapter, Qian Qianyi had originally followed the course of the classical prose restoration of the former and the latter seven scholars; Tang Xianzu before his death asked someone to tell Qian Qianyi to pay more attention to the literary works of Wang Anshi and Zeng Gong, and thus he gave Qian Qianyi a chance for transformation. Later, Cheng Jiasui recommended to him the literary orientation that Gui Youguang began with the study of the classical prose of the Tang and Song Dynasties, and traced back to that of the Qin and Han Dynasties. Qian Qianyi then decided to change his orientation, and believed that Gui Youguang was a literary master of an age, for he "based his ancient prose study on the classics and history works, and upheld readability and fluency as basic essentials". He had revised and rearranged the collected works of Gui Youguang, and hence Gui Zhuang, his disciple and the great grandson of Gui Youguang, spoke highly of him as a "meritorious man" of Gui's family. Gui Zhuang considered himself to be the successor of Gui Youguang's cause and even a descendant of Gui's family, and spent a lot of energy collating and editing the works of Gui Youguang, which helped extend the influence of the Tang-Song School of the Ming Dynasty on the literary circles of the Qing Dynasty.

At the beginning of the Qing Dynasty, Hou Fangyu, Wang Wan and Wei Xi were considered the three great masters, and their literary orientations were basically to respect the prose of the Tang and Song Dynasties. *The Synoptic Catalogue of The Complete Library of the Four Treasuries* made a comment: "For a time, scholars began to talk again about the literary rules and regulations since the Tang and Song Dynasties, and Wang Wan, Wei Xi of Ningdu, and Hou Fangyu of Shangqiu were considered the most elaborate." Hou Fangyu was the most distinctive of the three. He was originally an elegant young man, and delighted in writing parallel prose at the end of the Ming Dynasty; later, he threw away all his former works "to study the reasons why the masters Han Yu, Liu Zongyuan, Ouyang Xiu, Su Shi, Zeng Gong and Wang Anshi could emulate the writings of Sima Qian, and then to make every endeavor to realize the goal." (Xu Zuosu: Preface to *The Collected Works of Zhuanghuitang*) Like what Tang Shunzhi mentioned above, he thought there was a distinction of tangibility and intangibility between the writings of the Qin and Han Dynasties and those after the Han Dynasty; therefore, studying the prose of the Tang and Song Dynasties to attain a better level of classical prose was like reaching the other bank by sailing a boat, or stretching wings in order to fly strenuously, so he criticized the scholars who held the idea "A learner must follow the prose of the Qin and Han Dynasties" in the Ming Dynasty. "Isn't it absurd to want to give up the eight prose masters of the Tang and Song Dynasties, and leap over *Records of the Historian* and *The History of the Han Dynasty*, to reach the writings of the pre-Qin times? It is like crossing a river without rowing a boat, or planning to fly without stretching wings." (*A Letter to Ren Wanggu on Prose*) It can be seen that Hou's way of thinking was a continuation of Tang Shunzhi's view and the practice of Gui Youguang as well.

The mainstream of the writings in the Qing Dynasty is the classical prose of the Tongcheng School. Fang Bao initiated it, Liu Dakui inherited it, and Yao Nai spread it through his disciples all over the north and south.

People called it "Tongcheng Prose", because the three were all natives of the same place — Tongcheng. The Tongcheng School claimed the title self-consciously at the time of Yao Nai, who established the clear tradition of the school. Wu Minshu said in his "Letter to Xiao Cen on the Prose Schools":

> The Tongcheng Prose School, as it is called today, began with General-director Yao Jichuan (Yao Nai) in the reign of Emperor Qianlong. He claimed that he was an indirect disciple of Liu Haifeng, who was a disciple of Master Wangxi (Fang Bao), who was the predecessor of Yao's hometown. He again said Master Wangxi was a successor of Gui Zhenchuan of the Ming Dynasty. He compiled a book entitled *Categorized Selection of Ancient Writings*, which arranged the writings of Gui Youguang and Fang Bao directly after the eight prose masters, followed by the writings of Liu Dakui, and intended to demonstrate the orthodox of the ancient and present prose.

This literary tradition in the Qing Dynasty began with Fang Bao. He followed Ouyang Xiu and Zeng Gong in writing, and especially delighted in reading the *Records of the Historian* by Sima Qian. He shared the same interest as Gui Youguang. He was also a believer as well as an advocator of the traditional concept of the combination of writing and the way of Confucianism, and his own expectation was: "As for knowledge and conduct, I follow Cheng-Zhu, while for writing, I learn from both Han Yu and Ouyang Xiu." But his novelty was that he no longer repeated the old tune of the relation between the writing and the way of Confucianism, but established the new critical theory of prose with "substance and rules" as the core. Fang Bao studied carefully the classics of *The Spring and Autumn Annals*, the *Three Rites*, and *Records of the Historian*; his "substance and rules" came from his knowledge of classics and history works, and it seems that he stressed on the rules of prose organization and structure, etc. However, in *The Second Postscript to the Biographies of the Merchants*, he quoted texts from *The Zhou Book of Change* for an analysis of "substance and rules" and said: "Substance means 'content in writing', and rules refer to 'organization in writing'." The former in fact refers to the Confucian requirements of content in writing, while the latter indicates his focus on the detailed analysis of the texts of *Zuo's Commentary of The Spring and Autumn Annals*, *Records of the Historian* and *The History of the Han Dynasty*. He pointed out the characteristics of the texts: brief and detailed accounts, opening and closing, diction, sentence-making, etc. However, although Fang Bao stressed "rules", he thought "substance" was expressed through "rules", and to talk about "rules" was to discuss "substance". This kind of view of "substance and rules" is in fact a new elaboration of the concept of "the writing and the way of Confucianism", but the emphasis is on the study of the prose skills. It is a development of the literary concept.

The writings of Fang Bao are refined and clean. They are "excessive in rigor and substantiality, but fall short of grandeur and flexibility", which is closely related to his absorption in the study of the Confucian classics, though he considered *Zuo's Commentary* and *Records of the Historian* as "the most rigorous works of substance and rules". Wu Rulun commented that he "benefited greatly from his study of Confucian classics", so that he could be compared to Dong Zhongshu in the Han Dynasty and was close to Ouyang Xiu and Zeng Gong in the eight prose masters of the Tang and Song Dynasties. Fang Bao himself also affirmed that Gui Youguang did a better work in the respect of "organization in writing". In a word, although Fang Bao did not clearly proclaim the prose orthodoxy as explicitly as Yao Nai did, it can be seen clearly from his creative tendency and his emphasis of criticism that he had a thorough understanding of the classics and history books, the classical prose of the Tang and Song Dynasties, and the literary cause of Gui Youguang.

Liu Dakui was a pivot in the Tongcheng School, a link between the predecessors and the successors, but both his writing style and his literary conception went beyond the rules of Fang Bao. The writings of Fang Bao were refined and clean, while Liu Dakui's grandiose and surging. Wu Rulun praised his writing style as close to the free and swift vigor in *The Strategies of the Warring States*, and the talent display of Jia Yi, so we can see the tone of his writings was much different from that of Fang Bao. Liu

Dakui also showed a different literary flavor from Fang Bao, who inherited the prose tradition of the Tang and Song Dynasties and emphasized the prose of the Song Dynasty, such as the writings of Ouyang Xiu and Zeng Gong. Liu Dakui had a natural response to the scene of the prime Tang Dynasty: He compiled *Selected Poems of the Prime Tang Dynasty* and *The Orthodox of the Tang Poems* to respect the poems of the prime Tang Dynasty. Fang Dongshu said: "He selected particularly the poems lofty and refined to link with the poems of the seven scholars in the Ming Dynasty." (*Humble Opinions from Zhaomei*) This indicates he stood on the opposite side of the Tang-Song School. He thought that "the spirit" of an article could be embodied through "the rhythms of syllables" when they were being read aloud, and "the rhythms of syllables" depended on the choice of words and the structure of sentences. This view resembled the poetic comment of Hu Yingling, the disciple of Wang Shizhen of the Ming Dynasty, on the relationship between "genre, style, and tune", and "analogy, image and spirit". It seems that Liu Dakui shifted Hu's comment on poetry directly to his comment on prose writing. These all indicate that Liu Dakui could not be considered as an orthodox master of the Tongcheng School. Nevertheless, he was the master of Yao Nai, who organized and expanded the Tongcheng Prose School. It is more important that his many views had substantial influence on the Tongcheng writings following Yao Nai, though they were not in accordance with the rules of Fang Bao. For instance, his writing style was different from that of Fang Bao in the respect of grandeur and unrestrainedness, so in his discussion of the writings, he classified them into different styles, including the two most important styles: "grandeur" i.e. grandeur and unrestrainedness, and "ease" i.e. simplicity and remoteness. This directly led to Yao Nai's division of writing styles into the two main orientations of the firm *yang* (masculine strength) and the yielding *yin* (feminine gentleness) when he discussed the writing style. Yao Nai's own writing style on the whole is yielding, while in theory he affirmed the type of the firm *yang*. For instance, he praised the writings of the Western Han Dynasty as grandiose, intelligent, lofty and antique. Han Yu's writing obtained the meanings of the Han writers, while Ouyang Xiu,

Zeng Gong, even Gui Youguang became increasingly worse. Guan Tong, Mei Zengliang and Zeng Guofan, as the disciples of Yao Nai, all respected the style of grandeur, talent, unrestrainedness, which were quite different from the simplicity and conciseness at the beginning of the Tongcheng School. It is possible that this instance can demonstrate Liu Dakui's pivotal position between the predecessors and the successors, and between change and creation in the inheritance.

Yao Nai was the leader when the Tongcheng School became quite popular, and possessed the strong points of both Fang Bao and Liu Dakui. Yao Ying said in *A Brief Biography of Late Master Xibao* (*Yao Nai*): "The writings of Wangxi (Fang Bao) are plain but always uphold the Principlism. Haifeng (Liu Dakui) is brilliantly talented but maybe not erudite enough, and the master is good at both philosophy and writing." His theory also manifested such a quality of incorporation. At that time, the textual criticism was popular, which influenced the writing style. Weng Fanggang's poetics laid weight on learning while Yao Nai's theory of "philosophy, textual criticism, and poetry and prose" was a famous slogan of incorporating the philosophy of the Principlism with the textual criticism and the literature of the Qing Dynasty. Zeng Guofan said in very plain terms:

> The top Confucian and eccentric scholars in the empire advocated erudition. They collected all kinds of names and terms of a thing with all possible collateral evidence, and when they examined the source of a word, they could write over several thousand characters without stop. So they established another banner and called it Han study. They rejected absolutely the theories of the Principlism in the Song Dynasty and thought they should not exist, and their writings were jumbled with few important ideas ... He alone prevailed over all dissenting views, and held that none of the three — Confucian philosophy, textual criticism, and poetry and prose — should be neglected. The Confucian Principlism should be taken as substance, then poetry and prose could attach to it, and the textual

criticism could have a base. (Preface to *The Collected Writings of a Student of Ouyang Xiu*)

At that time, the textual criticism was popular, and there was a prevailing rejection of the Principlism of the Song and Ming Dynasties. The tradition of the classical prose had always emphasized the equal importance of the writing and the way of Confucianism, and naturally the way of Confucianism could not be discarded. Yao Nai's theory of "three in one" in fact was a compromise in the conflict between the Principlism and the textual criticism in the substance of prose, and it was an effort at defending the classical prose tradition. Yao Nai once saluted Dai Zhen, and was willing to be his student. This indicates his tolerance and acceptance of the new academic trend. When young, he learned the Confucian classics under the guidance of his uncle Yao Fan. All these belong to the aspect of "substance in writing". However, he was a literary writer after all, and his root was in the literary creation of poetry and prose. Later Zeng Guofan who dedicated himself to the advocacy of the Principlism criticized directly: "He had not learned the precision of the Confucian scholars of the Song Dynasty; therefore, although he had written more about prose writing, he had said little about the substance in prose writing."

Yao Nai's contributions in literature include his own writings and aesthetic differentiation of the firm *yang* and the yielding *yin* in literary criticism, and his conscious establishment of the classical prose tradition deserves a particular mention. In order to provide learners of the classical prose with a primary model textbook, he compiled *A Collection of the Classical Prose in Categories*, which traced back to the pre-Qin times and the Han Dynasty, and covered mainly the writings of the eight prose masters of the Tang and Song Dynasties as well as the writings of Fang Bao and Liu Dakui of the Tongcheng School. It excluded particularly the parallel prose of the Six Dynasties. The compilation of the book meant a reaffirmation in the new historical period of the tradition the Tang-Song School of the Ming Dynasty which was initiated to connect the writings of the eight prose masters of the Tang and Song Dynasties with the writings of the

Qin and Han Dynasties, and the inclusion of the Tongcheng School of the Qing Dynasty as a part of this tradition. Fang Dongshu had already said clearly of its significance: "Master Yao Jichuan compiled the collection of the classical prose after the eight prose masters: For the Ming Dynasty the writings of Gui Xifu (Gui Youguang), and for the Qing Dynasty the writings of Wangxi (Fang Bao) and Haifeng (Liu Dakui) are selected. He thought that this is the orthodox tradition of the classical prose." (*A Letter in Reply to Ye Puqiu on the Classical Prose*) Henceforth, the tradition for the classical prose in ancient Chinese literature has basically been determined, for from the rise of the modern vernacular movement to the replacement of the ancient Chinese language, the subsequent writings of the classical prose could only be regarded as a branch of the Tongcheng School, instead of an independent genre. For instance, the writings of the Yanghu School, though having its own name, was actually derived from the Tongcheng school. Its leaders Yun Jing and Zhang Huiyan were both the disciples of Qian Bojiong, who was the disciple of Liu Dakui, so they were the grand disciples of the Tongcheng School. Lu Jilu of the Yanghu School commented on their pursuit of the classical prose and thought it was the same as the Tongcheng School: "They traced back from Wangxi (Fang Bao) to Zhenchuan (Gui Youguang), Jingchuan (Tang Shunzhi), and Zunyan (Wang Shenzhong), and again to Luling (Ouyang Xiu), Meishan (Su Shi), Nanfeng (Zeng Gong), and Xin'an (Lü Zuqian)." (Preface to *The Collected Works of Seven Prose Masters*) This is the same way as the Tang-Song School going back to the classical prose of the Tang and Song Dynasty. Naturally, they had their own views, and made quite a few revisions and criticisms of the Tongcheng School. For instance, Yun Jing had a thorough knowledge of the pre-Qin philosophical works, and Zhang Huiyan treasured *The Anthology of Poetry and Prose* and was adept at writing the parallel prose when he was young. Therefore, they advocated both parallel prose and classical prose instead of neglecting completely the parallel prose of the Six Dynasties. They also thought a learner should begin from the study of the writings of the philosophers of the pre-Qin times to improve the way of learning. All these were insightful views. Wu Rulun commented on the writings of the Tongcheng School, and thought Fang Bao "benefited more from the Confucian classics" and Liu Dakui "benefited more from the history works." (*A Letter to Yang Boheng on the Collections of Fang Bao and Liu Dakui*) Yun Jing then advocated particularly the study of the philosophers of the pre-Qin times, and it was a rational supplement. Furthermore, all the ideas of the Yanghu School were absorbed in the later development of the Tongcheng School: Both Mei Zengliang and Zeng Guofan affirmed the orientation of studying the strong points of both the parallel prose and the classical prose. Moreover, Zeng Guofan compiled *A Selection of Classics and History Books and Philosophical Works of Various Schools*, which selected more articles from the classics, history books and philosophical works than *A Collection of the Ancient Prose in Categories.*

It was also a most prosperous time for the expansion of teachers and students in the Tongcheng School. Yao Nai's students Guan Tong, Mei Zengliang, Yao Ying, and Fang Dongshu were the four most famous figures. "So many students followed closely one after another like echoes of sound and shadows of people, or like fleabane following a wind and rivers flowing into a valley." (Preface to *A Sequel to A Collection of the Ancient Prose in Categories*) The Tongcheng prose style prevailed for a time. Among the Tongcheng masters, Mei Zengliang had the largest number of students and the greatest influence. He was on friendly terms with Zeng Guofan in the capital, and they made concerted efforts to enhance the prose style of the Tongcheng School. Zeng Guofan, with his political status, had a lot of followers, such as Zhang Yuzhao, Xue Fucheng, Li Shuchang and Wu Rulun, who were later known throughout the country. It was addressed as the revival of the Tongcheng School. Wu Rulun as a native of Tongcheng succeeded to Zeng Guofan's position in writing, and later he was appointed the general instructor of the Imperial College of the Capital, and had a great many students. With the change of the times, it was the two translators Yan Fu and Lin Qinnan (Lin Shu) who had the greatest influence in writing the classical prose of the Tongcheng style. The former introduced and translated the western works in social sciences, while the latter introduced and translated the novels of the Great Britain, the United

States of America and France, and compared the works of Charles Dickens with those of Sima Qian; they made historical contributions to the exchange between Chinese and western cultures. They were both students of Wu Rulun. This constituted the last glory of the Tongcheng School, and the Chinese classical prose as well.

If we view the rise, development and decline of the classical prose in a comprehensive and historical perspective, we may see that the classical prose movement of the Tang and Song Dynasties was the primary period, when the endeavors of Han Yu, Liu Zongyuan, Ouyang Xiu and Su Shi helped to establish the position of the classical prose as the basic paradigm of prose. It inherited the writings of the Qin and Han Dynasties, and passed down the tradition to the Ming and Qing Dynasties. Whether people of the later generations opposed it or supported it, they could not overlook it, because it had become the absolute historical background. The Tang-Song School of the Ming Dynasty and the Tongcheng School of the Qing Dynasty both confirmed their own historical significance in the classical prose tradition of the Tang and Song Dynasties. It can be said that the classical prose of the Tang and Song Dynasties is the same as the poetry of the Tang and Song Dynasties, and has became a classical model in the Chinese literary history; the Tang and Song times, same as the pre-Qin times, saw the establishment of classics in Chinese literature. The only difference between them is that the Tang poetry and the Song poetry are a pair of opposite and complementary types, while the Tang prose and the Song prose are in succession, one following another.

Appendices

I. Bibliography

Cai Juhou, *Cai Kuanfu Poetry Talks* 蔡居厚《蔡宽夫诗话》

Cao Pi, *On Scholars* in *On Classical Writings* 曹丕《典论·论文》

Cao Xuequan, *Shicang Selected Poems of the Past Ages* 曹学佺《石仓历代诗选》;

Shicang Selected Readings of the Tang Poetry 《石仓唐诗选》

Chen Banzheng, *Collection of the Best Ming Prose* 陈攽政《明文衡》

Chen Liang, *Selected Readings of Ouyang Xiu* 陈亮《欧阳文粹》

Chen Renxi, *Enlarged Choice Blossoms of Literature* 陈仁锡《广文苑英华》

Chen Shou, *Memorials of the Famous Officials in the Han Dynasty* 陈寿《汉名臣奏事》;

Memorials of the Famous Officials of the Wei Dynasty 《魏名臣奏事》

Chen Xie, *Miscellaneous Inscriptions* 陈勰《杂碑》;

Tablet Inscriptions 《碑文》

Chen Yan, *Records of the Best Song Poems* 陈衍《宋诗精华录》

Chen Zhensun, *Explanation to Zhizhai Catalogue* 陈振孙《直斋书录解题》

Chu Xin, *Complete Prose of 10 Masters in the Tang and Song Dynasties* 储欣《唐宋十大家全集录》

Du Yu, *Good Essays* 杜预《善文》

Duan Chengshi, *Youyang Miscellany* 段成式《酉阳杂俎》

Dugu Ji, *Collected Works of Piling* 独孤及《毘陵集》

Fan Ye, *The Book of the Later Han Dynasty* 范晔《后汉书》

Fang Dongshu, *Humble Opinions from Zhaomei* 方东树《昭昧詹言》

Fang Hui, *Quintessence of the Best Regulated Poems* 方回《瀛奎律髓》

Fang Xiaoru, *Orthodoxy of Prose* 方孝孺《文统》

Fei Yourong, *Postscript to the Collation of The Quintessence of the Tang Prose and Poetry* 费有容《斠刊〈唐文粹〉书后》

Feng Ban, *Dunyin Miscellanies* 冯班《钝吟杂录》

Feng Hao, *Comprehensive Annotations to The Collected Works of Fannan* 冯浩《樊南文集详注》

Feng Weine, *Records of Ancient Poems* 冯惟讷《古诗征》;
Records of Ancient Poetry《古诗纪》

Fu Xuan, *Collection of Sevens* 傅玄《七林》

Gao Bing, *Collected Comments on the Tang Poetry* 高棅《唐诗品汇》;
Standard Voice of the Tang Poetry《唐诗正声》

Gao Sisun, *Essence of Choice Blossoms of Literature* 高似孙《文苑英华纂要》

Gao Zhongwu, *Collection of the Talented Poets in the Restoration Era* 高仲武《中兴间气集》

Gong Mengren, *Selections of Choice Blossoms of Literature* 宫梦仁《文苑英华选》

Gu Tao, *Categorized Selection of the Tang Poetry* 顾陶《唐诗类选》

Guo Lin, *Supplements to The Quintessence of Tang Prose and Poetry* 郭麐《唐文粹补遗》

Guo Maoqian, *Collected Poems of Music Bureau* 郭茂倩《乐府诗集》

He Shang, *Zaijiuyuan Poetry Talks* 贺裳《载酒园诗话》

Hong Man, *10,000 Quatrains of the Tang Poets* 洪迈《万首唐人绝句》

Hu Yinglin, *Pond of Poetry* 胡应麟《诗薮》

Hu Zhenheng, *Complete Voice of the Tang Dynasty* 胡震亨《唐音统签》

Hu Zi, *Talks of a Reclusive Fisherman at the Tiao Stream* 胡仔《苕溪渔隐丛话》

Huang Kan, *Notes on The Literary Mind and Carving the Dragon* 黄侃《文心雕龙札记》

Huang Yongnian, *A Study on Historical Documents of the History of the Tang Dynasty* 黄永年《唐史史料学》

Huang Zongxi, *The Reading Text of the Ming Prose* 黄宗羲《明文授读》;

The Sea of the Ming Prose 《明文海》

Ji Yougong, *Records about the Tang Poetry* 计有功《唐诗纪事》

Ji Zhenyi, *Tang Poetry* 季振宜《唐诗》

Jiang Shaoyu, *Categorized Facts and Events of the Song Dynasty* 江少虞《宋朝事实类苑》

Kong Hai, *The Secret Repository as a Mirror of Literature* 空海（Kukai）《文镜秘府论》

Li Chonghua, *Poetic Talks at Zhenyi Studio* 李重华《贞一斋诗话》;

Zhenyi Studio Poetry Talks 《贞一斋诗话》

Li Ciming, *Reading Notes of Yuemantang* 李慈铭《越缦堂读书记》

Li Dongyang, *Lutang Poetry Talks* 李东阳《麓堂诗话》

Li Fang & Li Zhi, *Collection of Poems and Replies between Two Lis* 李昉、李至《二李唱和集》

Li Panlong, *Ancient and Modern Poems after Deletion* 李攀龙《古今诗删》;

Selected Poems of the Tang Dynasty 《唐诗选》

Li Tu, *Essence of Writings* 李涂《文章精义》

Li Yan, *Collected Poems in the Literary Garden of the Song Dynasty* 李蓑《宋艺圃集》

Li Zhao, *Supplements to the History of the Tang Dynasty* 李肇《唐国史补》

Lin Qingzhi, *Selected Quatrains of the Tang Poets* 林清之《唐绝句选》

Linghu Chu, *An Imperial Reader of the Poems* 令狐楚《御览诗》;

Collection Submitted for Imperial Reading 《选进集》（《御览诗》的又名）

Liu Ban, *Zhongshan Poetry Talks* 刘攽《中山诗话》

Liu Dakui, *Selected Poems of the Prime Tang Dynasty* 刘大櫆《盛唐诗选》;

The Orthodox of the Tang Poems 《唐诗正宗》

Liu Kezhuang, *Houcun Poetry Talks* 刘克庄《后村诗话》

Liu Shipei, *Lectures on History of Medieval Literature* 刘师培《中古文学史讲义》;

Miscellaneous Notes on Poetry and Prose 《论文杂记》

Liu Xun, *Generalities in Reclusion* 刘壎《隐居通义》

Liu Yiqing, *A Copy of Collection Forest* 刘义庆《集林抄》;

Collection Forest 《集林》

Liu Yuxi & Bai Juyi, *Collection of Poems and Replies between Liu and Bai* 刘禹锡、白居易《刘白唱和集》

Lü Benzhong, *Genealogy of the Poets of the Jiangxi School* 吕本中《江西诗社宗派图》

Lu Xun, *Note on Buying the Complete Collection of Philological Studies* 鲁迅《买〈小学大全〉记》

Lu You, *Notes from Old Learning House* 陆游《老学庵笔记》

Lü Zuqain, *Selected Works of the Three Sus* 吕祖谦《三苏文选》;
Collection of the Song Prose as a Mirror《宋文鉴》;
Cruxes of the Classical Prose《古文关键》

Mao Kun, *Prose Collection of the Eight Masters in the Tang and Song Dynasties* 茅坤《唐宋八大家文钞》

Mei Dingzuo, *Records of the Prose in the Past Ages* 梅鼎祚《历代文纪》

Ouyang Xiu, *Liuyi Poetry Talks* 欧阳修《六一诗话》

Peng Dingqiu, *Complete Collection of the Tang Poetry* 彭定求等《全唐诗》

Peng Shuxia, *Collation and Correction of Choice Blossoms of Literature* 彭叔夏《文苑英华辨正》;
Differentiation and Rectification of Choice Blossoms of Literature《文苑英华辩证》

Qian Qianyi, *Collected Poems of the Different Reigns* 钱谦益《列朝诗集》

Qian Zhenlun, *Supplement to The Collected Works of Fannan* 钱振伦《樊南文集补编》

Qian Zhongshu, *Selected Song Poetry with Annotations* 钱钟书《宋诗选注》

Qiu Chi, A Copy of Collections 丘迟《集抄》;
Concise Collection《集略》

Rui Tingzhang, *Collection of the Brilliant National Poets* 芮挺章《国秀集》

Shao Bowen, *A Record of Mr. Shao's Personal Experience* 邵伯温《邵氏闻见录》

Shen Deqian, *Different Choices of the Tang Poems* 沈德潜《唐诗别裁》

Shen Yue, *A Copy of Collection* 沈约《集钞》

Shi Jie, *Record of the Imperial Edicts in the Dazhong Xiangfu Period* 石介《祥符诏书记》

Shi Shan, *Wangyunlou Poetry Talks* 施山《望云楼诗话》

Sima Guang, *Memorial to Present History as a Mirror for Governance* 司马光《进〈资治通鉴〉表》

Sima Qian, *Records of the Historian* 司马迁《史记》

Su Tianjue, *Collection of the Yuan Prose in Category* 苏天爵《元文类》

Tan Yuanchun & Zhong Xing, *The Convergence of Poems* 谭元春、钟惺《诗归》

Tan Yuanchun, *Preface to The Collection of Classical Prose* 谭元春《古文澜编序》

Tang Shunzhi, *Collection of Essays* 唐顺之《文编》

The Quintessence of the Prose in the Tang and Song Dynasties 乾隆御定《唐宋文醇》

Wang Anshi, *Selected Readings of 100 Tang Poets* 王安石《唐百家诗选》;
Selected Works of the Four Poets 《四家诗选》

Wang Kaiyun, *General Introduction to the Parallel Prose* 王闿运《骈文概论》

Wang Ruoxu, *Hunan Poetry Talks* 王若虚《滹南诗话》

Wang Shihan, *Preface to the Basic Principle of the Anthology of Poetry and Prose* 汪师韩《文选理学权舆序》

Wang Shizhen, *A Collection of Samadhi of the Tang Master Poets* 王士祯《唐贤三昧集》

Wang Shizhen, *Postscript to the Unabridged Edition of The Selected Readings of 100 Tang Poets by Wang Anshi* 王世祯《跋王介甫唐百家诗全本》

Wang Shizhen, *Random Remarks from the Literary Circle* 王世贞《艺苑卮言》

Wang Zhi, *Talks on the Parallel Prose* 王铚《四六话》

Wei Gu, *Anthology of Literary Talents* 韦縠《才调集》

Wei Tai, *Poetry Talks in Seclusion at the Han River* 魏泰《临汉隐居诗话》

Wei Zhuang, *A Sequel to The Collection of Superb Subtlety* 韦庄《又玄集》;
Collection of Rinsing-Flower Poems 《浣花集》

Weng Fanggang, *Examples of Samadhi of Seven-syllable Poems* 翁方纲《七言三昧举隅》

Wu Guan, *Records of the Tang Poetry* 吴琯《唐诗纪》

Wu Mianxue, *Collected Poems of the Four Tang Periods* 吴勉学《四唐汇诗》

Wu Qiao, *Weilu Poetry Talks* 吴乔《围炉诗话》

Wu Weiye, *Meicun Poetry Talks* 吴伟业《梅村诗话》
Wu Zhizhen, *Collected Poems of the Song Dynasty* 吴之振《宋诗钞》
Xi Qiyu, *Collection of 100 Famous Tang Poets* 席启寓《唐百名家全集》
Xia Chengtao, *The Chronicle of Wei Duanji* 夏承焘《韦端已年谱》
Xiao Dezao, *Face-to-face Dialogue at Night* 萧德藻《对床夜语》
Xiao Tong, *Anthology of Poetry and Prose* 萧统《文选》;
Choice Blossoms of Ancient and Modern Poems 《古今诗苑英华》;
Choice Blossoms of Prose 《文章英华》
Xie Fangde, *Model Essays* 谢枋得《文章轨范》
Xie Lingyun, *Collected Poems* 谢灵运《诗集》;
Collection of Rhapsodies 《赋集》
Xin Wenfang, *Biographies of the Tang Talents* 辛文房《唐才子传》
Xu Jian, *Records of First Learning* 徐坚《初学记》
Xu Jingzong, *Collection of Essays and Poems* 许敬宗《文馆词林》
Xu Lian, *Collected Prose of the Six Dynasties* 许梿《六朝文絜》
Xu Xueyi, *Origins, Genres and Styles of Poetry* 许学夷《诗源辩体》
Xu Zhenqing, *Records of the Talks on Poetry* 徐祯卿《谈艺录》
Xun Chuo, *Ancient and Modern Five-Syllable Poems and Excellent Essays* 荀绰《古今五言诗美文》
Xun Xu, *Lyrics of Yan in the Jin Dynasty* 荀勖《晋燕乐歌辞》;
Songs and Poems of the Jin Dynasty 《晋歌诗》
Yan Kejun, *Complete Collection of the Prose of the Remote Ancient Times, Three Dynasties, Qin, Han, Three Kingdoms and Six Dynasties* 严可均《全上古三代秦汉三国六朝文》
Yan Yu, *Canglang Poetry Talks* 严羽《沧浪诗话》
Yang Shihong, *Voice of the Tang Dynasty* 杨士弘《唐音》
Yang Wanli, *Chengzhai Poetry Talks* 杨万里《诚斋诗话》
Yang Yi, *Xikun Collection of Chant-Reply Poems* 杨忆《西昆酬唱集》
Yao Chun, *Records of the Contemporary Prose* 姚椿《国朝文录》
Yao He, *Collection of Superb Subtlety* 姚合《极玄集》
Yao Nai, *Categorized Selection of Ancient Writings* 姚鼐《古文辞类纂》
Yao Xuan, *Quintessence of Tang Prose and Poetry* 姚铉《唐文粹》
Yao Zhenzong, *Textual Research on Book of the Sui Dynasty: Bibliography of*

Classics and Books 姚振宗《隋书经籍志考证》
Ye Mengde, *Shilin Poetry Talks* 叶梦得《石林诗话》
Ye Shi, *Selected Poems of the Four Lings* 叶适《四灵诗选》
Ye Wenzhuang, *Postscript to the Fragmented Version of Categorized Collection of the Tang Melody and Poetry* 叶文庄《书〈唐歌诗〉残本后》
Ye Xie, *Inquiry into Poetry* 叶燮《原诗》
Yin Fan, *Collection of Danyang* 殷璠《丹阳集》;
Collection of the Prominent Poets of Rivers and Mountains 《河岳英灵集》
Ying Qu, *Collection of Essays* 应璩《书林》
Yu Shinan, *The Collection of Beitang* 虞世南《北堂书钞》
Yuan Haowen, *Quatrains on Poetry* 元好问《论诗绝句》;
Tang Poetry in Music 《唐诗鼓吹》
Yuan Jie, *Collection in a Suitcase* 元结《箧中集》
Zeng Guofan, *A Selection of Classics and History Books and Philosophical Works of Various Schools* 曾国藩《经史百家杂钞》
Zeng Jili, *Tingzhai Poetry Talks* 曾季貍《艇斋诗话》
Zha Shenxing, *Supplements to and Annotations on the Poems of Su Shi* 查慎行《苏诗补注》
Zhang Biaocheng, *Shanhugou Poetry Talks* 张表臣《珊瑚钩诗话》
Zhang Duanyi, *The Collection of Gui'er* 张端义《贵耳集》
Zhang Jie, *Suihantang Poetry Talks* 张戒《岁寒堂诗话》
Zhang Zhixiang, *Categorized Collection of the Tang Poetry* 张之象《唐诗类苑》
Zhao Mengkui, *Categorized Collection of the Tang Melody and Poetry* 赵孟奎《分门纂类唐歌诗》
Zhao Shixiu, *A Collection of Two Wonders* 赵师秀《二妙集》;
Collection of All Wonders 《众妙集》
Zhao Yanwei, *Miscellaneous Collection of Yunlu* 赵彦卫《云麓漫钞》
Zhao Yi, *Oubei Poetry Talks* 赵翼《瓯北诗话》;
Reading Notes on the Twenty-Two Historical Books 《廿二史札记》
Zhao Yushi, *Notes after the Departure of Guests* 赵与时《宾退录》
Zhi Yu, *Collection of Literary Writings in Genres* 挚虞《文章流别集》;

On the Collection of Literary Writings in Genres 《文章流别志论》
Zhong Rong, *Grades of Poetry* 钟嵘《诗品》
Zhou Bi, *Composition Methods of the Three Genres of the Tang Master Poets* 周弼《唐贤三体诗法》
Zhou Bida, *Notes on the Beginning of the Compilation of Choice Blossoms of Literature* 周必大《纂修〈文苑英华〉事始》;
The Cause for Compilation of Choice Blossoms of Literature 《纂修〈文苑英华〉事始》
Zhu Heling, *A New Collection of the Writings of Li Yishan* 朱鹤龄《新编李义山文集》
Zhu Jing, *Collection of 100 Tang Poets* 朱警《唐百家诗》
Zhu Tingzhen, *Xiaoyuan Poetry Talks* 朱庭珍《筱园诗话》
Zhu You, *A New Selection of Essays by the Six Masters* 朱右《新编六先生文集》

Annotations on Bibliographies of Literature and Books in the Three Reigns of Our Dynastic History 《三朝国史艺文志注》
Bibliography of Books and Literature of the New History of the Tang Dynasty 《新唐书·艺文志》
Bibliography of Classics and Books of the Old History of the Tang Dynasty 《旧唐书·经籍志》
Biographies of Literary Scholars, History of the Ming Dynasty 《明史·文苑传》
Book of Poetry 《诗经》
Catalogue of Classics and Books in the History of the Sui Dynasty 《隋书·经籍志》
Choice Blossoms of Literature (wen yuan ying hua) 《文苑英华》
Chongwen General Catalogue 《崇文总目》
Classified Collection of Poetry and Prose 《艺文类聚》
Collected Explanations of the Records of the Historian 《史记集解》
Collected Writings from Taiyan 《太炎文录》
Collection Garden 《集苑》
Complete Collection of the Tang Prose 《全唐文》
Complete Library in the Four Treasuries 《四库全书》

General Anthology of Poetry Talks 《诗话总龟》
Great Canon of Yongle 《永乐大典》
Important Events Archived in the Imperial Library 《册府元龟》
Indexes to the Records of the Historian 《史记索隐》
Institutions and Regulations of Our Dynasty 《国要》
New Odes to the Jade Terrace 《玉台新咏》
Philological Study on The Songs of the South 《楚辞章句》
Sequel to the Draft of History as a Mirror for Governance 《续资治通鉴长编》
Simplified Catalogue of the Complete Library of the Four Treasuries 《四库全书简明目录》
Songs of the South 《楚辞》
Strategies of the Warring States 《战国策》
Synopses of the General Catalogue for the Complete Library in the Four Treasuries 《四库全书总目提要》
Taiping Imperial Encyclopedia 《太平御览》
Taiping Miscellany 《太平广记》
The Book of the Liang Dynasty 《梁书》
The third part of The Series of the Complete Library of the Four Treasuries 《四部丛刊三编》

II. Glossary

a hundred-one poem 百一 (bǎi yī) 19
admonishment 教 (jiào) 17, 24, 29
allegory 讽喻 (fěng yù) 25
anti-summons for reclusion 反招隐 (fǎn zhāo yǐn) 18
aspiration or sentiment expression 咏怀 (yǒng huái) 18
assorted imitations 杂拟 (zá nǐ) 18